HUNTERS OF HUMANS

by

V M Steele

Author of *The Scarred Wrists*

Published 1936 by

STANLEY PAUL & CO., LTD.
PATERNOSTER ROW - LONDON - E.C.4

Originally made and printed in Great Britain at Gainsborough Press, St. Albans by Fisher, Knight and Co. Ltd.

Library and Archives Canada Cataloguing in Publication

Steele, V. M., author
     Hunters of humans / V.M. Steele

Reprint. Previously published: 1936.
ISBN 978-1-896238-21-0 (softcover)

     1. Title.

PR6011.172H86 2017   823'.912   C2017-905070-2

Twin Eagles Publishing

Box 2031
Sechelt BC
V0N 3A0
pblakey@telus.net
604 885 7503

twineaglespublishing.com

THE THRILL OF THE HUNT

In her "Introduction" to The Sea Priestess, Dion Fortune says,

> People read fiction in order to supplement the diet life provides for them. If life is full and varied, they like novels that analyse and interpret it for them; if life is narrow and unsatisfying, they supply themselves with mass production wish fulfilments from the lending libraries. I have managed to fit my book in between these two stools so neatly that it is hardly fair to say that it falls between them. It is a novel of interpretation and a novel of wish-fulfilment at the same time.

In many ways, this is also true of *Hunters of Humans;* although it is not an "occult novel", it is at least as much a novel of interpretation as it is one of wish-fulfilment. Although it is certainly a romance, it is not really a thriller. It is more a police-procedural, but it might well be described as a "police-procedural of manners".

Hunters of Humans is the second novel that Violet Firth published under the name V. M. Steele. According to *The English Catalogue of Books*, the novel was first published (at 7s. 6d.) in February of 1936, and in a cheap edition (2s. 6d.) in March of 1937.

Like *The Scarred Wrists*, it includes Chief Inspector Saunders (thus nudging him toward an appearance as a "series character" in Hubin's *Bibliography of Crime Fiction*). However, at the end of *The Scarred Wrists*, Saunders has retired; in

Hunters of Humans, he is still quite active as a senior police-man. Nonetheless, it is clearly set "after the War," and very much in the atmosphere of the social changes occurring at that time.

Saunders and his subordinate, Austen, come down from London (by motorcycle) to investigate a suspicious rural death; they take rooms with Ann Studley (of all the possible surnames in Britain, one has to wonder why the author chose that one, given her experiences at the Studley Horticultural and Agricultural College) and her father, whose very reduced circumstances require them to take in boarders to make ends meet.

Ann and Austen provide the romantic interest, but the death in the local manor house (which belonged to Ann's family, before her father's intemperance forced him to sell it, and live in a small house that was Ann's mother's) provides the overall plot. Austen comes from a working class family, but almost finished a university-level technical education before being forced by family circumstances to go to work; he has brought sophisticated chemical testing processes into the force. One of the tensions between Ann and Saunders is their mutual anxiety about whether the other will take their class differences be insurmountable.

> "Ann's class was dying out; its day was over; there was no employment for it in a post-war, mechanized universe. Its children, when it intermarried with itself, were hard to rear. Saunder's type was dying out too, owing to better housing, better education and the passing of starvation wages. His sons, if he had had any, would have been like Austen. Austen's class was spreading hand over fist, absorbing Saunders, absorbing Ann; establishing new standards of aristocracy within itself—standards of vigour and efficiency and technical

iv

expertness."

"Blue blood has its points when it is really blue, but when it gets like watered claret, honest red blood is much to be preferred."

The death at the manor house was only recognized as suspect because the local doctor had been away when it happened, and a more up-to-date physician had become suspicious and reported the death to the authorities. It turns out that in fact the death was a case of poisoning, involving the use of foxglove to produce symptoms of heart disease to mask the later effects of potassium cyanide. (This novel was published a year or two before Agatha Christie's *Appointment with Death*, which also features digitalis poisoning, but through injection rather than through home-made foxglove extract.)

As the story unfolds, Ann comes to realize that the murderer is probably her father, and that he has probably murdered her mother and grandmother, using the same technique —one which has implicated her as an unwitting accomplice. This realization is another impediment to the developing romantic relationship, since Ann reasonably enough supposes that it might create difficulties for Austen to be connected with the daughter of a murderer.

The difficulties that arise between Austen and Ann put her under extreme stress, described in a comment that, in isolation, is utterly typical of Dion Fortune.

"Ann could not think. Her mind worked in a series of pictures, as minds do when life is driven down to its foundations."

The scene shifts to London, to court, and newspapers,

providing more occasion for tart observations about manners and customs, the foibles of attorneys and jurors, and the use of extra-judicial interventions by otherwise well-disciplined line police when their supervisors make it clear that they aren't noticing. The difficulties between Austen and Ann are resolved, as are the legal issues, and the replacement of an older, corrupt and decaying social order by a newer and more vigorous one is clearly under way.

* * *

As a novel, *Hunters of Humans* lacks some of the ease and focus of the other V. M. Steele novels: it is almost as though it were a first effort to tell a story that was both analytic and romantic. The narrative, analytic voice is much more present, and in fact there are really several strands of narration: the story of Austen and Ann; the story of the wily Saunders, whose passion is the game of hunting other human beings; and the story of the transformation of British society, both in the country and in the city, as different classes fall and rise.

There is also a stream of psychological, even psychotherapeutic, observation. It is hard, for example, not to wonder about Ann's belated realization of her father's activities, and her own involvement in them. It is as though she is living in a fairy-tale enchantment, as though compelled by an ogre in a dream. It is her involvement with Austen that begins to awaken her, to give her a way out of the ogre's cave.

At the same time, Austen is also under a spell—one of extended adolescence or immaturity, indicated not only by his intense focus on his work, but also in his odd status as a kind of beef-cake figure for press photographers, emblematic of a self-absorption that is only overcome when he is forced to deal with his relationship with Ann.

Finally, the narrator is well-equipped with tart observations about manners and customs, and the difference between the official and the actual (especially in legal matters), and an untroubled disregard for conventions (social and legal) when they do not align with the inner truth of a situation.

It would be interesting to know what the author intended. As Dion Fortune, Violet Firth wrote several statements about her occult novels. Unfortunately, if she wrote anything about the novels she published under the name V. M. Steele, it does not seem to have survived.

However, in her article, "The Novels of Dion Fortune" (reprinted in *Dion Fortune's Rites of Isis and of Pan*, Skylight Press, 2013), in the course of discussing her occult novels, she also described her own background as a writer, and it may be helpful to refer to some of those statements.

She describes herself as, "by temperament and training a journalist and fiction writer," and also mentions that

> ... a hard and exacting discipline, first of quality and then of quantity, ... furnished me with a literary style that was an absolutely pliable tool in my hand; rapid, effortless, requiring the minimum of revision, so that the first draft can generally go to the printers uncopied. In fact, constant unceasing paper-covering resulted in a facility that allowed my subconscious getting itself down on paper. Consequently my novels are drama-tised day-dreams. They are not written; they are lived and recorded. Everything is seen and heard exactly as if I were watching a play at the theatre.

She also states, "I would write novels anyway, even if I did not write occult novels," as indeed she did.

> I have a story-teller's imagination, and must write nov-els, whether they serve any useful purpose or not, in the

same way that a hen must lay eggs, for otherwise the poor creature would burst. But because I have a purpose in my life, which is the work of initiation organised as The Fraternity of the Inner Light, my novels have a purpose, which is the purpose of initiation. Therefore my novels have not got a purpose stuck on like a luggage label, after the dreadful manner of the allegorists, but spring from my purpose as the seed from the soil in which it germinates, into which it strikes its roots, and from which it draws its vitality.

The V.M. Steele novels are not occult novels, in other words, they do not embody explicit initiatory formulae. However, it may be possible to apply another remark to these novels.

We have, then, two types of novel—the novels of interpretation, and the novels of wish-fulfilment. Knowing this as a novelist, and also knowing as a psychologist the part played by the day-dream, I decided to put the two together and produce novels that should come as near to an initiation ceremony as possible; that is to say, it should produce in receptive persons something of the same result as produced by the experience of going through a ritual initiation.

And again, she states,

I have tried to make use of the dramatic form of the thriller-romance, as a vehicle for a mystic and cosmic interpretation. Read by a person who has it in him to respond, these stories will put him in touch with the corresponding cosmic factor through which his day-dream identification of himself with the hero who is put in touch with cosmic factors in the course of the story; in fact each story is the story of an initiation, and if the reader identifies himself with the hero, or herself with the heroine, they will be taken through that initiation as surely as a young sporting dog is trained to be coupled to an obedient and gun-wise beast who knows the words of command.

In the V. M. Steele novels, it is not cosmic factors but social factors and forces that are analyzed, and around which the thriller-romance is built. The novels use the vehicle of dual identification (with the male or female protagonist) to transmit, not cosmic initiation, but social initiation: awakening to a world in flux—and, even more, awakening through an empowering romantic relationship into an adult ability to deal with that world. Love and work: in this, at least, Violet Firth did not end up far from her psychoanalytic roots.

Richard Brzustowicz, September 2017

HUNTERS OF HUMANS

by

V. M. STEELE

Go, stalk the red deer through the heather,
Ride, follow the fox if you can!
But, for pleasure and profit together,
Allow me the hunting of Man—
The chase of the Human, the search for the Soul
To its ruin—the hunting of Man.
The Old Shikaree.

CHAPTER ONE

THE happenings that are chronicled in detective novels for the delight of crime fans are so remote from the everyday experience of most folk that when one occurs within their own circle of acquaintances, people jump at once to the conclusion that some natural explanation will be forthcoming after due investigation, and that the police inquiries are a mere formality.

Consequently, when Ann Studley read in the local paper, for the incident was not considered worthy of chronicle by the London paper, that the funeral of Mr. Gregory of Deepdene Hall had been stopped for further inquiries to be made into the manner of his death and that an inquest was to be held, she was not impressed with any sense of tragedy.

He had died suddenly of heart failure, and so an inquest was to be held. Well, both her mother and her grandmother had died like that, and her father had cheerfully informed her that she would probably go in the same way too when her time came, as heart failure ran in the family, and none of them made old bones. They had been spared an inquest, however, as the doctor, the old one, the predecessor of the one who had attended Mr. Gregory, had been visiting both his patients for some weeks before they died. Ann wondered why the present doctor did not do as he had done—take Mrs. Gregory's word for it that her husband was dead, and fill up the necessary forms. She was thankful that their doctor had not been so wrapped up in red tape, and noted Dr. Armitage's name as one to avoid if ever she or her father were in need of medical attention. Then she put the papers aside and got on with her housework; her father was not down yet—he was one of those individuals who get up when the spirit moves them.

Fortunately for all concerned he was his own master, selling on commission for various firms and doing a little bookmaking on the quiet—an activity which had brought him into collision with the local police; but his aristocratic appearance and dignified and charming manners had got him off with the bench of local notables.

His name, too, stood him in good stead in the district, for the Studleys, before they had fallen on evil days, had been lords of the manor. Francis Studley had been born in the big house, whose chimneys just showed over the trees across the little river that ran at the bottom of the garden, and which rejoiced in the euphonious name of Gug Hall. Thatched Cottage, in which she and her father now lived, was the last of what had once been wide acres, and had been inhabited by the bailiff. Her grandmother had lived there for many years after Gug Hall was sold at auction, tending the garden with loving care and rubbing beeswax into the lovely old furniture that had been her marriage portion, and so was spared when the bankruptcy swept away all else. Then, when her son's steady descent in life finally brought him to the end of all things, he had returned to her, bringing wife and child, and the three generations had eked out a narrow existence, precariously supplemented by Mr. Studley's earnings on commission, very little of which, however, found its way into any pocket but his own.

Hearing her father moving about upstairs, Ann prepared to take him up his breakfast, which consisted of a decanter of whisky, a syphon of soda, and some Thin Captain biscuits. Before she could accomplish her intention, however, he entered the room in his dressing-gown, and flinging himself into the deep arm-chair, picked up the paper without a word and began to read.

Ann put the tray at his elbow, and prepared to pour him out a hair of the dog that had bitten him overnight. She poured on, waiting for the expected "When," which was so long coming that he received a most amazing ration of whisky, even for him; but Ann knew better than to show any sign of hesitancy in the pouring of the spirit, which would have been interpreted as criticism and angrily resented in his present mood.

She went on quietly with her dusting and tidying and setting in order. They kept no servant, for Mr. Studley disliked having a woman from the village, alleging that they were inveterate gossips and would pick his character to pieces and spread his affairs all over the district, in which he was probably right. Ann, far from minding the work, enjoyed it, and also tended the garden with as much zest as her grandmother. Her father's somewhat shady reputation caused her to lead a very isolated life, and if she had not busied herself with domesticities, time would have hung heavily on her hands.

Her activities had stood her in good stead, moreover; for when her father's always uncertain income suddenly evaporated like snow in summer, she turned-to, and in spite of his indignant protests, let their spare rooms to visitors, obtaining a good price for them, as the place was within easy access of London for such as had a car. What she made during the summer kept them through the winter; and her father, discovering the arrangement to be economical from the point of housekeeping allowances, became reconciled to it, and even went so far as to introduce a visitor on his own account— a smart, heavily made-up lady who answered to the name of Mrs. Godfrey, though she answered to it so absent-mindedly that, although the initial G was clearly marked on all her *toilette* articles, Ann suspected that the name was not her real one.

When she was there Mr. Studley abandoned his usual habits of going out after lunch and coming in some time between midnight and dawn, and gave her the pleasure of his company. Ann suspected a romance; and owing to the furtiveness of the comings and goings of the lady, she suspected a husband; but she said nothing, for her father was an ugly man to cross, despite his surface charm. The alleged Mrs. Godfrey paid well, made herself very agreeable, and lavished presents on Ann, which were accepted with reluctance, her father daring her, on pain of his displeasure, to refuse them. Finally, however, Mrs. Godfrey came so often that Ann got used to her, though she never liked her; and when in the end she kept sufficient possessions for a weekend permanently in the bottom drawer in the spare bedroom, Ann accepted the situation with indifference.

Having allowed time for the hair of the biter to take effect, Ann thought it was well to beguile her father out of his black early morning mood, and began to make conversation. Seeing that he had just finished reading the local paper with apparent absorption, she could think of no better topic to open the ball than the inquest on Mr. Gregory.

"Where is Deepdene Hall, father?" she asked. "I have never heard of it about here."

He raised his head and gave her a sudden angry, suspicious look, as if she had asked some leading question on a subject he did not wish inquired into.

"Never heard of it either," he snapped; so she concluded that the hair had not yet had time to take effect and that she had better postpone her efforts to exorcise his dumb devil. If he did not know Deepdene Hall, it could not be a very conspicuous edifice, in spite of its fine-sounding name, for his commission salesmanship took him from door to door throughout the district—the district of which his forbears

15

had been lords of the manor—and the only persons who knew it as thoroughly as he did were the postmen and the police.

Presently she heard the car leave the barn that served as a garage, and knew that he had gone out to his day's touting, for that was all it was, and heaved a sigh of relief, as she always did when his presence was removed from the house. Nevertheless, there was a very curious bond between them in spite of his many drawbacks as a parent; a bond that often exists between mother and son, but more rarely between father and daughter. She felt that his petty rascality was due to the fact that he was a man without a profession, and life was more than he could cope with. She knew he had once held a commission in the Guards, but that had not lasted long. Concerning the manner of its ending she knew nothing, for he never referred to it, and neither had her mother or grandmother. She guessed, however, that it had ended suddenly, and badly, for once, when she was a little girl walking with him in Hyde Park, he had accosted a magnificent, military-looking gentleman as a friend, and had been snubbed for his pains.

Ann went tranquilly about her domestic duties, and when they were done, settled-down to her dressmaking. She had put the finishing touches to a summer dress of pale blue linen, cut square at the neck and short in the sleeve, of no recognizable fashion, and therefore never liable to look old-fashioned, and was giving it its final try-on, when she heard the click of the gate latch, and looking out of the kitchen window, saw a large, heavily-built man advancing up the narrow flagged path with a slow, heavy step that reminded her irresistibly of a policeman.

He was a man on the elderly side of middle age, and had the weather-beaten complexion of one much in the open air. But for his walk he might have been a farmer in his Sunday

16

best, but he had the indefinable air of a drilled man. This was no bearer of burdens, despite his slow, heavy walk.

Ann went to the door just as she was, in the new summer dress, and the sunny April day made it appear not too incongruous; so when she opened the door to the bucolic individual he was obviously struck all of a heap by the vision of feminine beauty that confronted him, to her great amusement. For Ann was a very attractive little person, and her flying cloud of wheat coloured hair and sea-blue eyes were set off to amazing advantage by the simple linen dress of robins' -egg blue, as she well knew, the minx, when she chose it, though there was no one but her father and the tradesmen to see it.

But the newcomer was not one readily to be put out of countenance.

"Good afternoon, miss," he said. "They told me in the village that you let rooms and 'ad a telephone. Have you got a couple of rooms to let for me and my man, and a sitting-room with a good strong table in it ?"

Ann replied that all these could be provided, and inquired how long he might be wanting to stay.

"That depends, miss, on circumstances over which we 'ave no control—unfortunately. We may only be a few days, or it might run into weeks."

Then terms were discussed. They would be out, he said, he and his man, a good deal, and would like sandwiches when they were away for meals. Ann wondered what sort of a lodger he would be, for he was obviously a man of the working classes, superior in his decent serge suit, but very different to the visitors she was accustomed to. Still, a let of some weeks in the off season was not to be despised in the depleted state of their exchequer, so she determined to make the best of him and his man, and if they did come home drunk—well, that was no novelty. He looked so very respectable, however, like a deacon of a chapel, that she thought it probable he could give her father points when it came to respectability.

"This is a bit of all right," he said with deep satisfaction when she showed him the rooms.

"You got some nice old stuff here, miss." His eye roved admiringly over the furniture.

Ann smiled. "Do you understand old furniture?" she asked, thinking that the clue to him might lie in the fact that he was a dealer.

"Can't say as I understand it, miss, but in my trade we pick up all sorts of knowledge, and none of it comes amiss. Now if you'd be so kind as to let me use the telephone, I'd be much obliged. And if you'd be good enough to show my man where 'e can put the side-car, I'd be even more obliged."

She took him along to her father's sanctum and gave him the telephone directory; then she went out to the gate to carry out the rest of his instructions.

The garden was so designed as to give the maximum of privacy. An impenetrable evergreen hedge protected them from the eyes of any chance passer-by down their narrow lane, and her father had recently replaced the low wicket by a high and solid gate of oak, despite her protests that the butcher was still unpaid. Consequently when she opened this gate she came without warning upon whoever might be outside it, and she was amused to see that the second stranger was struck even more of a heap by the vision in blue than his companion had been.

She on her side was not altogether unstruck by what confronted her, for as she came through the rose-covered arch she found herself within hand-touch of one of the finest-looking men she had ever seen, sitting carelessly in the seat of a large and powerful motor-cycle attached to a side-car, his long legs straddled out on either side of the heavy machine. His bearing, and the square set of his powerful shoulders, gave her the impression that he, like his companion, was a drilled man. He looked to her like the best type of cavalry ranker. Intelligent, clean-living, gentlemanly, but certainly not what her father would admit to be a gentleman. She thought he might be a trooper in the Household Cavalry on holiday, and she wondered what he was doing in the company of the bucolic individual who had just booked the rooms. On the back of the sidecar was permanently fastened a large case such as commercial travellers use; the motor-cycling kit the man wore looked well-worn, as if in regular use, and his bronzed face and hands also pointed to constant driving in all weathers. Well, it was none of her business so long as they paid their rent and did not make themselves a nuisance.

"Good afternoon," she said. "Your friend has taken the rooms, and asked me to show you the garage."

"Right you are, miss," replied the stranger with a beaming smile, evidently very anxious to ingratiate himself with the wearer of the blue frock. She saw that he was a good deal younger than she had at first imagined, not more than twenty-seven or eight, she thought.

"It would be best if you left your suit-cases here," she said. "It is a little way down the lane to the garage."

He removed from the side-car two suit-cases so large that she wondered however his bulky companion had been stowed away alongside them. Then he opened the case at the back of the side-car and took out several small but weighty boxes of brown varnished wood with brass handles, also a portable typewriter and a camera.

"If you like to jump in the side-car, I'll run you down to the garage," he said. "It will save you walking in the mud."

Now this was so obviously common sense that Ann could not very well refuse. All the same, she was furious with the young man for speaking to her as an equal. His companion

19

had at once recognized the difference in their respective social status, and addressed her respectfully, as a working man to a young lady; but this great lumping lout had evidently summed her up as the landlady's daughter, and he was of the class that is friendly with its landladies.

Bumping over the ruts prevented any further attempts at conversation, and the heavy doors of the shed also imposed a vow of silence until they had been dealt with. Then Ann said in her most dignified tones:

"I should be glad if you would put your sidecar well to the right; my father's car has to come in also."

"That ought to give him plenty of room," said the young man, bringing the combination to a standstill two-thirds of the way across the spacious barn.

"Will you put it right up against the wall, please," said Ann in her chilliest tones.

"He's got plenty of room there, miss, as long as he comes home sober," said the young man, viewing the ample floor-space: "What does he drive? A lorry?"

"No!" said Ann furiously. "A Baby Austin."

"Gosh!" said the young man. "What's he do with it when he parks it? Figures of eight?"

Ann was too angry to answer, but in the dim light of the shed he did not notice her disturbance. He gazed slowly round him, and observed the numerous gashes on the walls where Mr. Studley, returning badly bitten, had miscalculated the entrance.

"That his trade-mark?" he inquired, jerking his thumb towards them. "Then we'd better give him all the room there is," and he pushed his machine into the darkest corner, as if its deeds were evil.

"Now then, let's lock up and go home," continued the unwittingly offensive young man, fully believing he was making himself agreeable.

20

"You will be cold in that thin frock, though it's a jolly pretty frock."

"Oh, no, I shan't," said Ann, striving to keep her teeth from chattering, and marched ahead of him down the muddy lane at a pace that made even that young man stretch his long legs.

"Gosh, you've got a pretty place here!" he said as he followed her through the gate and saw the sunset light falling on the first of the spring flowers, gay in their old-fashioned profusion in the wide beds on either side of the flagged path.

When she showed him the bedroom he was to occupy he was even more emphatic in his admiration.

"You *have* got a nice little place here," he said. "I *do* like it." But she saw that he was looking at the bright cretonne curtains and not at the fine old furniture. He followed her down to the low-ceilinged dining-room, which she had assigned as their sitting-room, and there they found the older man comfortably installed in her father's armchair. He did not rise on her entrance.

"Now, missy," he said, "do you think you could do us a cup of tea?"

"Certainly," said Ann, unable to repress a smiling response to the good nature that twinkled in his little pig's eyes. "And I will also give you a fire. It turns cold in the evenings so near the river."

"So you're near the river, are you? Note that, Austen? We're near the river."

"Yes, sir," said the young man. "Shall I get the maps out?"

When Ann returned with the tea-tray she found the dining-table covered with large-scale ordnance maps, and there was a great pother getting the little gate-legged table out of the corner behind the, spinet. The young man, looking bigger than ever under the low, beamed ceiling, succeeded in extracting it, however, without wrecking anything. He moved remarkably quickly and lightly, she thought, for so large a creature. A man could have told her that his movements were those of a boxer.

"Now, miss," said the older man, "you would do us a service if you could point out Deepdene Hall to us on the map. We can't find it."

"Deepdene Hall?" exclaimed Ann in surprise. "Why that is the place where the man has just died. The man they are going to have an inquest on."

"That's right, miss, and I'm in charge of that business. Inspector Saunders is my name.—Chief Inspector Saunders, to be precise, of the C.I.D."

"Good Lord !" said Ann, and sat down on the nearest chair in sheer astonishment.

"Yes, miss. 'Tecs, that's what we are. And if you've been reading shilling shockers you know what to expect."

Ann caught the eye of the younger man, and she saw that he was watching her anxiously, as if to see how she would take this revelation of his profession.

"Dear me!" said she, "I had no idea I was entertaining anything half so exciting!"

Both men burst into loud laughter. They were evidently flattered by her attitude.

"Now, missy," said Inspector Saunders, "take a dekko at this map, will you, and see if you can find Deepdene Hall. Austen, pour out the tea."

"I haven't the faintest notion where Deepdene Hall is," said Ann. "I never heard of the place. I was asking my father where it was only this morning, and he did not know either. It ought to be in a narrow valley, from its name; but it sounds rather too like musical comedy to be a real hall. I expect it is a red-brick villa on top of a hill."

More deep-throated laughter from the two big men

greeted this. Ann felt that Inspector Saunders, probably for professional reasons, was just as anxious to be on friendly terms with her as young Austen was. But although she knew this, she could not help responding to his geniality; there was something very decent and kindly about him, with his little eyes twinkling so brightly at her through the steel-rimmed glasses he had mounted for the map-reading.

"We're a cup short," said young Austen, and Ann saw that a cup of very strong tea stood at her elbow as well as that of Inspector Saunders. "Where can I find another, miss?"

Ann saw that the Inspector was just as taken aback by this as she was, and was about to open his mouth and slay his subordinate. But the young man was so like a big, clumsy, Newfoundland puppy, so completely innocent of all offence, and so obviously delighted to be having tea with her, that she impulsively extricated him from his unsuspected predicament.

"If you will go down the passage," she said with a charming smile, "you will see a door on the left. That is the kitchen. And on the dresser you will see some cups and saucers."

Away trampled the big police officer, as pleased as a dog that is allowed to carry a basket.

"Very kind of you, I'm sure, miss," said Inspector Saunders in a low voice.

"Not at all," said Ann. "I'm delighted."

Austen came back with the cup.

"Now then, my lad," said Saunders. "Come round here and show us your landmarks."

He came round to the back of Ann's chair and bent over her shoulder, planting on the map a hand that covered several square miles.

"Here's Casley village and the bridge," he said, pointing with a thick brown forefinger to a dark patch on the map.

"Here is where the road we're on now turns off from the

main London road and crosses the river. Nasty bend there. Do you have a lot of smashes on that bridge?"

"No," said Ann, "we've never had one. It is so very bad that everyone is careful."

"Here is this house," continued Austen, and Ann saw that the whole of their ground, apple orchard, little wood on the river-bank and all, was clearly indicated on the large-scale map they were studying.

"Now then, according to what they told me at the Yard, Deepdene Hall ought to be about here," and he pointed to a spot on the opposite bank of the river practically opposite Thatched Cottage.

"It isn't," said Ann. "That's Gug Hall."

"Well now, missy," said Saunders, "do you think it likely that one of the *noovoo reesh* like Gregory would change the name of 'is house if he bought a place called Gug Hall? It ain't a pretty name."

"It would be cheek and impudence if he did," exclaimed Ann, firing up indignantly. "That's a very old name—Saxon, in fact. It is the same as Gog and Magog. It was good enough for us for four hundred years, so it ought to be good enough for him."

"So you know the place, missy?" said Saunders, looking at her curiously.

"I ought to," said Ann. "It was our old home."

Saunders looked at his subordinate, and Ann involuntarily looked at him too, and the man went as red as a turkey-cock underneath his tan as it suddenly dawned on him the kind of bricks he had been dropping.

"Well now, missy, do you think it likely that the name has been changed since this map was issued, four years ago?"

"I think it is unlikely it would have been done without my hearing of it, for father is constantly up and down the main London road where the gates are, and we should naturally

24

be interested if anyone re-christened our old home. In fact, it was only this morning that I was asking him about it and he said he had never heard of it. I think you will find that it is a newly-built house."

"They have been there two years, missy."

"Well, I don't know, Mr. Saunders, but you can easily find out, for they are sure to be on the phone."

Inspector Saunders laid his finger beside his nose and closed one eye.

"I am not phoning nobody; nor asking too many questions at the present moment. We always make indirect inquiries before we make direct ones. What's the good of telling the folk you're looking for that the C.I.D. are after them, and scaring the game before you've found the nest? This is why we are putting up on this side of the river and not on the other."

"Goodness!" exclaimed Ann. "Do you mean that you take the trouble to go six miles up the river to the bridge, and six miles back again on the opposite side, when you could put up in Datley, opposite the gates?"

"Yes, miss, I do. For if we put up at Datley, we scare the birds."

"What do you mean? Do you think Mr. Gregory was murdered ?"

"We don't know, miss; but your chief constable has asked us to find out, so 'ere we are. We aren't hunting anybody, and if we find the poor feller died in his bed natural, no one will be better pleased than we shall."

"What is this line across the river at the corner of your garden?" said Austen, laying a squaretipped, rather grimy forefinger on the map.

"That would be the weir," said Ann. "Listen, you can hear it running. There is a lot of water coming over it to-night."

They listened, and through the window that had been opened to let out the fumes of the lamps they heard the purl of running water.

"Sounds lovely, doesn't it?" said Austen.

"Yes," said his chief, "and so do the nightingales, and cock-sparrers, and bull-pups, and all the other pretty little creatures that sing in the spring. Now come along, we want to get to the bottom of this, so don't you side-track us. Now, missy, is it possible to cross the weir?"

"No," said Ann, "quite impossible. There is a very strong current over the weir. I have to be very careful when I am bathing not to go anywhere near it."

"There now, Jack," said Saunders, "there's a chance for you to have a dip."

"Not for me at this time of year, thank you, Chief. Too beastly chilly."

"No, it isn't," said Ann. "The river above here is shallow and broad for some miles, and it very quickly warms up if there is any sunshine. I have been in already this year. It is all right as long as you wait till the afternoon. It would be too cold for anything in the early morning, of course."

"We are forgetting our tea," said Inspector Saunders. "Jack, pour out another round. What time does your father get home, missy?"

"He is often late, Inspector," said Ann, suddenly drawing back into her shell at the mention of her father. She hoped to goodness that she was not going to be cross-examined about her father's doings by this man, who was so shrewd and persistent underneath all his geniality. But he saw her confusion and put her at ease.

"Don't you worry, missy, we're not after him. We only want to introduce ourselves and do the polite. 'E might think a couple of bachelors like us was going to run off with 'is daughter if we didn't. I just want to tell 'im we shan't be kissing you behind the gooseberry-bush while his back is turned."

Ann was not so sure. She thought that his companion would hardly trouble to wait even for the cover of a gooseberry-bush if given the slightest encouragement.

Inspector Saunders pushed aside the maps and gave his attention to tea and small talk, or so it seemed to Ann.

"You lead a pretty quiet life here, miss?"

"Not as quiet as you might think, Inspector," said Ann. "I fell in the river the day before yesterday, and you have turned up to-day. If I have any more excitements before the weekend, I shall have a nervous breakdown."

They roared with laughter.

"How did you come to fall in the river?" asked Austen.

"The bank gave way under me, and in I went. I was furious."

"Are you a good swimmer?"

"Pretty good. I shouldn't be here to tell the tale if I weren't. I was unpleasantly near the weir. That is how I know that nobody could possibly cross the weir," she added, turning to Inspector Saunders.

"I suppose a pretty young lady like you goes to plenty of parties and dances?" said Saunders conversationally.

"No," said Ann, "I very seldom go out in the evening; it is my father who is the gad-about. I have not been out in the evening since I went to the village concert at Christmas."

"Then perhaps you can tell me," said Saunders, "whether there- were any cars about these lanes between ten and ten-thirty on the night of Thursday the 12th. It's a Bugatti, an Italian car, that we are trying to trace."

"I don't think so," said Ann. "Not even my father's car, for it was being decarbonized. But I went to bed early, and my room is on the garden side of the house, so if a quiet car came down the lane after I had gone to sleep I mightn't hear it."

"Perhaps your father can tell us. I don't suppose 'e goes to bed as early as you do. Was 'e in that evening?"

"No, he wasn't. He came in, but he went out again."

"I dare say 'e got home again early enough to tell us whether anything was stirring in these lanes between ten-thirty and midnight."

"I couldn't say," said Ann. "I was asleep before he came in."

CHAPTER TWO

THE two detectives were very little later than Ann herself in going to bed, but although Inspector Saunders's snores were soon rumbling as steadily as running machinery, his subordinate turned and twisted in the narrow bed in the little pink and white room that had been assigned to him.

He knew perfectly well that he was like the moth to the candle, but was absolutely powerless to get a grip on himself. He was a man who was accustomed not only to discipline, but to a rigid self-discipline; but his eight years in the Metropolitan Police, one of the most strictly disciplined body of men in the world, went for nothing at the sight of a linen frock of robin's-egg blue.

As soon as it was light enough to see what he was doing, he got up and dressed, shaving as best he could with ice-cold water, for he had no wish to appear before the girl of his desires unshorn, and went down the creaking old stairs of the cottage as silently as a cat, despite his weight, by dint of placing his heels on the edges of the treads close up against the wall.

He went into the sitting-room that had been assigned to him and his chief. It was cold and unaired, and stank of last night's tobacco-smoke. The fire was out and the hearth strewn with his cigarette-ends and the dottle from Inspector Saunders's pipe. It was miserably cheerless, as only an untidy room can be in the grey light of dawn, but he did not notice the cold for he felt pretty sure that Ann would be about soon at her domestic duties, as there did not appear to be a servant, and his ears were on the alert, listening for her footstep. He would see her, and might even talk to her again. He would be very careful how he dealt with her, for old Saunders had very delicately but very thoroughly rubbed in the fact of the girl's social position, and that he must not be too free with her. But even so, half a loaf is better than no bread to a starving man, and he did not choose to think of what his state of mind would be when their investigation into the Gregory case was finished and they folded their tents like Arabs and moved away to the scene of some other crime.

He had never paid much attention to women, having joined the police when he was only twenty and being extremely keen on his work and the splendid opportunities for sport that the Force afforded him. Consequently, when the flood-gates went down, the tide carried all away, never having spent its strength in backwaters. In the instant that Ann had suddenly appeared before him, blue-frocked and golden-haired, he knew that this was his girl and he meant to have her.

And when at Inspector Saunders's command he had left his chair and come and bent over her as she studied the map, so close to her that her bright head was almost against his shoulder and she was practically in his arms, his emotions had gone completely out of control, and though he might see how dangerously bright the flame might be round which he was fluttering, he was absolutely incapable of keeping away from it. He knew that if there were any complaint about his behaviour towards the girl, there would be a very black mark against him at the Yard, and he was intensely keen on his career; but it all went for nothing as he hung about in the chill of the morning after a sleepless night, just watching for the flutter of her skirt.

He heard sounds of activity coming from the kitchen,

and immediately turned to the table in the window where the brown varnished boxes that travelled in their case at the back of the side-car had been deposited, and began to un-pack them. Out came a microscope of a very superior make, and its accompanying gadgets; likewise a camera and its gad-gets. Another case, when its cover came off, revealed rows of little phials and test-tubes, a complete miniature labora-tory. The portable typewriter and a few files completed the equipment. Austen sat at the table with his back to the door, making believe to fiddle about with his outfit, certain that sooner or later Ann would come in to do the room, and then she would have to say a few words at any rate to him, and he would be able to look at her and feel that she was near him. His heart was beating in anticipation as it used to beat before boxing contests when he was new to the ring. He heard quick light footsteps come down the passage, and the door opened and in came Ann with a broom in her hand.

"Hullo?" she said, "what are you doing here?"

She was so taken by surprise at seeing him when she con-fidently believed herself to be alone that she was completely off her guard, and spoke to him as one human being to an-other. He, for his part, was so entranced by the familiarity of her greeting that his head was going round as if he had had a punch on the jaw and he could not find a word to say to her, but rose up from his chair like a prehistoric beast out of its wallow, and stood helplessly before her. His confusion re-called her to the necessity for keeping the situation in hand, and she turned to the equipment on the table as being the easiest thing about which to make conversation and so break the embarrassing silence.

"What fascinating little bottles," she exclaimed, "and a microscope! This really is like the detectives I have always read about."

Austen stood so close to her that she felt like driving her

elbow violently into his waistcoat to teach him to keep his distance.

"I suppose you thought," he said, "that old Saunders ought to have had a violin and a hypodermic syringe and a dressing-gown ?"

"Well, hasn't he?" said Ann, "I shall be exceedingly disappointed if he hasn't."

"You'd be worse disappointed if he had. He knows as much about music as a cow, and as for dope—well, he can hardly be got to take a glass of beer when he's on a job."

"What do you do with all these fascinating little gadgets ?" asked Ann, genuinely interested, for she was a keen crime fan during the long winter evenings when she read in bed. In his enthusiasm for his craft the man forgot his excitement and embarrassment, and became rational, for the time being at any rate.

"I can do all sorts of things with them," he said. "Test for blood-stains and tell you what kind of blood it is, bird, beast or human; and I can tell you what kind of dust we find in a chap's pockets or on his hat, and what kind of mud is on his boots. Or if we find something odd in a bottle, I can generally form some idea as to what it is, and that saves a lot of time when you are out on a case, for otherwise you are always sending things away by post to the central laboratory and are often held up till you get the answer."

"How awfully interesting," said Ann. "So this is what they teach you to do when you go to Scotland Yard ?"

"No," said Austen smiling, "it is what I taught them to do. This equipment is all my own idea, and there are half a dozen others like it now, and I have taught the chaps to use them. I should have been an industrial chemist if my old dad had not fallen off a scaffolding. I had got as far as my Inter B.Sc. when I had to turn round and hunt a job at short notice. I couldn't make use of my scholarship any longer because I had nowhere to live when the home broke up, and mother had to have all the compensation because she was an invalid. I was half-way to nowhere, and all I had to offer was my size. I did not see the fun of being a navvy, so I joined the police."

"And when you got there, they made you a detective because you had studied chemistry?"

"Well, not quite that. I had two years in the uniformed force before I got my chance."

They were both so interested that they had forgotten how cold it was, and Ann's broom rested in her hand unused.

The man poured it all out as if his life depended on explaining himself to Ann, who listened like the wedding-guest to this strange breath of a wider life that was blowing into the narrow confines of her existence; her mind nourished on Sherlock Holmes and Dr. Thorndyke, quite able to appreciate the subtleties of his explanations.

"There had been some vitriol-throwing in a model dwelling in one of the back streets of Paddington when I was in Division F. I was on the stairs keeping order while the C.I.D. men were going through the flat of the girl who was supposed to have done the throwing, and I heard one of the 'tees say, 'There' has been some funny smelling sort of hair-wash in this bottle.' And the other fellow said to him, 'We'd better send it to be analysed.' And I put my head round the door and said to them, 'You don't need to do that if you will let me pop out to the chemist on the corner and get some litmus paper; I'll soon tell you if it was acid or not'; and it so happened that my super was there, though I hadn't seen him, or I probably shouldn't have dared to put in my spoke with the 'tees, and he recommended me for the C.I.D., which is the plum of the force, in my opinion."

"And did you catch the woman who had thrown the vitriol?"

33

"You bet we did. But it was knowing right on the nail what had been in that bottle which made all the difference. For we should not have dared to arrest her until we knew, and if we had had to wait to send it to be analysed, she would have vanished like a fish in a pond."

At that moment a distant church clock struck seven and Ann pulled herself together.

"This won't do," she said. "Inspector Saunders said he wanted breakfast at eight."

"Am I in your way here?" asked Austen.

"You are not in my way," said Ann, "but I am afraid you will not find it very comfortable while I am doing the room. Won't you come along to the study? There is a heating-lamp there, and it will soon get warm."

Austen, looking rather crestfallen, for he had hoped to chat with her, and maybe lend a hand while she did her housework, followed her down the passage that ran the length of the house, past the kitchen, and on to a door at the far end.

She opened the door, and then recoiled back into his arms as if shot and snatched the door shut behind her; but not before he had seen, lying on the sofa in a huddled heap, a man in evening dress looking like a dilapidated waiter. There was no need for the experienced police officer to ask what was the matter with that man. He was too obviously dead drunk.

Ann was too upset to realize that Austen was holding her in his arms, and he had the sense to release her and shepherd her gently down the passage into the kitchen before she came out of her daze.

She sat huddled on the hard kitchen chair into which he put her, and looked up at him miserably.

"You have a hard row to hoe," he said in a low voice.

"It's not too bad," said Ann, struggling desperately to

34

pull herself together and put some sort of a face on the matter. "He doesn't often get like this. In fact, I've never seen him like this before. I know he takes more than is good for him, but this—this is exceptional."

At that moment the kettle providentially boiled over and Ann rose to attend to it.

"Shall we have a cup of tea ?" she said.

"I'd love it," said Austen.

There was no time for more than a hasty cup, drunk by Ann as she went about her work, for she did not wish to give Inspector Saunders a late breakfast upon his first morning in the house.

"Do smoke if you want to," said Ann.

Austin grinned. "And advertise to old Saunders that I'm hanging around your kitchen?"

"Would he mind ?"

"Goodness knows what the old blighter'd mind. Depends which side of the bed he gets out on. Anyway, there is no point in leading him into temptation."

Ann suddenly glimpsed a fresh difficulty in dealing with Austen. The slightest sign of resentment towards him on her part, and he would be in trouble with his official superior. And then it dawned on her that what he had seen through the half-open door of the study effectually prevented her from putting on any airs with him. How could she, the daughter of that degenerate wreck, reduced to letting lodgings in order to keep a roof over both their heads, hold herself superior to the clean-living police officer of unblemished character? Sickly she realized that Inspector Saunders, with his doubtful aitches and exceedingly plebeian manners, was probably a far better father than Francis Studley, and that his daughters would have an infinitely better chance in life than she had. She picked up a basket of kindling and went hastily down the passage to the dining-room.

35

Austen, left alone, hardly heard her go, so deep was he in his thoughts. The discovery of what her father was like put a different complexion on the whole matter. The girl might have been born to a very different position to his, as Inspector Saunders had rubbed into him until he was raw, but her father had already brought her down pretty low, and he would bring her lower yet before he had finished. He himself had got an assured position, and pay that many a black-coated worker would not have despised. He knew that he was considered at the Yard to have a brilliant future opening up before him as the acknowledged leader of the younger school of detectives, an estimate from which his forceful nature saw no reason to dissent. Why should he look upon himself as the moth with the flame? The girl was by no means out of his reach under the circumstances. Times had changed since Inspector Saunders had formed his opinions. The working classes, thanks to universal education, had come up; and the upper classes, thanks to Lloyd George and the War, had come down, and the younger generation were beginning to meet and mate. He was quite aware that Mr. Studley would expect to be addressed by him as sir, and would address him as Austen; but it seemed to him that if he were very careful not to give offence in the early stages, and moved very slowly until the girl got used to him, his chances were by no means negligible. He knew that he had had a dashed sight better education at his council school than she had had at her private school. He also had no false modesty about his personal appearance; his photograph, both in uniform and with as little on as possible, was in great demand with the health and strength magazines. His quarters in the police barracks were one mass of cups, medals and shields. He considered that, man for man, he was a match for anyone she was likely to find in her own class. He also had seen that she was a keen crime fan, and that his profession had a glamour for her.

Consequently, when Inspector Saunders descended to his breakfast, he found awaiting him a subordinate clothed and in his right mind, which was more than he had expected from the way the lad had been capering round the girl the previous evening. He was exceedingly relieved; for not only did he not want any disciplinary complications with a subordinate for whom he had a very genuine affection, but he would have been exceedingly sorry to see the boy burn his fingers. They had not worked together for six years without his discovering that underneath the mask which discipline imposed on him, the younger man had a hot and passionate nature, and took things hard. He wouldn't mind the lad having a bit of fun, so long as the young lady or her father did not turn rusty; but he very definitely did not want a serious affair on young Austen's side, because with a young lady like that there could be nothing doing for him; and then there would be the devil and all to pay if Jack took it hard, as he certainly would, if Saunders knew him; and he would be very sorry to see a good man dish his career for the sake of a woman. They weren't worth it.

So Inspector Saunders lapped his tea from his saucer in peace, for his subordinate no longer watched the door like a cat at a mousehole, but was behaving like a rational being.

Presently they heard a slow, shuffling tread go down the passage and laboriously mount the stairs.

"That's the old man, I expect," said Saunders. "Sounds a bit shaky on his pins."

"He was as tight as a drum last night," said Austen.

"Did you see him?"

"Saw him this morning. His door was open and I couldn't help seeing him. He never got up to bed at all. Slept on the sofa in his study."

"Nice for the girl," said Saunders. Austen did not comment.

"Ann," came a voice from upstairs.

"Yes, father?" they heard Ann's clear tones replying.

"Who does that side-car belong to that is in the garage?"

"To the visitors who are stopping here."

"Visitors?" cried the fractious voice. "Do you mean to say you have got some visitors here?"

"Yes, father," they heard Ann reply. "Two men."

"Two men?" the voice expressed unutterable exasperation. "Are they respectable?"

"I don't know, father; we shall have to wait and see."

"Gee, that's one for us, Chief!" exclaimed Austen, and they both shook with noiseless laughter, for they knew that Ann knew they could hear what was being said, and was guying them.

"She's a sport, that lassie," whispered Saunders. "She likes a bit of fun. But don't you go too far, my boy, we don't want the old man on our track."

"Do you mean to say you took these men in without asking who they were?" came the acidulated tones from upstairs.

"Oh, no, father," Ann's voice was like honey.

"Well, who are they?" rasped the man.

"Detectives, father."

There was a dead silence upstairs, and they heard a bedroom door close softly.

"That's put the fear of God into him!" exclaimed Saunders. "What's the old boy got on his conscience?"

"Plenty, from the looks of him," said Austen. "But it is unlikely to be the Gregory case."

"Now what grounds have you got for saying that, my lad? Because the girl is a nice girl is no reason for saying the old man mayn't be an old—. Surely you know by now that the firm we work for expects us to trust nobody and suspect everybody? We'll just put him through the sieve as a matter of routine."

But it did not prove to be an altogether easy matter to get Mr. Studley on to the sieve. For elusiveness he gave the famous Pimpernel of the classics points and a licking. He got up after the detectives had gone out, and he came in after they had gone to bed, and the days went by and they never caught a glimpse of him. Inspector Saunders did not wish to appear to be seeking him out, and so, in his own expressive words, put up the game before he had located the nest; which, being translated, meant to scare the criminal into flight before enough evidence had been pieced together to make it safe to arrest him; neither did he wish to waste a working day hanging about until the sluggard should bestir himself, especially as the sluggard would probably take a turn for the worse in such circumstances, and become safely bed-ridden. He knew that Mr. Studley, being impecunious, was unlikely to do a bolt even if guilty, unless he had definite reason to feel himself suspected, so Saunders got on with the job of combing the district to see if he could trace where certain articles had been purchased, which the experts told him had played a part in the tragedy. So far his efforts had not met with any success.

He was also trying to learn if anyone had been seen coming or going in the neighbourhood of Deepdene Hall on the fatal night. Its proximity to a main arterial road made this a difficult matter; but the fact that the grounds were walled and there was a lodge at the gate somewhat narrowed the range of the quest. A car could not have come in unnoticed, but a cycle or a foot-passenger might have done so, for the gatekeeper and his family retired early and slept the sleep of the just.

The field of research was further narrowed by the river, which, though not wide, was both deep and swift at that point. The nearest bridge was six miles up-stream, and there was no bridge down-stream, nor any other mode of crossing till you came to the ferry at its mouth, where it joined the Thames. No one could cross by the ferry without the assistance of the ferryman, who had ample opportunity, in sculling his skiff across, to take note of his passengers. Austen had been dispatched to visit this worthy, and had drawn blank.

The bridge at Casley was immediately opposite a public house, which was "chucking out" at the time when the murder took place, and there had been knots of loungers outside it, none of whom had seen anything suspicious. All cars crossing the bridge had to take the bend by the public-house at a foot-pace owing to its dangerous nature, and the loungers had been able to tell the detectives exactly who had come and gone—three lots of young people from a party, all well known in the neighbourhood; two doctors, and an elderly commercial traveller who did not travel in that district, but always came home that way for his week-ends and was known to everybody by sight. Austen patiently traced everyone of these and got their fingerprints; his method being to hand them his professional visiting-card and inquire whether they had seen the faithful Bugatti, which appeared to haunt the scene of all Inspector Saunders's cases; and after they had replied in the negative, as they naturally would, for the Bugatti only existed in Saunders's imagination, to recapture his card, a feat at which long practice had made him extraordinarily expert, the card simply vanishing into thin air without the victim noticing it.

The taking of finger-prints, however, was something of the nature of needle-hunting in haystacks, for the murderer had been discreet enough to wear gloves. Despite this, however, the Finger-print Department at Scotland Yard had still got a shot in its lockers; for the C.R.O. (Criminal Record Office) has a memory as long as that of the Recording Angel, and in its archives was the information that this was not the first time that men had died as Mr. Gregory had died, suddenly and horribly by poisoning with cyanide of potassium, a poison rarely used for murder because it acts so quickly that the victim dies in the presence of his murderer, and sometimes dies noisily.

If any of the finger-prints associated with any of those cases were found among the specimens taken among the associates of the Gregorys, the person owning them would be asked to give a very comprehensive and detailed account of his comings and goings, and from that inquiry much might transpire.

Scotland Yard keep the finger-prints associated with unsolved poison mysteries when they throw away the finger-prints of burglars by dozens, because a poisoner, having got away with it once, and having enjoyed the thrill of the power of life and death, can seldom resist the temptation to try his luck again. Juries will not convict in murder cases if they can help it, for when they look at the face of the man sitting quietly in the dock so near to them, they feel no better than murderers themselves when they think of him being hanged by the neck till he is dead. Many more murderers would get convicted if hanging were not the only punishment for murder. It is the irrevocableness of the punishment that worries juries. Circumstantial evidence has got to be very, very strong before they will accept it, and when the evidence is scientific and consists in the behaviour of chemicals in test-tubes, it is beyond their comprehension and carries no conviction to their minds. Consequently, it is a very careless poisoner indeed who does not get the benefit of the doubt, juries not realizing that when they will not take the responsibility of condemning one man to death by hanging on the evidence of a government analyst, they are probably condemning two or three others to death by torture.

CHAPTER THREE

AUSTEN privately thought that it was a waste of energy bothering with Mr. Studley. It was not an easy matter to get his finger-prints, as it was hardly possible to introduce oneself to him by handing him a visiting-card after residing in his house for the best part of a week, and random finger-prints are seldom satisfactory in a house cleaned by such as Ann, and Saunders did not wish the wide-awake Ann to see them peppering the woodwork and then photographing it, and so have her suspicions aroused and warn her father.

But Saunders was in no hurry. He had the infinite patience of the experienced detective. The bird would not flit so long as it was left alone, of that he was confident. The only thing, he had to fear was suicide. Police officers hate losing a prisoner by suicide; they feel it reflects on them professionally and are strongly prejudiced against justice being done in this manner, regardless of the saving in expense to the taxpayer.

Saunders did not expect suicide on the part of Mr. Studley, however, even if he were the guilty party (and it was by no means certain if he were; in fact, it was in many ways unlikely, for he was on the wrong side of the river for the job); it is a notable fact that poisoners very seldom commit suicide; they have had too much opportunity for studying death at close quarters to fancy it when applied to themselves. Moreover, poisoning is a coward's job, and to do away with oneself requires courage.

Saunders decided not to hurry Mr. Studley. All the same, he would not be sorry to see the last of the case, for he did not at all like the way his subordinate was hanging round Ann. She was a very nice young lady; he had nothing against her; in fact, he had taken a decided fancy to her, and thought that she reciprocated, judging by the way she joked and laughed with him and looked after his little comforts as if he had been her father.

There was always a bright fire when he came home on a chilly evening, with his enormous carpet-slippers toasting in front of it. Austen despised slippers, and if his feet were wet, walked about in his socks till they dried; but Saunders was getting on in years and liked a little luxury. Sausage and mash made a frequent appearance in the menu after she had learnt of his partiality to it, and so did fish and chips for the same reason. Tea was brewed at all hours for his consolation and refreshment, and Inspector Saunders could drink Mr. Studley under the table when it came to tea. But in spite of all the amenities of his billet, Saunders would be thankful to see the end of the case, for the last thing he wanted was trouble with Austen, with whom he had worked amicably for years.

Without Austen, he would have been lost, for he had got used to relying on him. He himself was the old-fashioned type of thief-taker, a lineal descendant of the Bow Street runners. Son of an agricultural labourer, he had tramped up to London, sleeping under hedges, and been accepted into the Metropolitan Police on the ground of his fine physique and decent, honest face. His education had been of the scantiest. His literary attainments were limited to scratching out epistles that were kept as curios by the recipients; his reading was limited to the *Police Gazette* and the daily papers.

He was accurately described by Austen, however, when he told Ann that his revered chief was as cute as a wagon-load of monkeys. He also had the knack of getting the best out of the men under him, as witness Austen's affection and respect for him, and had brought generations of young detectives up in the way they should go. He was a very senior inspector indeed, but would never see superintendent's rank because of his lack of education and general roughness of demeanour, for the modern police officer of the higher ranks is by no means a rough diamond.

Saunders was a survival of an age that had passed away, but a highly respected and privileged survival, and they let him have Austen to be his Abishag and keep his ancient feet warm, for he could not have coped with modern detective methods single-handed. Austen, for his part, was well content to work with Saunders as second fiddle, though he could easily have demanded to lead his own orchestra, for promotion had been speeded up in the force recently, and Austen's qualifications from an educational point of view were exceptional, and just what was wanted in the rapidly developing art of the scientific detection of crime.

It was Saunders who had broken him in as a cub, however, when the young constable was picked out from the ranks, as he had told Ann, and given his chance to prove himself; and it was to Saunders he owed each successive chance that had come his way, for Saunders was an admirable nurseryman of subordinates if he detected any promise in them. If he managed to float off on his own, with a cub of his own, he thought that the old detective would have to take his long-overdue pension, which would break his heart. Austen, therefore, had determined to make no effort for any further promotion till the old man retired of his own accord, which could not be long now. Meanwhile, he got through Saunders the pick of the big cases; whereas, as a junior detective working on his own, he would have had to fiddle about with petty larcenies, which would bore him very much indeed.

So the arrangement suited both parties; and divisional superintendents, who had been licked into shape by Saunders in the days of their youth, and even greater luminaries, who owed not a little to the shrewd old officer's advice, let the old boy go his own way, especially as his way nearly always led someone else to Dartmoor or Portland, or other eligible residences at His Majesty's disposal. Detectives are born, not made, and the police staff college can do no more than put a polish on suitable material.

There were not many men at the Yard who could equal Saunders in natural capacity as a thief-taker; there were still fewer who could equal Austen in his scientific methods of criminal research; put the two together, and throw in Saunders's enormous experience and Austen's energy, and the combination was unrivalled. So the "powers that be" returned thanks to their Maker and let it alone to get on with its job.

A large part of a successful detective's equipment lies in a curious sixth sense, a combination of experience of crime and criminals, knowledge of human nature, native shrewdness, and a curious capacity to sense the "feel" of any individual with whom he is brought into contact, all churned up together in his subconscious mind and delivered on the surface as a kind of flair that bears more relation to the powers of the bloodhound, to which he is so often likened, than to any merely human capacity. Detectives rely on this quality in themselves, and their superiors trust it in an experienced man, to a far greater extent than the writers of crime fiction realize; and this sixth sense, together with pure chance, and the dogged perseverance and tireless patience which give chance an opportunity to operate on the law of averages, play a bigger part in bringing criminals to justice than any fanciful methods, to the success of which the criminal has himself to contribute by doing or being something quite out of the ordinary. If an "omnibus" volume of crime stories be read from cover to cover, it will be found that all the crimes possess more or less "fancy" features; whereas in the daily life of a professional detective, crimes are monotonously identical according to their various types, and outstanding features are few. So monotonous are they, that in five cases out of six he can turn them up in a card index and see who has done the job, for professional criminals are so stereotyped in their methods that they might almost be said to hang out a board with their name on it when doing a job, in the same way as decorators at work on a house. All the detective has to do, after using the index, is to find his man; and this generally only necessitates a call when he is at home in his usual haunts. Better and brighter crimes are badly needed if the Yard is to live up to detective fiction. The only time it lies awake over crime is when the amateur turns professional and brings a little intelligence and imagination to the job. But usually, owing to his lack of knowledge of the ropes of the underworld, he gets caught out before he has time to "play himself in."

It was because the Gregory case was obviously not a professional job—murder seldom is—and because it had been so carefully thought out that the alibis of every possible suspect were of cast-iron, that Saunders and Austen were detailed for it. It was the complete lack of evidence which showed that they were dealing with a foeman worthy of the best steel that the Yard could produce. It also showed that no prentice hand was at work. It is a maxim in criminology that poisonings never come singly. Once the poisoner has discovered a satisfactory technique, he deals death light-heartedly for any fancied slight or remote risk. Saunders suspected that the death of Mr. Gregory was not the first of its kind to come from the same hand; but as the Gregorys were comparatively recent corners to the neighbourhood and had previously lived in London, it was very difficult to know where to start looking for the other corpses.

Saunders's resources at the moment were practically limited to flair and luck, and if these failed him, he would have to go home with his tail between his legs, which he hated. The only thing he hated worse than this was to arrest an innocent man.

So far he had seen no one he had fancied as a likely starter, with the possible exception of Mr. Studley, whom, to be strictly accurate, he had not seen at all. But his suspicions had been roused in the first instance by the sudden subsidence of that gentleman when his daughter had shouted the information at him that there were detectives in the house. Secondly, the extreme elusiveness of their host could hardly be looked upon as normal. The natural thing for a man to do, who had to be out all day, leaving a young daughter alone in the house with two strange men, was to have a look at those men and see what sort of chaps they were. In fact the natural instinct of any man was to want to know who was under his roof. Saunders could not attribute this coyness on the part of Mr. Studley to anything save a guilty conscience. And yet a conscience can prick very actively when guilty of many things besides murder.

Mr. Studley might have been doing nothing more desperate than selling tickets in a sweepstake, or have a wireless without a licence, or even be running a mild form of long-firm swindle, which seemed very probable from what he could hear of him in the village. Because a chap bolts like a rabbit at the sight of the man in blue, it does not follow he is guilty of an indictable offence; least of all of an offence that would be worthy of the powder and shot of such a big gun as Chief Inspector Saunders, the doyen of the C.I.D. Saunders would no more have pursued the investigation of the robbery of a hen-roost which he might have chanced upon in the course of his work, than any other member of the general public. He would have loftily informed the local police of his observations, and left them to get on with it, without even deigning to offer advice.

He cared nothing for the shysterings of the boozing Mr. Studley. His host was safe from him even if he committed petty larceny under his very nose.

It was simply a kind of mulishness, which disliked having the fixed habits of years upset, that made him determined to put Mr. Studley through his sieve along with the rest of the county; for when Inspector Saunders felt himself baffled, he was given to making inquiries simply for the sake of making inquiries, with a kind of reflex action, just as an infant's hands clutch anything they touch. Many of his successes were due to this habit, though he stoutly attributed them to be pure brains, and could generally think of something which, in the light of what came out under cross examination at the trial, he could twist into a clue. Austen, the more intellectual, better educated man, would have abandoned the case long ago for lack of intelligible clues—provided, of course it had been an ordinary case with no Ann in it. As it was, the young detective would have found clues, or pretended to find them, in the moon or the bottomless Pit.

Saunders knew perfectly well he was being jollied along by Austen with his pseudo-clues—clues that his keen-minded subordinate would not have looked at twice when in his sober senses. But Austen was not in his sober senses these days, and Saunders was worried about it. The fellow was hanging round the girl far too much. Her father would kick up a shine sooner or later; ought to have done it long ago if he had any notion of the duties of a father according to Inspector Saunders's lights. The girl herself had been inclined to jib at first, but he was not so sure what she was up to now. Austen was a darned good-looking chap, even if he were of plebeian origin. Saunders was a shrewd observer of human nature, and very little in the way of emotional reactions escaped his little pig's eyes, even when he shut them, as he generally did for forty winks after meals.

He could see that Ann carefully avoided looking at Austen. He could see that Austen never took his eyes off Ann. He guessed that Austen must have the run of the kitchen, because on one occasion when Saunders had wanted tea when Ann was out shopping, Austen had made it, and known exactly where to put his hands on everything, even to Ann's best tea-spoons.

Saunders wondered what Ann was getting at, and felt righteously indignant with her. She ought to know better than to play about with a chap like Austen. Austen was too good a fellow to be messed up. He had not lived and worked with the young detective for years without learning that Austen left women severely alone. Consequently, he would get it in the neck when his time came. Saunders had never seen Austen carrying on like this before. He was thoroughly uneasy about it, partly because he had a very genuine affection for the lad and did not want to see him hurt, and partly because he knew what an unholy mess it would make if there were a rumpus over his subordinate's behaviour towards the girl.

Saunders had a vision of Ann having enough of her plebeian admirer and putting him in his place, and he knew what Austen's temper was like when he got upset. She might find it useful enough to have a hefty young man to get the coals in for her (Saunders had heard bumpings from the coal-shed at the same time that he had heard clinkings of crockery from the dining room), but she might not find things quite so pleasant if Austen got out of hand and let himself go. He was no la-di-dah university man in whose mouth butter would not melt. The fair and aristocratic Ann would probably hear a few home-truths she would not care about if she played with Austen and then dropped him.

In fact, Saunders suspected, she might not find it particularly easy to drop him. He was a pertinacious beggar with an excellent opinion of himself. Saunders saw himself let in for all manner of trouble if he could not control his subordinate.

He seriously cogitated whether he should give Ann a talking-to; tell her that she was playing with fire, and Austen was the sort of chap who would explode on her hands if she did not mind what she was about. Knowing Austen as he did, and his usual avoidance of all forms of philandering, he was afraid that the lad was taking things seriously, and would get badly hurt. It was inconceivable to him that Ann would take Austen seriously. Saunders cursed all women, individually and collectively, and thanked his stars he had always had the sense to avoid them.

He even thought of shifting his digs to another village, so as to remove Austen from the temptation of propinquity, but he was reluctant to do so until he had had the elusive Mr. Studley through his sieve and learnt whether there were any real cause for his suspicious behaviour. As soon as he had done that, he promised himself, he would hand in his checks at the Yard and pronounce the Gregory poisoning case an unsolved mystery, and, since the firm of Saunders and Austen had failed to solve it, an insoluble one.

Finally his patience was rewarded, but not until the detectives had been at Thatched Cottage nearly a fortnight, the Yard was getting restive, Austen was calling Ann by her Christian name, and Ann herself blushed pink if Saunders even mentioned Austen to her casually, as he did occasionally to watch her reactions.

Mr. Studley was feeling so sick and giddy after the previous evening's debauch that he even partook sparingly of dog-hairs that day, being alarmed at the condition to which he had reduced himself, and when the detectives returned in the evening he was not out in his car as he normally would have been, but sitting huddled up in his dressing-gown over the study fire. Ann at work in the kitchen with the door open for ventilation, for the room was low, heard Inspector Saunders go heavy-footed down the passage and knock at the study door and her father's voice bidding him enter. Then she saw the big bulk of Austen pass the half-open door like a shadow. She shot out into the passage, seized him by the sleeve and dragged him into the kitchen.

"What are you doing to my father?" she demanded of him, fierce as a little tigress.

"Nothing—nothing. It's only routine. We put everyone through the sieve as a matter of course for what we can get out of them. That's how we build up our cases. You went through it yourself the first night we were here. Didn't you see what the Chief was driving at? And you haven't got an alibi, either, let me tell you! Put that in your pipe and smoke it. Now let me get on with my job."

He gently detached her fingers from his sleeve and went cat-footed down the passage towards the door of her father's study. Then he opened a note-book, and began to take down in shorthand what was going on within. Ann sat down miserably on the bottom step of the stair and gazed at his boots. He gazed at her hair and had difficulties with his shorthand.

Politenesses and comments on the weather were still being exchanged when they took up their positions. Then they heard Inspector Saunders get down to business. Ann, in the light of her experience of his methods knew how he was going to work, and admired his cleverness. Her father, she could tell by his voice, still thought they were exchanging blandishments.

"You must find this weather trying, sir, getting about the country the way you do, and with your poor health."

"No, oh no," replied Mr. Studley patronizingly. "It makes no difference in a closed car. It is not like your open side-car, where you are exposed to every wind that blows. And in any case, I have no choice. My work obliges me to be out at all hours. You see, I have, among other things, an agency for agricultural supplies, and I have to catch my customers, in many cases, after their day's work."

Ann wished he had not replied to questions before they were asked, as if he knew he were suspect and had to clear himself.

"Yes, indeed, sir. No one knows what irregular hours mean better than we do. No trade union hours in our trade. Now, sir, I believe you can simplify my job a lot for me, if you would be so kind. Could you tell me whether a small, high-powered car of foreign make, probably a Bugatti, has been going about these lanes at night recently?"

"Not to my knowledge," said Mr. Studley.

"Now could you show me on this map where Deepdene Hall is. We can't find the place."

"It is not very far to seek," said Mr. Studley. "You can see its chimneys across the river from the bedroom window. It used to be called Gug Hall, but when Gregory bought it he changed the name to Deepdene Hall. The old name had no associations for him, and it is undeniably ugly."

Ann looked at Austen in blank amazement at this statement, but his face was expressionless.

The dialogue continued.

"Your daughter tells me you were at home on the night of the 12th, Mr. Studley—"

A low cry escaped from Ann as she saw the trap. Austen scowled at her angrily and raised his finger for silence.

"—Did you hear any shout, or the sound of a struggle, from across the river?"

"I am afraid I was not in the house the whole of the evening. I went down to the Black Horse, the inn in the hamlet half a mile from here. I had a little business to transact with a man who is, unfortunately, given to frequenting such places. I left there when it closed at ten o'clock and returned here. I tried to phone Watts's garage about my car, which was being decarbonized, but could not get through, the line was dead. So I walked up half a mile the other way, to the village of Dinton, where the garage is, and made my inquiries in person."

"And you did not see anything of the Bugatti in the lanes?"

"Nothing at all."

"Nor hear its engine-note? Do you know the engine-note of a Bugatti, sir? It is very distinctive when it is travelling at speed."

"Not to identify it. One can hear the cars on the main road fairly clearly on a still night, and they are constantly passing. I could not undertake to pick out the sound of one from among the rest of the noises."

"Thank you, sir. I don't think I need worry you with any more questions. I see you are looking tired. Bed is the best place for you if you have got a chill on you, sir, if you don't mind my saying so. Perhaps you will be good enough to keep your eyes and ears open as you go about the country, and let me know if you pick up anything of interest?"

Austen caught Ann's eye and jerked his thumb commandingly towards the kitchen door, and she took the hint and crept silently away before Inspector Saunders had finished discussing remedies for chills with her father, and had trampled heavily down the passage back to his sitting room with the silent-footed Austen at his heels.

CHAPTER FOUR

ANN sat gazing into the fire in the kitchen trying to piece together what she had heard and penetrate its significance. The behaviour of Austen, stealthily spying on her father, had thoroughly alarmed her. Did they suspect him of murdering Mr. Gregory? She was greatly puzzled by the fact that he had denied all knowledge of Deepdene Hall to her, and had kept his counsel about such a mutually interesting matter as the change of its name. Why this secretiveness? She felt sure his duplicity would go against him with the detectives, whose deep voices she could hear across the little hall of the cottage, presumably discussing the case.

She was truly thankful that her father had been able to produce such a cast-iron alibi. With his car being decarbonized, it was obvious that he could not have left the Black Horse when it closed at ten, and gone six miles up and six miles down the river to Gug Hall, and got to the garage at half-past ten, which was the hour at which Mr. Gregory had been found dead.

And then it suddenly occurred to her that it was not a cast-iron alibi for anyone who knew the district. When Inspector Saunders had asked her whether it was possible to cross the river by walking on the weir, she had replied in the negative, and it had never occurred to her, excited as she was by the unexpected incursion of detectives into her quiet life, and the heavy breathing of Austen almost in her ear, to mention the stepping-stones just below the weir. Not many people knew them in the district, a few of the ancients, maybe, who had worked at Gug Hall in the old days, and had made use of them for coming and going between the big house and the bailiff's cottage. They were not readily observable by a stranger, now that the path that led to them was overgrown, for they ran diagonally across the river, being partly natural and partly artificial, and anyone observing the river from above, where it ran in a miniature gorge, would never suspect the sudden reef of rocks that stood up in it round the next bend and hidden by trees. Ann saw at once that the presence of the stepping-stones knocked the bottom out of her father's alibi, for he could easily have crossed to Gug Hall, as it would always be called in the district, murdered Mr. Gregory, and still had time to show himself at the garage as he had said, and as the detectives would no doubt verify in the morning.

Ann sat gazing into the fire and trying to assess the significance of this discovery. It never occurred to her to consider the possibility of her father's complicity in the murder, if murder there had been, and even Inspector Saunders had not appeared very certain upon this point; and she came to the conclusion that her father, who was no better than he should be, and had already been in trouble with the local police over betting, had probably been in some sort of sordid mischief again, which he did not wish to be dragged into the light of publicity.

* * *

Meanwhile the two detectives were piecing together the bits of their jigsaw puzzle.

"Well, my lad?" said Inspector Saunders to his subordinate, "what do you think of what the fellow had to say and the way he said it?"

"Don't like his alibi, sir."

55

"Neither do I, my lad. Too darn perfect. And why did the fellow tell the girl he knew nothing about Gug Hall and the Gregorys when he knew all about 'em?"

"I doubt if there's much in that, sir. He's drinking like a fish, and if she asked him when he was half-sober, as he was this morning, he might have answered like that out of pure cussedness. It may, of course, mean that he knows more than he cares to tell; but on the other hand, it may just be a tipsy man's silliness. How many chaps have you and I seen behave suspiciously who had had no more to do with a job than the man in the moon?"

Saunders looked at his subordinate curiously. How was it that Jack Austen, usually so shrewd, could not see how ugly that alibi began to look when you picked it to pieces. Why, of all nights, should the exceedingly elusive Mr. Studley be at home on this particular night? And by his own choice, for you choose when you will have your car decarbonized; it is an operation for a chronic, not an acute condition. He had his alibi slick and ready for the one night in the year when it was going to be needed, and he volunteered it before he was asked for it. Inspector Saunders did not like the look of it at all, and wondered that Austen was not giving tongue on the trail with his usual celerity.

Then he remembered the girl. If young Austen were really keen on the girl, as he sincerely hoped he wasn't, it was going to complicate matters considerably. Austen, during the six years they had worked together, had had one or two spasms of pity when his sympathies had been roused over a case, and this Inspector Saunders considered a most debilitating weakness in a detective. If Austen started trying to shield old Studley for the girl's sake, he would not be pulling his weight in the case. Saunders had nothing against Mr. Studley, except that fishy alibi which he himself had provided, but he was a very experienced detective, and a born thief-taker, and he had summed up Francis Studley as being in a blue funk and trying to drown it in drink, with disastrous consequences to his nerve and morale. If old Studley kept on drinking, and Austen kept on palling up to the girl, whatever there might be in the affair would come out sooner or later. One thing was quite certain, however, if either the girl or Austen smelt a rat, they would both draw in their horns. It would not be safe to ask a man of Austen's temperament to try and pump the girl he was sweet on. On the other hand, he was pretty certain that if Austen learnt anything definite, he would not be disloyal to his cloth. The best thing would be to let the case hatch with its own heat; give young Austen plenty of disciplinary rope, and let nature do the rest. He was sorry for the boy, he stood to burn his fingers properly over the girl; but a career as a successful detective does not tend to cultivate any abnormal development of the tender sentiment of pity, and as long as Austen did not disgrace his teacher by dishing his career, Saunders was not disposed to take a reasonable amount of heartache too seriously. "Men have died, and worms have eaten them, but not for love." The boy would get over it, and possibly become a confirmed bachelor like himself, which was a pleasing prospect to the childless man, who in his secret heart was making something of a son of the young officer he had trained in his craft so successfully.

So Chief Inspector Saunders, with his little pig's eyes twinkling mildly, said to Detective Sergeant Austen, who was gazing into space with a beatific expression on his face:

"The old boy has probably been getting into a bit of mischief, as you say. Running after women, most likely. Unsatisfactory sort of cuss, but probably no real vice in him."

"That's just how I summed him up," said the young detective, obviously relieved. He was still more relieved that Saunders did not tell him to make any inquiries at the garage, apparently thinking the alibi not sufficiently important to take seriously. Old Studley was probably trying to save his face over some wretched barmaid; let him save his face if he wanted to; it was of some use to him, and of none to anybody else.

"I had no end of a song and dance with the girl while you were interviewing the old man," he said at length.

"You did, did you? What bit her ?"

"I think she made up her mind you were going to arrest her respected parent then and there. She saw me padding down the passage like a burglar, and she pounced on me and hauled me into the kitchen and pretty nearly put a gun to my head; wanting to know what we were up to with the old chap. She seems to be fond of that tank of a father of hers. No accounting for tastes, is there, sir?"

"He wouldn't be my fancy," said Saunders. "What happened then?"

"I tried to smooth her down. Told her it was just routine. I thought it was, I did honestly."

"Well," said Saunders dryly, "I hope you'd have done the same even if you hadn't."

"Then she followed me out into the hall, and I had the devil's own job to make her keep quiet. I couldn't turf her out because the old boy would have heard us arguing, and that would have spilled the beans properly. So I let her stop, and glared at her whenever she showed signs of getting out of hand."

"Where is she now?"

"Hopped it into the kitchen when she heard you saying good-bye to her parent."

"Then you'd better hop after her and calm her down. Tell her we wouldn't have her pa as a gift. I don't want no young women having hysterics while I'm about."

Austen did not need to be told twice. He found Ann in

58

the kitchen sitting on a hard chair in front of the fire. There was no other chair available, so he sat down on the table without waiting to be asked.

"I thought I'd come and put your mind at ease," he said. "I saw you thought we were after your father, but honestly, it was just routine. I asked old Saunders point-blank if he had any suspicions of your father, and he said no. He doesn't care two hoots about him. We are not even bothering to go up to the garage and verify his alibi."

Ann's relieved face told him how acute her anxiety had been. "I was awfully worried," she said, "when I heard him telling two different stories about Deepdene Hall. I couldn't think what he was driving at. But then I remembered that he was nearly as bad as he was the other morning when I asked him, and he probably said it just to annoy."

"That's what we thought," said Austen; "we did not take him seriously. He's probably attending cock-fights or something. There is a lot of that going on nowadays, and he'd feel an awful fool if he were hauled up in front of the beak for cock-fighting. He just wants to be let alone; that's all that's the matter with him."

A slow, uncertain foot came down the passage and paused outside the kitchen door, and Mr. Studley came in, looking like death. He surveyed the man and the girl in silence, and a sickly smile spread over his ashen countenance.

"Good evening, sir," said Austen, leaping off the table and coming smartly to attention.

"May I introduce myself? Detective-Sergeant Austen, working under Chief Inspector Saunders. The Chief sent me along to set your young lady's mind at rest. I am afraid we scared her when the Chief asked to see you. She had made up her mind we meant to run you in. I've just been telling her that we never thought of any such thing. It's just our usual routine. We draw the net through the whole district, just on spec', and see what turns up."

"Then you have not got any definite clues yet, Sergeant?"

"Nothing definite, sir. There are always all sorts of things that might be clues, but when you come to investigate them, there's generally nothing in it. We are just working our way systematically through them."

Ann admired the diplomatic way in which he had told her father neither yes nor no in answer to his question. The more she saw of these men, the more she realized their skill and technique. The detective novels could not touch the real thing.

"You're looking badly, sir," said Austen. "Can I get you a chair? Is there another chair here, Miss Studley?"

"No, there isn't," said Ann. "He can have this one." And she went and perched herself beside Austen on the table. Her father lowered himself slowly and painfully into the chair she had vacated; he looked at the two of them as they sat side by side, the man and the girl, and he smiled his curious smile again. A kind of smile Ann had never seen before. Austen had, however.

"Gosh," he said to himself. "Isn't he like Armstrong, the poisoner!" Then he spoke again: "Look here, sir," he said, "if there is a chemist anywhere near here, I'll get you something that will put you right in two tweaks of a puppy-dog's tail."

"I doubt it, my lad," said Mr. Studley.

"I don't, sir," said Austen. "I am a pretty good hand at that sort of thing."

Ann was astonished to see her father and the policeman exchange what looked very much like winks.

"Thanks, my lad," said Mr. Studley, "I'd be very glad of it."

She heard Austen go down the path whistling gaily. He sounded exceedingly happy, she thought. As the sounds of the motor-cycle died away in the distance, Ann looked up and found her father still watching her with the curious smile that made her feel so uncomfortable.

"A very smart young fellow," he said. "The police have improved since the days when I was young and collided with them occasionally. Board-schools and all that. However, I expect underneath you would find what Kipling calls the 'raw, rough ranker.' "

Ann was surprised to find how much she resented her father's disparagement of Austen.

"I can never rid myself of the idea," he went on, "that a detective's work is dirty work. After all, what is he but a spy in civil life? There may be some romance round the work of a spy in war-time, when he risks his neck, but I am afraid I cannot appreciate the halo of romance with which detectives are surrounded in books.

"I used to know a man very well who had been a chief constable, and he told me you would not believe the amount of 'framing up' that goes on among the English police. It isn't so bad with the local police, but these C.I.D. chaps are terrible. They daren't go home without their prisoner. He said he had as much trouble keeping the C.I.D.s from arresting the wrong man and framing a case against him as he had in catching the criminal."

"Mr. Austen did not seem very hopeful about catching anyone in connection with the Gregory case," said Ann.

"Then all the worse for honest men, for they have got to have somebody. This young fellow may be all right, but that other pig-eyed chap would stick at nothing, if I'm any judge of men."

Ann was used to her father's disparagement of his fellow-men, but she was inclined to agree with his estimate of Inspector Saunders. She herself had felt the pressure, though carefully modulated in her case, of the iron hand inside the genial velvet glove of the elderly detective. He might be a kindly man in private life, and she thought he was, but she felt quite sure he would go over his best friend like a steam-roller if his duty required it.

"And the young chap will probably have to do what he is told, though it's no fault of his," Mr. Studley continued. "I believe the discipline in the Metropolitan Police is simply iron. If they find they can't break a man's will in the first year, they chuck him out. Hastings told me that they write out for a bobby what to say in evidence, and make him learn it off by heart and recite it when he goes into the witness-box; and you can tell that is so from the mechanical, wooden way in which they give their evidence. I know you are a detective fan, my dear, but I can't say I see them with any halo of romance around them. I know too much about them." He sighed deeply, and seemed sunk in gloomy meditation on the iniquities of the police force in general, and the C.I.D. in particular, till Austen returned with a bottle in his hand, when he welcomed him with a cordiality that belied his recent expression of distaste.

Mr. Studley coughed and spluttered over the dose the young detective mixed him, but in ten minutes he looked a different man.

When Ann arrived down next morning, she found the kitchen fire lit and the coal-scuttle filled.

"I thought I might as well make myself useful," said Austen. "I'm an early bird. I can't sleep after it gets light."

They made tea and drank it together: He did not seem to have much to say for himself this morning; his steady stare embarrassed her, for he seemed to watch every movement she made, so she cast about for something to say, and found nothing more mutually interesting than his work. So while she made the toast and fried the bacon, she learnt something of the methods of the Criminal Investigation Department from first-hand sources, and they struck her as being surprisingly different from the methods of the story-book detectives.

"Our best friend is the common informer," said Austen. "We generally know who has done a job, but to prove it to a jury is another matter."

"Then you don't work out your cases by long trains of reasoning from clue to clue."

"Not as a rule. We work from a number of short ends. We apply common sense rather than any fancy sort of psycho-analysis. Put yourself in the other fellow's place, and you get a pretty good notion of what he has done and how he did it."

"What are the most difficult criminals to catch?" asked Ann.

"Amateurs," said Austen. "Especially if they haven't planned things much, but have acted on impulse. It's a jolly difficult thing to prove who did the job when a chap has been slogged on the head with his own poker and no one is missing from the district. It is when the criminal begins to gild the lily that he finds himself in the soup. That's always the trouble with the educated amateur, he tries to be too clever and so draws attention to himself. And the professional is so darn careless he simply walks into our arms. Do you know, Miss Studley, that the thing that has hanged more men than anything else is their alibis? Bust up an alibi, and the fellow is as good as jugged. But if a chap sits tight and says he can't remember where he was on a particular evening, what can you do with him? You may suspect, but you can't prove; whereas, if he produces an alibi that isn't the genuine article we can generally shoot it as full of holes as a cullender. That's our speciality."

"What are the most difficult kinds of crime to detect?"

asked Ann, as he seemed disposed to lapse into silence and staring again.

"Well, I think they are poisoning cases," said Austen, "but then I suppose a chap always thinks his work is the most important cog in the machine."

"Do you specialize in poisoning cases?"

"As much as anyone can specialize in anything at the Yard. I am supposed to have a persuasive way with juries in poisoning cases. It is the devil's own job to get twelve British grocers to accept the evidence of an expert chemist; but I have got the knack of telling the tale most convincingly, and they believe me when they chuck out the evidence of the expert witnesses."

Ann remembered her father's words about the framing of cases by the C.I.D., and experienced a sudden feeling of revulsion for the young detective, who talked so cheerfully of hunting his fellow-men to the gallows.

"Do you think Mr. Gregory was poisoned?" she asked.

"I mustn't talk about my cases, Miss Studley; but I am here, so you can draw your own conclusions."

Ann carried the breakfast into the dining-room, and was affably greeted by Inspector Saunders.

"I hear a great deal of talking going on in the kitchen, missy," he said. "I gather you are attending lectures on the detection of crime."

Ann felt herself getting pink. "Well, it's very interesting," she said. "I have read so many detective novels that I consider myself a connoisseur of crime."

Saunders jerked his thumb towards the miniature laboratory on the table in the window.

"Proper Dr. Thorndyke, ain't he? Now if that young man of mine hadn't had his mind polluted by reading crime fiction, and had taken the heavy end of the log in detective work, and done the lifting, instead of taking the light end

64

and doing the grunting, there's no saying to what heights he might have risen."

Ann watched Austen preen himself in the sunshine of his superior officer's elephantine badinage, which evidently indicated approval. Subordinates are not chaffed unless they are in good standing.

"Now then, Jack, eat your breakfast," continued Inspector Saunders. "We must make an early start. I want you to run me up to the Yard, but I won't ask you to fetch me back, as I shall be doing a bit of work at the C.R.O., and I don't know when I shall be through with it, so you can take the day off. I leave him in your care, missy. See he doesn't get into mischief; he's a bad lad when he's turned loose."

Ann looked highly embarrassed at the idea of having the infatuated Austen on her hands for the day; and he for his part looked so absolutely blissful that Inspector Saunders had all he could do to keep a straight face.

They were undergoing one of those fugitive heat-waves that the English spring occasionally manages to produce, and when Austen got back from his run to Town he said to Ann:

"I say, Miss Ann, what about a bathe? Is the water really as warm as you say it is ?"

"Yes," said Ann, "it will be warm enough after all this sunshine, and you won't feel the cold wind because of the trees. I will show you the bathing-place and tell you what to steer clear of."

Austen's face fell. "I say, aren't you coming too? I shan't bathe if you don't. Come on in; it will be lovely on a day like this. I shan't bite. You'd be used enough to mixed bathing if you went to the London baths."

Ann adored bathing, and would, in fact have gone in herself if he had not returned so soon. (She wondered what speed he had done on the return journey; Saunders would not put up with high speeds when he was aboard), so she allowed herself to be beguiled against her better judgment, and when she came down wrapped in her gay bathing-cloak, she found Austen standing in the sunshine in his blue swimming-suit with the badge of the police sports association on the breast, looking a most magnificent specimen of manhood and twice the size he did in his clothes. Deprived of her heels, she was well below his shoulder.

They went silently down the path through the orchard, both a little embarrassed at the unconventional situation in which they found themselves, and when they reached the bathing place, Ann whipped off her cloak and dived with a single movement.

Austen came in with a dive that hardly rippled the water.

"Swim upstream," she called to him. "Never swim downstream from here; it is much too close to the weir."

They swam upstream a little way, but not very far, for the current was strong, and they had to swim three yards for every one they progressed. Then they drifted down on their backs with the current.

"I say," said Austen, suddenly rolling over in the water, and coming towards Ann with a fast racing stroke, "have you ever had your life saved?"

"No," cried Ann, divining his intention and darting away, "and I don't want to. I'd much sooner drown in comfort."

He laughed and came after her, moving half a dozen yards to her one, and she felt herself gripped under the arms and pulled on to her back. She knew better than to struggle, and so swallow water and choke, and she lay passive but furious as he pulled her on to his chest and swam with strong kicking strokes towards the landing place and deposited her on the shelf of rock at the water's edge.

"I want the Albert medal," he said, laughing.

Ann scrambled out of the water.

"I'm cold," she said. "I shan't stop in any longer," and made a dive for her cloak and bundled it round her.

"I'm not coming out just yet," called Austen. "I want to have a look at that weir. Old Saunders is quite convinced you can get across on it," and he started to swim downstream.

"Mr. Austen!" shrieked Ann. "You mustn't! It's frightfully dangerous," and she ran along the bank parallel with him, her cloak flying out behind her.

Now Austen had never seriously thought of going near the weir, but he was furious with himself for having lost his self-control so far as to fool about with Ann in the water, and the idea of running a certain amount of risk and pitting his strength against the current had simply been a way of "letting off steam." Ann, had she realized it, was doing the worst possible thing by running along the bank and shrieking at him. If she had walked off and left him to drown himself if he wanted to, he would have come out immediately, for the water was unquestionably very cold. Her extreme concern as she crashed through the bushes regardless of scratches, for she knew only too well the dangers of that weir, he in his overwrought state took as a personal tribute, and swim down to that weir he would if he died in the attempt. Being a Londoner, he had done all his swimming in baths or swimming-pools, and he did not understand river-bathing. He had not taken half a dozen strokes, however, before he realized the reality of the danger and the reason for Ann's frantic screams, and set to work to battle his way to the bank in good earnest.

No ordinary swimmer could have done it, but he held championships among a picked body of men, and foot by foot he won his way to the side.

But when he got there, he was no better off, for the bank was of clay, and though not high, it was very slippery and there was nothing to lay hold of. Desperately he turned and began to fight his way upstream towards the landing place, Ann moving along the bank just above him and striving to reach a hand to him, which he dared not take for fear of pulling her in.

He felt himself becoming exhausted; the uneven struggle could not go on indefinitely; it was only a matter of time till he went over that weir; he wondered what was at the bottom of it. Rocks, probably, from the look of the banks.

Suddenly he saw Ann dart ahead a few yards and sink on her knees with her arms clasped round the trunk of a sapling that grew right on the edge of the bank, and extend one leg down towards the hurrying water. He saw what she intended. If he could reach and grasp her foot, and the tree held, and she was not dragged from her hold by his weight, then he had a chance.

But, God! If he pulled her in! For a moment he was about to throw up his hands and go over the weir, but the instinct of life was strong in him, and he could not give up without fighting to the bitter end. If he felt her slipping, he could always let go. Inch by inch he struggled over the short space that separated him from her, feeling his strength gradually giving out, till at last the slender white foot came within his reach and he grasped it.

For a moment or two he just hung on, recovering from the struggle. Then he heaved himself up in the water and gripped the white webbing belt that encircled Anne's waist with one hand, and like lightning shifted his grip from her ankle to the tree with the other, feeling at the same time for a foothold on the bank, and by good luck finding it.

They hung thus for what seemed to Ann endless hours, she and the tree crushed together in a grip like the hug of a bear as the man hung on for dear life. Then he gathered strength for the final effort, and heaved himself on to the bank, dragging Ann with him. He staggered a few feet away from that treacherous edge, still dragging Ann on her knees, and then dropped like a log, pinning her under him, and lay still.

* * *

When Austen raised his head and gazed at the sky, he could not for the life of him imagine where he was. When he saw a girl with blood on her breast crouching beside him, he concluded there had been a riot, and groped round vaguely for his helmet and truncheon, for a policeman without his helmet is like a limpet without its shell. Then memory returned to him and he rolled over on to his side and gazed at Ann. As he moved she gave the sharp scream of pain that he had learnt to know so well in his patrol days when he took charge in a street accident.

"Ann, what's the matter? Are you hurt?" he cried sharply.

"It's my foot. You're lying on my foot," moaned Ann.

Austen sat up hastily and examined the foot. His wide experience of injuries, both in the street and on the sports field, enabled him to say with as much certainty as a surgeon that the ankle was neither fractured nor dislocated; but most of the skin was off it, and it looked an alarming sight at first glance, and was probably very painful.

"Can you manage to stand on this foot?" he asked her.

"Yes," said Ann, "I am sure it's not badly hurt, just skinned. Look, 1 can move it quite freely," and she waggled her toes at him.

"Then come along," said the man, "and let us get up to the house before we are chilled."

He rose stiffly, and they went slowly up the path, Ann limping on her sore foot, and Austen's arm round her, supporting her.

When they got to the house he turned to her and took

both her hands in his, as they stood dripping on the mat.

"I don't know what madness possessed me," he said. "Forgive me, Ann, I took leave of my senses." His voice broke. "I won't bother you more than I can help. Have patience with me." He bowed his head over her hands. "I owe my life to you," he said, and turned and went hastily to his room.

CHAPTER FIVE

IT took Ann some time to get sticking-plaster and cotton-wool on to all her cuts and scratches, for the tree had scraped her breast cruelly, and the webbing belt, as Austen dragged himself up by it, had bruised her waist. He had been standing by the smouldering kitchen fire for some time when she at last came down, trying without success to warm himself, and was looking very grey and drawn.

"Come into my sitting-room," said Ann. "There is a good fire there; I stoked up before we went bathing."

He followed her silently to the little room overlooking the garden that she called her own, too dispirited to be cheered even by this mark of favour; and abandoning his usual custom of watching every movement she made, gazed moodily into the fire as she blew the logs into flame with a pair of bellows. She studied his face as he lay back in the deep chair, utterly indifferent to his surroundings, and thought he looked deadly ill.

"I don't believe hot tea is going to be enough for you," she said. "I wish I could get at dad's whisky, but he keeps it locked up."

"If that is the only difficulty, we can soon get it unlocked," he said. "Let me have a look at the cupboard."

She took him into the study and showed him the cellarette in the sideboard, and he took a bunch of skeleton keys out of his pocket and unlocked it as nonchalantly as its rightful owner.

"I will present him with replacements to-morrow," he

said. "This is an emergency. I am going to be ill if I don't get warmed up soon."

Ann produced lemons and a kettle and brewed hot toddy, of which they both partook, and life soon began to take on a more normal complexion. Austen did not seem disposed to talk after his exertions, and presently fell asleep in his chair, and Ann, made sleepy by the toddy and the hot room, curled up like a kitten in a corner of the sofa and did likewise.

When she awoke, the early spring dusk was drawing in, and the fire had died to embers. Austen still slept, and cautiously she put fresh logs on and coaxed them into flame with low breathings of the bellows. He stirred uneasily, but did not wake; he had learnt to sleep by day in a cubicle, with all the noise of the station house going on around him. Ann returned to her corner and curled up again, well enough content to be quiet with her own thoughts, which were many, and not without interest.

As the logs burnt up, Austen's face came clearly into view in the light of the flames. She wondered what age he was. When she had first seen him, before she had come into his life to worry him, she had put him down as twenty-five or six, but sleeping the sleep of exhaustion, he looked nearer to forty than thirty. Life in the police is hard, and young men, taking responsibility, soon look mature, and mature men past their prime. Although the Metropolitan Police recruit lads of twenty, it is a rare thing to see a boyish face under a helmet. The previous case in which Austen had been engaged had concerned a series of robberies from warehouses, and necessitated a lot of night work, exposed to the weather, and it had exhausted him. It is never easy to re-establish the habit of sleeping at night when once it has been broken, and with the night work and his worry over Ann, Austen had been sleeping badly. In fact, this was the first deep sleep he had had since she had suddenly appeared before him in the gateway and so utterly disorganized his life. The use of a little arithmetic enabled her to put him down as twenty-eight. If he had joined the force when he was twenty, as he had told her, and if he had been in it eight years, as he had told her father, the result was a foregone conclusion.

Curled up there in the firelight, Ann began to do some very serious thinking. There could be no doubt whatever about Austen's feeling for her, nor about his intentions if she gave him the least shred of encouragement; and Ann, who was an honest little person, realized that, whether she meant to or not, the young detective had had no reason to complain of lack of encouragement. She had let him hang around the kitchen and share her early-morning tea; she had slipped unconsciously into the way of treating him not merely as an equal, but as a friend; Christian names had been used in the excitement of the escape from drowning; she had a distinct recollection of shrieking, "Jack, Jack!" as she had run along the bank and sincerely hoped his ears had been too full of water for him to hear. Then there had been this crowning indiscretion of going swimming with him; and here he was now, asleep in the chair in her own little sanctum, and very much at home there. If by any evil chance her father came back unexpectedly, there would be a terrible rumpus, for the lower Mr. Studley sank himself, the more highly did he value his family prestige. If he discovered the man he had called a raw, rough ranker asleep in his daughter's boudoir, she felt pretty sure he would spare no pains in getting him into trouble with his superiors.

Ann also wondered exactly what Inspector Saunders would think of the situation. She had sensed the friendship that existed between the two men, and she had also sensed the fact that although discipline might not obtrude, it was never far absent. Austen automatically came to attention when Saunders spoke to him, and although he chaffed his chief pretty heartily upon occasion, it was only after Saunders himself had started the ball rolling. Austen never took the initiative with him in anything. If Saunders did not give the command that the tea should be poured out, Austen left it to stew in the pot.

Ann was perfectly satisfied that her father would be implacable on the subject of Austen in any shape or form; she also thought that Inspector Saunders would give the pair of them short shrift if he saw anything that offended his sense of propriety, and she suspected that a deaconlike person such as himself would have very strict views on the subject. She thought that, although Austen's swimming-suit might go on the line, hers had better dry in the privacy of her own bedroom.

But apart from the question of getting into hot water with authority on both sides of the family, there was the question of Austen himself. Underneath the impassive exterior imposed on him by the training of his service, she could easily see that he was a hot-blooded man; his feeling for her was stormy, and she guessed that his anger would also be stormy. But apart from any question of his righteous indignation if she treated him badly, she knew it would hurt him horribly if she led him on and then drew back. He might be a man of the lower classes, but he had his feelings, and probably they lay nearer the surface than those of a man who had been brought up in the public school tradition. He had told her that his grandmother was Highland Scottish, which explained his size; and she knew that the Gael, although he may be self-contained, is seldom placid. Austen, she had already seen in her dealings with him, was quickly up and down, going to extremes in both directions. Decidedly, this was a man who would have to be handled very carefully and she began to wonder whether backing out was still open to her without serious unpleasantness.

Then she began to ask herself how she felt about him. As she had hung over him from the bank as he battled with the water and watched him slowly become exhausted, something was being torn up by the roots in her very soul; the only other occasion when she had felt like that was the first time she had seen her father drunk. She asked herself how she was going to feel when the Gregory case came to an end, as it must inevitably do in course of time, and Austen went away. She admitted that she would miss him horribly, and life would be a terrible blank. In some curious way she seemed to feed upon the strong emotion he was constantly pouring out upon her; she had found herself counting the hours until the sidecar would be heard returning down the lane in the evening, and just to have him around gave her something that made her life bud and blossom. Inspector Saunders had thought her a very pretty girl when he had first seen her, but he had concluded as the days went by that he had done her less than justice, and that she was worth travelling a long way to look at; in fact, he had never seen anything quite like her, and he couldn't blame the boy, save officially, if he lost his head and made a fool of himself.

Ann asked herself what she would do if, when the Gregory case was finished and the time came to leave, Austen asked if he might keep in touch with her. If she answered in the affirmative, he could only interpret it in one way, and if she subsequently refused to "complete the deal," would have a very just cause for reproach. She also shrewdly suspected that if she said no, and gave him his *congé*, she would shortly be feeling as her father felt when his supply of whisky gave out. She knew how he resorted to a hair of the dog that had bitten him, and she saw herself in desperation sending for Austen back again, with the query as to whether he would come. He was, she suspected, as proud as Lucifer, and where his pride had been humbled would not easily forgive, and still less easily forget.

It was while she was engaged in these cogitations, without having arrived at any conclusion, that the door opened and Inspector Saunders entered.

"Phew!" he said. "Some folk don't believe in ventilation!"

Austen shot out of the chair and sprang to attention at the sound of his superior's voice. Saunders came farther into the room, and as the fire flared up, the whisky bottle at Austen's elbow caught his eye.

"What's this, Austen?" he said. "You know my rules. If you work with me, you'll do your work on water, same as I do."

"Sorry, sir," said Austen, fingers to trouser seams, as immobile as a statue.

"Oh, Mr. Saunders!" cried Ann, "that's not fair! I gave him the whisky. He was nearly drowned over the weir. He was unconscious on the bank for ages."

"I'd never drink spirits for pleasure, sir," said Austen, "they're just medicine to me."

Saunders did not reply, but struck a match and lit the lamp and looked at his subordinate. Accustomed to gauging the physical fitness of the men under him, as all those who administer discipline must be, he saw that Austen was just coming out of the acute stage of shock.

"So you've been in the wars?" he said, his grim demeanour relaxing.

"Yes, sir," said Austen, dropping from "attention" to "stand easy" with a sigh of relief.

"Miss Studley half-drowned, too?" he inquired, with the air of making polite conversation that Ann had got to know so well. She saw at once that he was trying to find out if they had so far forgotten themselves as to go bathing together, and she did not intend that he should obtain any information on this point.

"No, thank goodness," she said, "I was on the bank. I had to pull him out. If I had been in the water, too, we should neither of us be here to tell the tale."

"I owe my life to her, sir," said Austen. "I was a darn fool and went too near the weir, although she shouted to me not to. There's no doubt about it whatever, no one could get across that river on the weir, and precious few could swim it."

Inspector Saunders, his mind at ease on the subject of the proprieties, lowered his bulk carefully into the chair that Austen had vacated. Austen, after an inquiring glance at Ann, went and sat beside her on the sofa. It seemed to her that they were constantly being put up together to be stared at, like two love-birds on a perch, but somehow she no longer resented it. The long minutes when they had clung together on the edge of eternity had left their mark, and the clock could never be set back.

"Inquest is fixed for Tuesday, Jack," said Inspector Saunders.

"Good," said Austen.

"Well, missy," said Saunders, turning to Ann, "You are what is called a crime fan, aren't you? Would it interest you to hear the inquest?"

It was his intention to watch Ann as the evidence was being given, and judge from her demeanour whether she knew anything or not, but neither she nor Austen suspected this and thought it was a thrilling idea. Saunders, watching their enthusiasm with amusement, concluded then and there that the girl knew nothing and suspected nothing about the murder, but the invitation having once been given, could not very well be withdrawn. He wondered how the girl would like the inquest when she saw it. He suspected her enthusiasm depended upon her ignorance of the nature of such functions in real life, and thought it would be a good thing if all crime novels were burnt by the public hangman. Austen, he knew, was so case-hardened that it never occurred to him that he was enthusiastically taking his girl to see fellow humans hunted to death in the same spirit that he would have taken her to the pictures. Saunders had a shrewd suspicion that he might not be particularly popular with either party after his suggestion had been tried out in practice. He made up his mind that he would use the evening after the inquest to run up to London to see his superiors at the Yard, and let Austen smooth the girl down as best he might. Hysterical females were the one thing that really ruffled Inspector Saunders. He infinitely preferred Bolsheviks with bombs.

He had begun to suspect, also, that Austen's chances with the girl were not as hopeless as he had at first thought, and he calculated that if he left them alone together, and it fell to Austen's lot to console her if she had been upset by the inquest, the lad would find her in a very amenable mood to chance his luck. After the first pang of jealousy and dis-appointment, when he saw the man who was like a son to him being taken away from him by the inevitable woman, Saunders began to be extremely flattered that a girl with the breeding of Ann Studley should consider a policeman as an eligible suitor. He knew that the whole standard of education in the force had been enormously raised since he had joined it as a raw clod-hopper back in the nineties, but it certainly meant something if the higher ranks could aspire to marry the daughters of earls and dukes, for he had looked up Mr. Studley's pedigree, and found it peppered with coronets. In-stead of the bachelor flat he had thought they might share together after Austen gained senior rank—discipline would not permit of it before—he began to imagine Ann being left in his care at Imber Court while Austen competed for cups and other trophies at the police sports, and how she would compare in looks and style with other policemen's wives. He saw Austen, with the help of her influence, even becoming commissioner, the first ranker to do it. The appointment of outsiders to the highest posts in the police has always been a sore point.

So mellowed was he by these reflections that they all spent a most matey evening in Ann's room, the excuse being that the fire was out in the detectives' appointed sitting-room.

CHAPTER SIX

THE next day was Sunday, for which Austen was thankful, for his battle for life in the river had taken it out of him, and the roar of the weir and Ann's screams had rung in his ears all night and prevented him sleeping. He could not be sure whether Ann had actually used his Christian name in her excitement as she ran along the bank; at midnight he made up his mind that she had, but as the sky began to turn grey he came to the conclusion that she had not. When he got up in the morning he not only knew for certain that she had not, but also that she never would, and that the weir might have its points as a swimming-pool for despairing lovers. Austen was apt to be like that before he had had his breakfast if the previous day had not gone well; but after Ann had blushed as pink as a rose at the sight of him, and he had seen two cups sitting matily together awaiting the early morning tea, he came to the final decision that Ann was as good as his. Austen's final decisions on the subject of Ann were rather like Patti's farewell concerts.

The Sabbath forenoon was spent by Saunders sitting in the garden in his shirt-sleeves reading the Sunday papers. It was spent by Ann in preparing the Sunday dinner. It was spent by Austen in getting under Ann's feet like a puppy as she tried to get on with her work. How it was spent by Mr. Studley, none of them knew. He got up in reasonable time; in fact, for him it might be said that he was up with the lark. He kept Ann on the run, to Austen's indignation, until he was immaculately turned out in a suit of summer grey in honour

80

of the early heat-wave to which Saunders was presenting his shirtsleeves in the garden, while watching his host out of the tail of his eye; and finally departed for an unknown destination in the Baby Austin, whose weather-beaten and generally dilapidated appearance was in striking contrast to the Sabbath smartness of its driver.

Ann had a fairly good idea of one call he had made, at any rate, in the course of his outing, for as she was laying the tea on a table under the apple-tree, she saw a portly female figure coming out through the French windows of her little room and, swearing inwardly, she hastened across the lawn to greet her Aunt Maude.

Aunt Maude was a determined survival of the old regime when the upper classes had the upper hand, and people like Saunders and Austen knuckled their forelocks and knew their proper place, and Ann was not at all sure how she would like being asked to meet them at tea. She thought, however, that Aunt Maude's manners and sense of *noblesse oblige* would be proof against a contretemps. In this, however, she had reckoned without Mr. Studley.

Aunt and niece duly exchanged embraces without much gusto, and Aunt Maude subsided gracefully into the large basket-chair that Austen had lugged out for Saunders. not considering it safe to trust the fat, old six-footer to a deckchair. Austen, watching from behind the sprigged muslin curtains of his little bedroom, cursed the old trout with the whole of his extensive vocabulary and fretted at his spoilt Sunday afternoon. He could not hear what was being said, but he judged from the finger-waggings and Ann's mutinous countenance that the visitor was a relative, and that Ann was getting a wigging. The word "policeman" uttered by the trout in terms of extreme horror, came up to him, and he guessed what the wigging was about, and hated her, himself, and the whole world (with the exception of Ann), with a deadly hatred.

Aunt Maude, seeing the tea-table, had jumped to the conclusion that Ann must be expecting her, having been warned by her father and instructed to prepare for a visit; it never occurred to her that her niece might be entertaining the policemen to tea. She supposed they had their meals in the kitchen or the potting-shed. It pleased her to see the delicious cakes that had been prepared for her, for she was a lady who liked attention. She therefore modified the opening gambit she had prepared, which was just as well, for Ann was an independent little person, and would stand no nonsense from Aunt Maude or anyone.

"I do not think your father will be back to tea, dear," she said. "He told me he was going on somewhere else."

"Oh?" said Ann. So she owed this visit to her father. It must be something very pressing that would induce him to call on Aunt Maude, whom he hated like poison and would have dropped altogether, save that she sometimes paid his more pressing debts, and it was understood she had left her little income, such as it was, to Ann. No one in his family ever left anything to him, which was a very sore point. Still, he had always been able to manage Ann, who seemed to have a soft spot for him somewhere, which came in very useful at times, though he found it intensely irritating when he was half sober.

"I hear from your father that you have got visitors in the house?" said Aunt Maude. Ann's lodging-letting was a very sore point with her, for she was intensely proud, and would have much preferred her niece to starve with dignity.

"Yes," said Ann. "Rather interesting visitors. The two detectives from Scotland Yard who are trying to find out what Mr. Gregory died of. They won't say so, but I am sure they think he has been murdered."

"Indeed?" said Miss Studley. "Well, I think it is disgusting."

Ann could not be quite sure what she thought was disgusting: the murder of Mr. Gregory, or detectives as lodgers, or lodging-letting in general.

"Your father is very worried about you," continued Miss Studley.

"Indeed?" said Ann, in her turn. She wondered what in the world was worrying her father, and found it hard to believe that it was her personal welfare. One of the bitterest ingredients in the soup that Mr. Studley was making of the life of his young daughter was that though she still cared for him, it was only too obvious that he cared nothing whatever as to what became of her.

"Yes, dear. He is very worried about the way you are behaving with one of these detectives."

Ann felt herself going as red as a peony. "I think he might have said so to me himself," she said, "instead of telling tales to you."

Miss Studley bridled. "He thought that a woman's hand was needed, dear, and I think he was quite right." It was a job after her own heart.

"Oh, my God!" said Ann to herself. "This is vomitaceous!" How she hated Austen at that moment!

"Can't you get rid of them?" said Miss Studley.

"No, I can't," said Ann. "We need the money."

"Your father wishes them to go," said Miss Studley.

"Then why can't he say so?"

"Because he sees that you have made up your mind, and nothing he said would have any effect." This sounded like a quotation, thought Ann.

"They would have to go if he told them to. Let him chuck them out himself, if he wants to be rid of them. I'm not going to do any more of his dirty work."

"How dare you speak of your father like that!"

Ann might defend Mr. Studley tooth and nail to outsiders, but she would tolerate no pious pretences from his own sister, who knew perfectly well what he was like, but always declared it was his wife's fault.

"Now look here, Auntie," said Ann, "I have got to keep a roof over our heads because father can't. These men are very nice men, ever so much nicer than the Territorial officers, and he never minded them."

"I have nothing against the men as men. I have no doubt they are perfectly respectable. Policemen have to be. What your father objects to, and what upset me very much when I heard of it, was that you should have got yourself talked about with them."

"There is no one to do any talking if father doesn't," said Ann.

"That is not the point," said Miss Studley, shifting her ground at this home thrust. "The point is your own behaviour as your father's daughter—as a Studley, Ann. It is very foolish of you to behave as you are doing. After all, a man is a man, even if he is a policeman."

"I think I had better go and get tea," said Ann. "I left the kettle on the fire. It has probably boiled over by now." And she walked away across the little lawn with a very straight spine, putting her small feet down very firmly. Austen, watching from behind his curtains, took heart of hope when he saw that walk. Ann's back was obviously up, and it wouldn't be up if she were taking her wigging lying down.

Ann made the tea, collecting another cup and saucer, and bore it out on to the lawn.

"Tea's made!" she called, in her clear voice, as she crossed the hall. Saunders and Austen were clearly to understand that they were included in the tea-party, and if Aunt Maude did not like it, she could lump it.

Saunders, lurking in the dining-room and surveying the

visitor through the curtains, winked one eye to himself and did not budge. Jack could lead off in this figure. It was his job to do the dirty work. He could tackle armed gunmen. Let him tackle this.

He heard the stairs of the old house protesting as six foot three of brawn and bone came down them as if it meant business.

Austen looked exceedingly smart in his Sunday suit of double-breasted Navy blue. Miss Studley, glancing up with a start to find him standing over her, thought he must be young Manby-Lisle, home on leave from India, and what a fool Ann was to dish her chances by playing about with policemen. She was speedily disillusioned, however.

"Auntie, this is Mr. Austen," said Ann; Austen bowed.

"Good afternoon, officer," said Miss Studley.

"Good afternoon," said Austen, and sat down.

If Ann chose to introduce him as an equal, he certainly was not going to play policeman to her aunt.

Saunders approached with his stately waddle, and Miss Studley unfurled a pair of lorgnettes and surveyed him. Austen was thankful these implements had not been used on him. He was certain he could not have kept a straight face.

"Good afternoon, madam," said Saunders, taking charge of the tea-party, as if it were traffic. "Inspector Saunders is my name. Chief Inspector Saunders, to be precise," and proceeded to lower himself into a deck-chair.

"Look out, Chief," cried Austen. "It won't stand you. Here, take this one, and I'll have a cushion on the floor."

"Ah," said Saunders, straightening up laboriously, "we have to be careful where we sit when we're getting on, don't we, madam?"

Ann could have embraced him. Even the lorgnettes could not cope with this. Aunt Maude, for once, had bitten off something socially that she could not chew. The Metropoli-

85

tan Police, individually and collectively, have a well-developed superiority complex, by means of which they control traffic and crowds without resort to force. It is only police with an inferiority complex who are always relying on their batons. She was confident that Austen and Saunders between them would disperse Aunt Maude.

She knew Austen well enough by now to know that his wooden police face meant either anger or laughter, it was impossible to say which. She sincerely hoped he saw the funny side of Aunt Maude, and was not hurt by her treatment of him. Unfortunately, however, he was hurt, and badly hurt. In the ordinary way snubs, oaths and flattery were all one to him, but where Ann was concerned, he was acutely sensitive. Saunders, who knew him better than Ann did, viewed the situation with anxiety. Austen was an explosive individual when ruffled, and could give back-chat to divisional superintendents on occasion. He had no wish to take part in a social baton charge on a Sunday afternoon. So he took his stand at a strategical point in the conversation and metaphorically put on white armlets. Auntie would stop or come on as he directed.

Ann began to make conversation re sugar and milk, and Saunders beckoned her on and held up Austen. Austen rose from his cushion with the lithe movement Saunders had often watched when an armed desperado had to be taken by surprise. Saunders cast hastily about in his mind for some remark that would take the place of a police whistle, but Austen only handed Aunt Maude a cup of tea, for which she did not seem very grateful.

Beyond that one "Good afternoon, officer," which was about as insulting under the circumstances as any words that could have been framed by human lips, Aunt Maude had not opened her mouth except to put something in it. Saunders looked at Ann, and saw that she was wearing a pleasant social smile, but that on either cheekbone burnt a scarlet spot. He did not want Ann to start a brawl, either, and was casting about once more for suitable remarks when Ann ignored his traffic signal and started off on her own account.

"How is Lady Birchington, auntie?" she inquired sweetly, speaking only to her aunt, and ignoring the two men. Saunders wondered what in the world was coming. Was she going to play her aunt's game, and freeze them out? If she did, he thought Austen would murder her.

"Lady Birchington is very well, dear, thank you," cooed Miss Studley, greatly relieved at the way Ann was taking things.

"I suppose you heard that what she said about Miss Dean was all a pack of lies, and she had to give a written apology?" continued Ann.

"My dear Ann !" exclaimed the scandalized Miss Studley, who had done her fair share in spreading the rumour about Miss Dean, and was very lucky not to have been threatened with a libel action herself.

"I don't know how you can put up with her," went on Ann. "She had got a mind like a cesspool. She ought to put chloride of lime on it."

Miss Studley went purple. Saunders heard Austen give his deep, baying laugh, and glared at him to be quiet. Trouble was coming, and he did not want his subordinate involved in it. Ann was obviously on the warpath.

"And Colonel Carter," she went on, "do you remember how he used to try and kiss your maid whenever he called? Isn't he a dreadful old man? Why ever do you let him come to the house ?"

Miss Studley went livid.

"And Canon Long, he—" began Ann, but got no further. Miss Studley's face was like a Scotch plaid, and Ann stared at it in amazement, thinking she was going to have a fit.

"How dare you speak like that of my friends!" she exclaimed, in the strangled voice of extreme fury.

"Well, auntie," said Ann, with the utmost politeness, "If you expect me to tolerate your friends, I think you ought to be prepared to tolerate mine."

Miss Studley rose, gathered up her sunshade, her gloves and her handbag, and crossed the lawn like Nemesis going to fetch help.

"Cor!" said Inspector Saunders, gazing at Ann in speechless admiration.

"Yes," said Ann vindictively, "and she'll have nearly an hour to wait for the bus, and she will have to stand on her two flat feet, because there is nothing to sit on."

Austen laid himself flat on his back on the grass and exploded into helpless laughter.

"Shut up, you fool!" growled Saunders, planting a toe in his ribs. For Miss Studley must still be in earshot, and he knew from his youthful memories of the squirearchy that it was safer to insult than laugh at a woman of her type. He reckoned that the unforgiveable sin had been committed that afternoon, and that Ann had burnt her boats behind her.

Austen rolled over out of reach of Saunder's toe, holding his side. "Ouch!" he said. "Don't kick me there, Chief, it hurts. That's where I got biffed when we bagged Six-shooter Sam. You're treading in his footsteps."

Saunders surprised a look of concern on Ann's face, and decided in his own mind that Jack was well away with it.

CHAPTER SEVEN

THE next day was the eve of the inquest to which Ann was looking forward as to a party. In fact, it was to be something of a party, for Saunders had been at pains to inform his assistant that he himself would not be able to look after Ann, and she must be in his care. An arrangement at which Austen by no means demurred. He had asked Ann if she would have tea with him at the local cafe after the show, as he candidly called the inquest. He explained that although he would not be required to give evidence at the present juncture, he had to attend such functions out of respect for the corpse, if not for the coroner, for whom he seemed to have his full share of a policeman's hatred and contempt; for the police regard coroners as sportsmen regard jays, which by their chattering outcry warn game of their presence.

As she was washing up the breakfast things, Austen shyly approached Ann with his best blue jacket over his arm and asked her if she would be good enough to repair a seam which had come unstitched. Though recent events had broken down barriers and drawn them very close together, they had also made them very shy and self-conscious with each other. Austen could not forget that he had held Ann in his arms, and Ann could not forget that she had been there.

Ann took the jacket in hand, and finding something hard which prevented her from effecting her repair, fished about in a fold of the lining and discovered a pair of handcuffs, which thrilled her to the marrow.

Now whatever perverse star it was that watched over the

fortunes of Ann and Austen, and had so nearly succeeded in drowning them the previous day, again rose above the horizon, and the devil entered into Ann, and she took a length of lingerie ribbon from her work-basket and tied a neat bow of pale blue to each wristlet and replaced the handcuffs where she had found them. She thought that the next prisoner Austen arrested would get the shock of his life.

She gave the coat to Austen when she met him in the hall on his return that afternoon, for she did not wish Inspector Saunders to know of the transaction. Austen, however seemed to feel no embarrassment on the subject, but tossed his coat over his arm and joined his superior officer in their sitting-room.

Suddenly Ann heard guffaws from Inspector Saunders, and the door flew open and out came Austen with the decorated handcuffs in his hand.

"You little cat!" he said. "You're going to be arrested for this!"

Ann darted through her sitting-room and out of the French window, feeling like a hen streaking across the barnyard, pursued by the rooster. She heard the crash of an overturned chair as the big man negotiated her little room, and out came Austen after her, flushed and laughing, with a wild look in his eyes. Behind him laboured Inspector Saunders, as if he expected murder to be done and meant to prevent it.

Ann ran like a hare, though she knew she had not got the slightest chance of making good her escape from Austen. She ran so well that they had left Saunders far behind and were at the bottom of the orchard before he caught her. He gripped her round the waist, which had been badly bruised by her belt as he had clung to it for his life during his battle with the river. She screamed, not the usual squeal of the captured flapper, Ann would have scorned that, but a genuine cry of pain because he was mauling her bruises, and that scream was again the worst thing she could have done, for if the man had been out of hand before, he was beside himself now.

He held her tightly to him from behind, blind to the strength he was using, snapped the handcuffs on her wrists, and then kissed her roughly, just as Inspector Saunders came up.

Ann saw at once that Saunders was really angry, but Austen was too excited to know or care, and would not let Ann go, but tried to kiss her again.

"Ow, you beast!" cried Ann. "You're busting my ribs. Let me go!" And she kicked him on the shins, again showing her ignorance of male human nature.

"Steady, Austen, you're hurting her," said Saunders, whose practised ear told him that Ann's cries were not mere coyness, but genuine cries of pain. But Austen was past all remonstrance, and they wrestled together in rough horse-play, Ann kicking, and biting his wrists, and trying to hit him on the nose with the handcuffs, nearly as excited as he was.

But Inspector Saunders took the situation in hand, and the voice they heard was that of the police officer controlling crowds, authoritative, but not provocative.

"Come, come, this has got to stop. It is going beyond a joke. Keep still, miss. Don't struggle, you are only making him worse. Now, Austen, pull yourself together, you are hurting the young lady."

They fell out of their clinch, and began to feel sheepish. Ann's hair looked as if she had been through a bush backwards, and Austen was bleeding from a cut on the bridge of his nose, where she had managed to hit him with the handcuffs.

Inspector Saunders stood and looked at them for that long minute of silence which is more effective than any third degree.

"Austen," he said at length, "if anything like this ever happens again, I shall report you. Miss Ann, this is just as much your fault as his. You ought to have more sense than to provoke a man like that. No, I don't want explanations. I want to hear no more about it. Silence, Austen. (As Austen started to come to Ann's defence.) My dear, pull your dress down and tidy your hair."

"I can't," said Ann. "I'm handcuffed."

"Austen, take the cuffs off her at once."

"I can't, sir, the key's in my other suit."

"Then, my dear, you will just have to walk back to the house under arrest, and I must say I think you deserve all you've got, but I hope for all our sakes we don't meet anyone."

Which pious hope was not justified, for on the threshold they met Mr. Studley, surveying the wreckage of Ann's room, where Austen had charged through it like a bull.

"Here's a pretty kettle of fish, sir," said Inspector Saunders as cheerfully as if nothing had happened. "The young lady has been playing with my handcuffs, and has got them on and can't get them off; and we can't get them off, either. Austen, you go and see if you can find a key in my room."

Austen, who was now as white as he had previously been flushed, took the hint and vanished.

Mr. Studley smiled a sour smile and said no word.

"Very alarming for a young lady, sir," Inspector Saunders laboured on.

"Very," said Mr. Studley. "I thought I heard screaming, and so did a man working in the road. I suppose it is the stolen whisky that has capsized your understrapper," and he turned on his heel and went into the house.

Austen came back with the key of the handcuffs, and Saunders released Ann without a word.

"Now, my lass," he said, "you go up to your room, and

92

don't let me see you again to-day." And Ann crept away, not daring to meet their eyes, feeling as if she had been well whipped.

Ann was in a terrible state of mind because she feared her foolish prank had got Austen into serious trouble, and that Saunders would report him and he would be punished. As a matter of fact, it was far more serious than either of them suspected, for Saunders, with the peculiar instinct of an experienced police officer, had for some time past been viewing Mr. Studley with ever-increasing suspicion, and making inquiries about him, unknown to his subordinate, and the more he inquired, the more suspicious he became, for the man's reputation was more than dubious; but so far there was nothing to connect him with Mrs. Gregory, which was the link he was really seeking. He had discovered that she went away for frequent week-ends, but during these week-ends Studley had always been about the district as usual.

Nevertheless, he would not lift his nose from the trail, but followed blindly, like a bloodhound, a scent that no eye could see. He was convinced that sooner or later the handcuffs that Ann had decorated with blue ribbon would close upon the wrists of her father, and he saw things looking very awkward for himself and his comrade if Mr. Studley retaliated by putting the worst possible construction on the incidents he had witnessed, as Saunders was certain he would. The thing that had finally clinched his belief in Studley's implication in the murder of Gregory was his peculiar attitude towards the three of them. He made no attempt to deal with Ann as his daughter, either by reproving her, or reproaching Austen, or complaining to him about the behaviour of his subordinate. His attitude seemed to be, "Take her and keep her, she is evidence against you." Saunders felt pretty sure that Studley regarded the affair as a weapon in his hand, and was tacitly daring the detectives to take any steps against him. To the credit of the spirit of the force be it noted that it never entered Saunders' head to call off the hunt; he only speculated what sort of unpleasantness he and Austen would be in for, and how they could contrive to wriggle out of it.

With admirable tactfulness, Saunders made Austen drive him half across the county and stood him supper at a pub, with much beer, putting aside for once his rule that police work is best done on water. Austen was almost ready to weep with mortification, and unrequited love, and God knows what else, but the beer and some fatherly advice soothed him. Saunders kept his anxieties to himself, and encouraged Austen to talk about his troubles, a most efficient safety valve; and by the time he brought the young detective home he was restored to his right mind and master of himself.

Ann, as she was filling her hot-bottle in the kitchen, saw Austen's face come round the door, half-smiling and half-ashamed of himself, and poured hot water over her fingers.

"Are you angry with me, Puss?" he said.

"Have I got you into trouble?" she asked anxiously, an interesting variant on the Eve-and-apple theme.

"A bit. It doesn't matter. It will blow over. Tell me you aren't too angry with me, Pussy."

"Why do you call me Pussy? I never said you could."

"Because you are such a little cat. That is your punishment for your outrageous behaviour. You have got to answer to the name of Pussy henceforth and forever. Good-night. I must hop it. The Chief said I could put my head round the door and apologize to you, but he dared me on my life to come in."

"A lot of apologizing you have done!" thought Ann to herself. "You are as pleased with yourself as a dog with two tails, if the truth were known. I don't understand men. They always do the exact opposite to what one would expect."

* * *

The inquest was fixed for two o'clock in the afternoon, and Austen, after taking Saunders in the sidecar to the little country town where it was being held, came back for Ann. She had learnt enough of police work from her reading of shockers to know that he was a plain clothes man, and would not put in an appearance at the inquest in helmet and beetle-crushers; consequently she was unprepared for the official manner Austen assumed when they disembarked from the sidecar in the crowded market-square, and he took the salute from all the assembled constables, gave the policeman's salute to a couple of inspectors, and cleared a way for their passage through the crowd, with the habitual authority of a uniformed man.

Their progress naturally attracted a good deal of attention, and Ann heard cameras clicking all round her; for Austen, with his magnificent physique and outstanding personality, was always good newspaper "copy." He and Saunders had been engaged together in a number of sensational cases, and their respective personalities had caught the newspaper men's fancy. Saunders always turned surly when anyone tried to interview him, but Austen was as good as any Press agent in the delicate art of handling reporters and obtaining from them the exact publicity that was desired, and no more. He was also shrewd enough to know that pressmen could be powerful allies if ever he were in hot water with his official superiors; consequently he humoured his journalistic friends to the top of their bent; posing for them picturesquely whenever they desired it; regarding their favour as a kind of fire insurance, and finding himself able to command the services of a corps of by no means inexperienced amateur detectives whenever he might require them.

Ann, who was accustomed to a rather boyish Austen

lumbering around the little house at her heels, or an Austen deferring to, and being ordered about by, Inspector Saunders, suddenly found herself confronted by an Austen that was altogether new to her; a decidedly imposing Austen, who was being worshipped open-mouthed by all the young constables, to whom he represented the ideal of the new police.

Austen was totally indifferent to the attention he was attracting, for point-duty during his uniformed days had long since cured him of all self-consciousness in public. Ann was first rather startled and then, to her surprise, rather flattered. There was a kind of pride of uniform among the police; they seemed to consider themselves a superior breed, condescendingly shepherding the helpless and foolish beings dependent upon them for safety. They represented the majesty of the law, and the law was at that moment coming into action in all its majesty to inquire how, why, and wherefore one of its subjects had come to an untimely end. Ann, shepherded by Austen through the obedient crowd that made way for their passage, felt that she, too, was within the sacred circle of the majesty of the law. She was obviously regarded by the police as their property, as being on their side. There was a kind of intimate affability about the large men who made the crowd make way for her that she had never seen before. She thought that the pet goat, which marches in front of the Welch Guards, must feel as she felt.

* * *

"I feel like royalty," Ann whispered to Austen, and he laughed delightedly, for he had been wondering uneasily how the daughter of a hundred earls (according to Saunders), would like being seen out with a policeman, even if he were not in uniform.

Once in the court, which was much smaller than Ann

expected, they were ushered into a seat behind the little party of waiting witnesses, a seat reserved for the police witnesses. Ann saw Sergeant Ashcott and Constable Geary sitting stolidly side by side at the other end of the bench, and did not recognize them at first without their helmets. They gaped when they saw her in the company of Austen, and nudged each other. Among the knot of witnesses she saw a man whose face she knew, and who looked like a butler. Also a hospital nurse in uniform, and a lady in a widow's veil which completely hid her face, and whom she took to be Mrs. Gregory.

There was a buzz of conversation in court, for the coroner had not yet taken his seat. Sergeant Ashcott whispered to Austen that the coroner had been entertaining the government pathologist to lunch, and they could expect him when they saw him.

Austen began to murmur in Ann's ear.

"I had meant to tell you last night how the land lay so that you would understand all the fun of the fair. Don't for God's sake give anyone a hint that I have told you anything. I am not supposed to talk about my cases, especially when they are still *sub judice*, but I want you to know that we are after Mrs. Gregory and an unknown man whom she is supposed to have been carrying on with. We don't think she actually gave Gregory the poison, she has a cast-iron alibi for that, but we think she was an accessory before the fact. You will find the cross-examination of her fascinating."

Then the coroner came in, and the business of the afternoon commenced, Ann settling down in her corner to watch it, feeling exactly as if she were at the theatre. It never entered her head that the woman by whose cross-examination she was expecting to be thrilled would go to a living death if she failed to keep her end up; and that her lover, who might possibly even be sitting in the limited portion of the court

97

available for the public, would be sent to the gallows. Subconsciously she felt that they would all be going home to their teas after they had played their parts and the show was over.

The first witness was the butler, who had heard a cry, and hurrying to see what was the matter, had found his master horribly contorted, and an instant later, dead. He described the grisly details with gusto, and Ann saw Mrs. Gregory stir uneasily in her seat. These details awakened memories of the deaths of both her grandmother and mother. Just so had they died. That was a point in Mrs. Gregory's favour, thought Ann. Thus did people die of heart-disease. She knew, for she had seen.

Then came Sergeant Ashcott, who had been summoned when it was found that life was extinct, and he repeated some of the butler's details, but impersonally, as if he were an auctioneer's man describing a washstand. Ann, who, being an experienced crime fan, was following the trail with avidity, learnt nothing fresh from him save that the deceased had been drinking a cup of cocoa at the moment of his death, and that the Sergeant had taken away under his arm the eiderdown on which the cocoa had been spilt, and was greatly elated by the coroner's compliments on this action.

Odd how coincidences occur, thought Ann, both her mother and grandmother had been drinking cocoa when they had the final seizure that terminated their illnesses. She thought that cocoa was probably bad for the heart, and determined to avoid it herself in future, for her father often said to her when he was irritated with her, "Thank God, you won't make old bones, none of our family ever do." She also determined that she would break Austen of his habit of getting her to make him a cup of cocoa last thing at night. She suspected it was only an excuse for a gossip.

The doctor who had attended Mr. Gregory during his last illness was now going into the witness-box. He explained that he had shortly before attended the deceased for a broken collarbone, resulting from a fall while hunting, and he was then perfectly sound in wind and limb. The condition of Mr. Gregory's heart had puzzled him when he was called in the second time, and he had asked, nay, pressed, for a consultation; but Mrs. Gregory had taken up Christian Science, and was opposed to it, though she had no objection to his continued attendance upon her husband; in fact had herself sent for him repeatedly at all hours of the twenty-four, whenever her husband's condition showed the slightest sign of exacerbation. Consequently, no specialist had seen Mr. Gregory prior to his death.

When asked to give his opinion concerning the state of Mr. Gregory's heart, he said the condition was such as is produced by overdoses of digitalis. Had he prescribed any digitalis? No, he had not, and in response to his questionings, Mr. Gregory had assured him that he was not taking any other medicines than those prescribed, save the mildest of health salts. He also described the appearance of Mr. Gregory's body, using, however, long Latin names for his description, and Ann thought how much better unpleasant things sounded when called by Latin names than by Saxon ones. Then followed more messy details, for the third time, and Ann was becoming slightly bored. That was heart disease, all right, those precise things had happened with both mother and grannie. Ann knew. She had had to clean up.

"And why," said the coroner, "are you of the opinion that death was not due to heart disease?"

The doctor gave his reply in technical language, and Ann was none the wiser.

"To what do you attribute the death?"

"The symptoms are consonant with death from a poisonous dose of cyanide of potassium."

Cyanide of potassium? That was the stuff one took wasps'

nests with, thought Ann.

"One could hardly take less than a poisonous dose of cyanide of potassium," said the coroner, ironically.

Then came an expert from London, who had done the post-mortem on Mr. Gregory's remains, and he confirmed the diagnosis. Then another expert, who had analysed the remains of the cocoa in the cup and the stain on the eider-down, so thoughtfully preserved by Sergeant Ashcott, who preened himself while this evidence was being given, and was again complimented as a smart officer. This expert, too, had found cyanide of potassium in bulk.

"Enough to kill an army corps'" as he picturesquely put it.

He was followed in the witness-box by the nurse who had come in to look after Mr. Gregory during his last illness at such times as his wife was away from home, as she fairly frequently was for short periods, visiting her sister in London. She was obviously horribly frightened, and could hardly give her evidence, and it took all the tact and patience of the coroner to elicit that she was in the habit of putting a night-tray, with the cocoa ready mixed, at Mr. Gregory's bedside, so that he could heat his own milk in an electric saucepan and make it when he wanted it. He was by no means bed-ridden, she explained, though he never got up before noon, on doctor's orders. When the coroner told her that no blame could be attached to her, she burst into tears and had to be helped from the box by three large constables. It was only then that Ann began to realize that the performance she was witnessing was not a theatrical one. The poor little nurse's sobs were heartrending. Ann began to feel uncomfortable.

Then Mrs. Gregory went into the witness-box, and there was a murmur and stir in court, which was immediately quelled by the constables. Her thick black widow's veil was down over her face, completely concealing her features, and she took the oath in an almost inaudible voice.

"Will you kindly put your veil back so that we can see your face, Mrs. Gregory?" said the coroner in his pleasant voice. She did not comply.

"Please, Mrs. Gregory," coaxed the coroner.

"I have been in great grief," came the muffled voice. "I would sooner not."

"I am afraid I must insist, Mrs. Gregory," said the coroner.

Slowly and reluctantly the woman raised the veil from her face and flung it back over her hat, and Ann found herself gazing straight into the eyes of Mrs. Godfrey, her father's friend, the regular week-end visitor at Thatched Cottage, who now stood there in the coroner's court as Mrs. Gregory, the wife of the dead man, suspected of being privy to the murder of her husband. And the police were after her, and also after an unknown man, her lover, whose hand it was that had given the actual poison—and this unknown man was—?

Ann knew who Mrs. Godfrey's lover was. She was neither blind nor a fool. But it was impossible! Her imagination refused to accept it. Then she remembered her mother and her grandmother had both died in exactly the same way as Mr. Gregory. If it were true of him, that he had been murdered by means of cyanide and digitalis, it was true of them also. Ann's mind went completely blank. All she could think of was a scene in a sunlit wood, on the bank of the little river where Austen had so nearly lost his life, and herself climbing among the bushes, gathering foxglove leaves—gathering foxglove leaves!

Mrs. Gregory's blazing eyes glared at Ann like the eyes of a mad-woman, daring her to identify her. But Ann was too dazed to do anything but stare back in blank bewilderment, her mind refusing to take in the significance of the scene before her.

As from a great distance she heard the voice of the coroner trying to command Mrs. Gregory's attention. The woman withdrew her eyes from Ann, and the girl's brain slowly began to work once more as that hypnotic stare was removed. Mrs. Gregory's replies were inaudible where they were sitting, and the police witnesses began to get bored and stare about the court, and Austen whispered in Ann's ear:

"Isn't she in a blue funk!"

Ann did not gaze about the court; she stared at Mrs. Gregory, unable to turn away her eyes, and Austen, watching her out of the corner of his eye, was delighted to see that Mrs. Gregory's evidence was fully coming up to expectations so far as fascination went.

But Ann was seeing more than Mrs. Gregory's face. Behind her rose a series of pictures. She saw herself on a sunny spring day such as this, going into Watson's the chemist's, and old Mr. Watson filling up the entries in the poison book with the information that she wanted cyanide of potassium in order to destroy wasps' nests. Three times she had done that, and each time some one had died of a heart attack shortly afterwards—her mother, her grandmother, and now Mr. Gregory.

Then she saw a picture in a botany book she had used at school, the picture of a foxglove plant in colours, and under it was written, "Digitalis purpurea, the common foxglove."

There was a fair being held not far from the coroner's court, and the windows being open because of the mildness of the day, the sound of the steam-organ attached to the roundabout came clearly to her; it had only one tune, and as soon as it got to the end of it, began again at the beginning in an endless circle of melody, and the tune it played fitted itself to the rhythm of the words, "Digitalis, digitalis," and Ann could see nothing of the crowded and hushed court, but only herself in the wood, gathering foxglove leaves.

Gradually her mind cleared and she began to take in the evidence that was being given. Mrs. Gregory had recovered her self-confidence now, and was speaking clearly. The coroner, Ann could see, was pressing her hard, insisting on answers, and in none too gentle a tone, for Mrs. Gregory had evidently tried to be evasive.

He was questioning her chiefly about the dates of her visits to her sister in London, and asking her how she could remember so exactly when she had been there, over a stretch of years. She replied that she kept a diary. Could she produce it? Yes, out it came from her underarm bag, a small purse-diary: And the volume for the previous year? Yes, that was produced, too, from the same voluminous receptacle. The coroner examined them, and seemed satisfied. All the same, he did not give them back to her; and when she rather snappily asked for them, for she had recovered her self-confidence by now took no notice.

Finally Mrs. Gregory was allowed to get down from the witness-box and her sister took her place. She did not carry Mrs. Gregory's heavy layer of make-up, and her colour was ghastly and her eyes were like those of a hunted animal. Yes, her sister had stopped with her at her London flat on the dates aforesaid. How did she know? She, too, had kept a diary, produced both volumes, without waiting to be asked. The coroner thanked her, and took them from her, and let her get down.

Then the coroner turned to the jury, and in a quiet, conversational tone, using simple, coloquial language, recapitulated the case to them, and explained the meaning of the technical evidence. Ann understood it all now; she saw plainly that digitalis (or foxglove, she added mentally) could produce symptoms that looked like heart trouble to most people, but would not deceive a heart specialist. Dr. Armstrong had

103

once been house physician at a heart hospital, and he knew a very great deal about hearts, and it was his special knowledge which had made him suspicious, weeks before Mr. Gregory had died, that there something wrong. If it had not been that Mrs. Gregory, because of her interest in Christian Science, had persuaded her husband not to go up to London to see one of the famous specialists Dr. Armstrong knew, they would have had the advantage of a second opinion, and the bereaved family would have known for certain what was the matter with Mr. Gregory, and his life might have been saved.

He hoped it would be clearly understood that he was in no way blaming Christian Science for this death. It had nothing whatever to do with it. Mrs. Gregory had never shown any interest in it until her husband's illness was nearing its end.

Then the coroner turned to the question of the cyanide of potassium. It was a poison easily obtainable in country places by anyone who was known to a chemist because it was commonly used for destroying wasps' nests and unwanted dogs and cats. The source of the cyanide of potassium found in Mr. Gregory's cocoa, however, had not been traced.

He explained to them very clearly and carefully, using non-technical language, how a death from cyanide of potassium could be distinguished from a death due to a heart attack. Ann understood him perfectly. How terribly obvious it all was when it was put to you like that!

He told them there were three possible verdicts they could bring in. Death by misadventure, if they thought Mr. Gregory had taken the cyanide accidentally. Death by his own hand, in which case they must decide whether he was in his right mind or not when he did it. Death by someone else's hand, which was murder. They were not required to say, and, in fact, they must not say—that was for the police—who they thought had done it if they decided that Mr. Gregory had been murdered. They must return their verdict in one of the three forms that he had given them. The case was now In their hands.

They clumped out in their heavy country boots, small tradesmen and farmers, Ann knew most of them by sight, and the crowded court relaxed and began to whisper.

CHAPTER EIGHT

"SLIPPED through our fingers," Ann heard Austen say in her ear. "But did you ever see anyone look quite so guilty? And wasn't her sister scared too? But we couldn't catch 'em out. They are away with it, whatever the verdict may be. I wonder how soon we shall hear wedding bells? I think I shall have to attend and see who the bridegroom is ."

Ann felt that she must pull herself together and put a brave face on the matter. Austen must suspect nothing until she had time to think over quietly all she had heard and really find out what it meant. She must not come to hasty decisions. She might be all wrong, and it would be a terrible thing to cry murder at her own father and then find she was mistaken, for a charge like that, once made, is never really shaken off. She must show an intelligent interest in the proceedings, but not too much.

She did not dare lift her face to look at Austen, and fortunately she had a wide-brimmed hat on.

"The little nurse was just as scared as Mrs. Gregory, it seemed to me," she said.

"That's a different kind of scare; we get to know them so well," said Austen. "Poor little soul, she went through hell, though."

The police constables had departed. They were alone in their corner of the court; the light of the brief spring day was fading, and there was a considerable amount of noise from innumerable low conversations and people moving about, and Ann thought it was an excellent opportunity to try and get some further information out of Austen so that she would know better how matters really lay. She felt like Delilah coaxing the secret of his strength from Samson, but she promised herself that she would not betray the confidence of the young police officer, but merely learn the position for her own information, for she saw that she had to walk very, very warily.

"Have you got absolutely no clues ?" she asked. "Are you going to stop looking for the murderer? Does it mean that you and Mr. Saunders will go away?"

"Would you be sorry if we went away, Puss?" said the whispering voice in her ear, as Austen tried to look under the brim of her hat.

"I would hate to have you go away without finding out who murdered Mr. Gregory."

"You think he was murdered, then?" asked Austen, successfully side-tracked by her red herring, and anxious to learn how the evidence had impressed a non-technical listener.

"I *know* he was murdered," said Ann, and an emphasis crept into her voice against her will that made Austen prick up his ears.

"What makes you think that, Puss ?"

"Who could listen to the evidence and doubt it?" Ann evaded.

"You may find the jury doubt it," said Austen with a sigh. "Juries are amazing things, especially in murder cases. Capital punishment puts them off their stroke. They won't convict if they can help it."

"I suppose if the jury brings in a verdict of not guilty you will pack up and go home?" said Ann conversationally.

"They won't bring it in quite like that, Puss; they aren't trying anybody. The coroner's court only has to find out what the fellow died of. If they find it's natural causes, or suicide, then, as you say, we shall pack up and go home, unless

107

some very drastic fresh information comes into our hands; but that is unlikely in this case, because they are not professional criminals, and there is no common informer to rely upon. When regular criminals are at work, the informer is as common as rain in summer."

"Why do people turn informer? What makes them give their friends away?" Ann felt her breath coming quickly as she asked this question.

"All sorts of motives. The fellow who gave Browne and Kennedy away did it because he wanted to run straight and Browne wouldn't leave him alone. Criminals give each other away wholesale because they want to keep in with us. A fellow knows we are after him for something not too desperate, and he spills the beans on someone else, a card of a higher value, as it were, and we open our fingers a little, and the smaller fish slips through. We know we can always find him again when we want him. That, I think, is the commonest reason for turning King's evidence; but the old Chief always says that as long as a fellow has a girl he's bound to be nabbed, because he's either so keen on her that he goes to see her when he ought to be lying doggo; or he has a row with her, and she gives him away out of spite."

Ann felt sick at heart when she heard this accurate diagnosis, and realized how closely it applied to herself. If she did not turn common informer, her father was safe. If Austen had not had "a girl" (horrible expression!), he would not now be betraying his duty and talking about the case to her, the murderer's daughter, of all people, and she might have let the cat out of the bag without knowing it.

"Does no one ever give a criminal away out of an abstract sense of justice?" she asked.

"I've never known it done," said Austen.

The light was steadily fading as they talked, and someone turned on a pair of table-lamps up by the coroner's desk.

The small circle of shaded light threw their own corner into even deeper shadow, and Austen took a chance, and slipped his arm round Ann's waist. She stiffened as if burnt, and his heart stood still. Had he over-reached himself? Then he felt her relax and lean up against him. He pressed her closely to him, unable to speak; and they sat for a while in silence, save for the sound of Austen's breathing, as he breathed quick and deep, as if running.

To Ann it seemed that the one point of stability in her crumbling universe was Austen's love for her. Social distinctions went by the board. Much good her aristocratic relations had ever been to her. They were, for the most part, a shifty, unstable lot, like her father, and she hoped to goodness that she took after her mother's family and had missed the Studley taint, otherwise she was not much catch for anybody. She had had her fair share, too, of young sprigs of nobility to whom her Aunt Maude had introduced her, anxious for her niece's future; but these, while perfectly willing, nay, anxious, to flirt indefinitely with the desirable Ann, and to go to any lengths that she would permit, had no intention of marrying her. Poor lads, they could not; they had to marry money.

It seemed to Ann, when she got to know Saunders and Austen, that she had escaped from a theatrical scene filled with gimcrack pasteboard figures, and come out into the honest light of day, among trustworthy, solid humans, with whom she felt safe. She was far more at home with rough old Saunders than with her aunt's precious colonels and canons, who were liable to kiss parlourmaids, and Ann, too, if they got the chance. Blue blood has its points when it is really blue, but when it gets like watered claret, honest red blood is much to be preferred.

Ann's class was dying out; its day was over; there was no employment for it in a post-War, mechanized universe. Its children, when it intermarried with itself, were hard to rear. Saunders's type were dying out too, owing to better housing, better education, and the passing of starvation wages. His sons, if he had had any, would have been like Austen. Austen's class was spreading hand over fist, absorbing Saunders, absorbing Ann; establishing new standards of aristocracy within itself—standards of vigour and efficiency and technical expertness. The more vigorous of Ann's class were settling down into it and accepting its standards; the more intelligent of Saunders's class were being licked into shape by State education and pushed into it, likewise to be absorbed. The less vigorous, the less intelligent of both classes were going to the wall and becoming extinct because they got no chance to reproduce their kind—vide Miss Studley, that soured virgin. Likewise Mr. Studley, whose sole attempt was Ann, who was now being taken from him by Austen.

When Ann cuddled up to Austen in the shadowy corner of the coroner's court, forgetting her caste and surrendering to his manhood, she was justifying Darwin of his wisdom, though she had not thought it out in terms of sexual selection, adaptation to environment, or survival of the fittest. She had not thought at all, poor child. She simply knew that in her desperate need and terror Austen's arm was strong about her; that he was big and masterful and manly; and that, anyway, she liked him; and liked him more and more as she got to know him better. It was no use for Aunt Maude to argue with that.

So they sat close together in the gathering dusk, while the jury debated and Mrs. Gregory snuffed smelling-salts and gulped ominously from time to time; both infinitely comforted by the touch of the other. It is not perfect love that spoils a man's work, but imperfect love that hammers him to pieces.

When Ann recommenced her third degree, Austen was

in a state when he would have bent his head to be shorn of his strength for the asking.

"Have you absolutely no clues?" said Ann.

"Well, Puss, we have, as a matter of fact. We've got some quite good ones, only for God's sake don't ever give a hint of it."

Ann's heart stood still, and she waited for his next words, hardly daring to breathe.

"We know exactly how the job was done, and we know the exact time when it was done. We also know the motive. Mrs. Gregory was carrying on with some fellow who was not content with carrying on, but wanted to marry her for her money—Gregory's money, to be precise. Knowing all this, it is simply a matter of keeping at work in the district with a tooth-comb till we light on some likely chap and ask him to give an account of himself on the night of the 12th, between ten and ten-thirty. Our field of research is cut exactly in half for us by the river. Whoever did the job must have been on the Datley side of the river, because he could not have got across at the bridge by Casley without being seen by the loungers outside the pub; and he did not cross by the ferry, because I've seen the ferryman, and we know what the river is like for swimming in, don't we, Puss?"

"My God!" thought Ann, "the steppingstones!"

The constriction in her throat nearly choked her, but she managed to say: "How do you think the—the murderer did it?"

"The fellow came in at a gate in the garden wall near the river, to which he had a key. He went up to Gregory's bedroom through a French window in Mrs. Gregory's sitting-room, which has a Yale lock on it for some unknown reason, and to which he also had a key. He shoved the cyanide in Gregory's cocoa, which was standing ready mixed, but not made, and he came out the same way. He did it between ten

111

o'clock, when the nurse put the tray there, and ten-thirty, when Gregory died, and he jolly well knew the ins and outs of that household, and he's no amateur."

"How do you know he did all this? How do you know he's not an amateur?"

"We've found marks at all those places, Puss. The hinges and lock of the door in the wall had been recently oiled, and oiled from inside, too, so that implicates someone in the house. Then there were the marks of a labourer's hob-nailed boots on the path, right away from the door to the French window."

"Then it was a labourer who did the job?" asked Ann, breathing a sigh of relief.

"No," said Austen, "that is exactly what it wasn't. It was a fellow who had bought the boots for the job; so that tells us that whoever it was, it wasn't a clod-hopper. It was someone in a different position who wanted to direct attention away from himself, and that's the thing that hangs more murderers than anything else. If they only wouldn't gild the lily, most of 'em would get away with it."

"But how do you know this? How do you know the man who wore the hob-nailed boots wasn't a labourer?"

"Well, Puss, you know the way a clodhopper galumphs along, don't you? He's stiff in the joints, and lurches from one foot to another when he walks and comes down flat-footed. He puts his feet wide apart, partly because he's stiff, and partly because he's accustomed to walking over rough ground. This fellow tittuped along on his toes like a City gent, and he had either got abnormally large feet for his height, or an abnormally short stride; moreover, the boots were brand new, and at several points on his way from the gate to the window he tripped over his own feet, but not on his way from the window to the gate, by which time he had got used to his new footgear. No, Pussy, everything points to its not being an

112

agricultural labourer. We are looking for a shabby-genteel individual five foot seven in height, who takes size eight in shoes; who has come down in the world and had got a bad record. Luckily for your parent, the river wipes him out."

"Yes," Ann agreed faintly, and then added hastily lest a pause in the conversation might prove embarrassing: "How do you know he has come down in the world?"

"Well, Puss, that old mutton-dressed-as-lamb with a stucco frontage isn't any particular catch, is she?"

"And—and how do you know he has a bad record?"

"Because of the workmanlike manner in which he did the job. That's not the first corpse he's polished off with cyanide and digitalis. All the same, Puss, nothing but luck will enable us to land him. Bad luck for him or good luck for us. He's had one bit of bad luck in his doctor, who knew more about hearts than most. A wonky heart for a few weeks, and a final seizure, would have satisfied most G.P.s. It now remains to be seen where his next bit of bad luck will come from. Mrs. Gregory, most likely. That woman will have the high-strikes in the near future, if I'm any judge of females; and when she loses her nerve she may blow the gaff, or drop a brick, or get a conscience, or any old thing. She's no Lady Macbeth."

"But—but how about finger-marks?" asked Ann, the crime fan.

"Blighter wore gloves, Pussy. First thing they do nowadays, thanks to the popular interest in criminology."

Ann heaved another sigh of relief, but Austen went on:

"That doesn't bother us unduly, however, because we are certain he's an old hand, and it's ten to one we have already got his prints at the Yard. We are quietly getting the prints of everyone who has ever been associated with the Gregorys to the umpteenth generation, and if one of 'em matches anything we've got, well, he'll have to explain himself."

"I suppose you have examined a lot of people's finger-

113

prints?"

"Puss, I should think we've examined the entire county! There's no stopping old Saunders once he starts, but even he can't go on for ever. I don't mind telling you, Puss, that if it hadn't been for you, I should have been dead sick of this case long ago and voted for home. It's a mystery to me why the Yard haven't called us off before this."

"Then—then you haven't got a theory?"

"Only what I've told you, Puss. We're running blind, trusting to luck at the moment; but that's good enough for us. We always say that Sergeant Chance and Constable Luck are the backbone of the Force, and it's perfectly true. They've dished a dashed sight more criminals than any fancy Thorndyke touches."

"But—but how much longer will you keep on? When will you give up and go home?"

"I don't know, Puss. The Chief is going up to London with Sir William Bruce, the Home Office man, after we've heard the verdict, and he will talk the case over with the powers that be, and they will decide whether he keeps his nose to the trail or seeks pastures new; and we, Puss, unless you've changed your mind, go and have tea. I could do with some tea, couldn't you ?"

"I could!" said Ann fervently.

Then the coroner came back, the jury reappeared in their box, someone switched on the lights, Austen dropped Ann like a hot coal, and the words, "Wilful Murder" rang through the court.

They went out by the back alley by which they had come in, thus avoiding the crowd, and Austen took advantage of the darkness to put his arm round Ann again; not round her waist, he couldn't reach it, the disproportion in their heights was too great, and to whisper to her:

"Pussy, I'm so happy!"

And he held her to him so closely that she tripped over his feet, and he had to let her go in favour of a more dignified and practical mode of progression.

They were the first to arrive in the cafe in the square, opposite the Town Hall, in whose back regions the coroner's court was situated. Austen immediately took possession of a little table for two beside the door, where the air was fresh after the stuffiness of the crowded court, but this advantage was somewhat offset for Ann by the crowd of loungers who gathered round the door and stared at Austen, evidently guessing that he was connected with the case:

They saw Mrs. Gregory and her sister get into a magnificent car and drive away, a photographer's flare lighting up the whole scene with a horrible publicity.

"She's got luck, has that woman," commented Austen, "It remains to be seen whether it will hold."

The cafe filled up rapidly as people came out from the inquest, all of them looking at Austen and herself with interest. They had probably seen them sitting together in court, and Ann wondered how much they had been able to see of the position of Austen's arm.

"Hullo, Puss, you're looking very white, what's the matter?" asked Austen, seeing Ann's face for the first time in the brightly-lit cafe.

"I've got a headache," said Ann, and she had. "The court was very stuffy."

"I'm awfully sorry, Puss, I'm afraid courts always are. I'm too used to them to notice it. A cup of tea will soon put you to rights. It was worth a headache to see Mrs. Gregory wriggle in the witness-box wasn't it? Didn't you find it interesting? I think the cross examinations are fascinating. I never get tired of them."

Ann admitted that she found it very interesting, which was indeed the truth. The merry-go-round was still grinding out 'Digitalis, digitalis', and she thought she would never get the sound out of her ears till her dying day.

As she was pouring Austen out his tea she glanced up, and saw her father standing in the doorway looking down at them. The tea went all over the tray and Austen grabbed at the pot, crying, "Puss, look out!" Then he looked up to see what had startled her, and saw Mr. Studley. He also saw that he was in that dangerous state of drunkenness when a man has lost his self control, but is not incapable and helpless. The expression on his face was terrible. Austen had seen many men stand up to be sentenced, but he had never seen anyone look worse than this.

The crowd in the tea-rooms, fresh from the inquest and recognizing Austen who was a much-photographed man, sat as still as mice, scenting drama. Not a teaspoon clinked. Studley, oblivious of the sensation he was making, leant up against the door-post and stared savagely at his daughter and her companion.

"Well, Detective-sergeant Austen," he said at length, with that careful deliberation of drunken men when their speech is failing them, "Seducing my daughter?"

Austen rose to his feet and faced him, and Ann made certain he was going to strike her father. Then she saw him, as she had so often seen him before, change from the man into the police officer.

"That is a very improper remark, sir," he said, "I am only doing my duty and carrying out my orders. Inspector Saunders wished the young lady to be in court, and instructed me to bring her."

"And to take her to tea afterwards?"

"Yes, sir, and see her home safely."

"And chase her all round the garden and kiss her? And steal my whisky and drink it?"

The silence in the cafe could have been cut with a knife.

"Those are very improper observations to make, sir, I should go home if I were you, sir. If you have any complaint against me, you can report it in the proper quarter."

Ann knew that her father was trying to make Austen lose his temper, but if there is one thing more than all others which it is difficult to do with an experienced police officer, it is that. Austen looked like one of the statues from Easter Island that decorate the front steps of the British Museum.

Ann had taken to heart the lesson Inspector Saunders had taught her when he told her to be quiet and not struggle with Austen, and she thought that if her presence were removed, her father would be much less likely to go to extremes. Silently as a shadow she slipped from her seat, unnoticed by either man, and vanished among the cars parked in the ill-lit square.

She found the bus that ran down the London road to Datley just ready to start, boarded it, and was soon being carried away from that town of ill-omen. Neither Baby Austin nor sidecar overtook her during the two miles to that village, and she wondered how the dispute in the tea-rooms had ended.

Her father was in the habit of making drunken assaults on anyone who annoyed him, and no one hit him back, though he had been summoned several times, for to hit a man of his age puts the assailant hopelessly in the wrong; consequently he had escaped the thrashings he so richly deserved. But Ann knew that if he even lifted his hand to Austen, Austen would run him in, which, she thought, would be a very salutary lesson for him. Her cheeks burned when she thought of his words in that crowded cafe, with everyone listening.

She left the bus when it stopped near the gates of Deepdene Hall, and saw how little excuse her father had for his pretended ignorance of the change of name, for it was painted in large black letters on the white gate, as if the place were a boarding-house.

She went down the path at the side of the high garden wall till she reached the river bank, and then turned to the right and walked a few yards. But when she came to the place where the first of the stepping-stones stood amid the swirling white water, her nerve failed her. The light was very bad, practically dark; the river was high, and some of the stones might be under water. Although less than a hundred yards from her home as the crow flies, she was twelve miles away by road, with no other means of conveyance than her two tired feet.

She stood desperately on the bank. A misstep in the dark meant certain death, and there was a bend in the middle of the line of stones that was very misleading. Dared she try? And if she tried, could she manage it? Should she go back to the village of Datley and try to get some kind of conveyance? No, a thousand times no, after the scene in the cafe. Besides, everybody would want to know what she was doing in Datley, the scene of the murder. And it might come out about the stepping-stones, and then her father's alibi would be gone. No, she must cross by those stones, or, alternatively, make those twelve miles on foot before dawn in her high-heeled shoes and thin linen dress if she wished to keep her secret. Her heart failed her at the prospect.

Then it suddenly occurred to her that the moon was full, and would be up shortly, and then she would have plenty of light for the crossing. She had a good nerve, and did not fear the undertaking as long as she could see what she was doing; but to try to cross in the dark was sheer madness, and she ought to have realized it before she set out on the bus; but she was so distraught with the whole business that she was almost incapable of thought.

She settled down on a rock to wait for the moonrise. She was miserably cold, for the temperature drops quickly at sunset in the early part of the year, even if the day has been warm. Fortunately the high wall of the garden of Deepdene Hall was just behind her and sheltered her from the wind. Her coat she had been unable to obtain when she fled, for it was locked up in the case at the back of the sidecar where the miniature laboratory travelled—the laboratory that enabled her lover to recognize bloodstains and bring men to the gallows, she thought to herself, with a bitter laugh.

Then, above the purl of the swift-running water, someone else laughed—a horrible hyena laugh, with no mirth in it—peal after peal—and then turned to such shrieks that Ann's heart stood still with horror at the sound. Then she heard the noise of a window being hastily shut, and the cries were muffled. She could not imagine what this awful outcry in the quiet countryside could be. And then it suddenly dawned upon her that it was Mrs. Gregory having hysterics. She was close up to Deepdene Hall, under its very walls, in fact. And she was sitting on the very spot by which her father had passed upon his dreadful errand exactly a month ago. Yes, it was a month ago to the day, and he, too, would have had a full moon to cross the water by; that was probably why that time was chosen. It was no sudden impulse that had caused him to deal death to a fellow-being. Everything had been carefully thought out; his alibi, Mrs. Gregory's alibi—everything. Ann remembered how the coroner had tried to shake that alibi, but in vain. It was too perfect. What Austen called a cast-iron alibi, and viewed with such suspicion.

Supposing her father came again by this dark and dangerous way to see his mistress and rejoice with her at their escape, and make plans for their future happiness! How long would he tolerate Ann's presence on earth under the circumstances? A grown-up daughter is a tiresome thing in a second marriage. He had often told her that death would come to her early, and through heart-failure, and she knew what heart-failure meant in his terminology now. He had threatened to murder her every time he had said those words, and he had said them frequently lately. She turned and crept away into the bushes like a wounded animal and hid herself.

It never occurred to her to betray her father; to hand him over to the justice he so richly deserved. Between them was that curious tie of father and daughter, which has its analogue in the bond between mother and son, though it is rarer.

"If I were hanged on the highest hill,
    (Mother O' mine, O mother O' mine),
I know whose love would follow me still,
    (Mother O' mine, O mother O' mine)."

When she was small her father had made the greatest pet of her and she had been his constant companion; and although his steady degeneration from a normal that was never any too good had brought him to a point when he was incapable of feeling any but the baser passions or caring for anyone but himself, and she fully realized that he no longer had any scrap of affection for her—in fact, might be said to hate her in proportion as he realized how he had failed and disgraced her—something deep in Ann's heart clung to him steadfastly, without shadow of turning; and this was a thing that neither Austen nor Saunders, from their different points of view, had reckoned with. They looked for her to behave logically and reasonably; but these things of the deeper emotions are not logical and reasonable, they are instinctive, and we can neither account for them nor control them. Had Austen known it, the yielding of Ann's body to the pressure of his arm, which had sent him to the seventh heaven, was a farewell.

Ann crouched on the roots of a large tree in the endeavour to keep her body from the wet earth. The terrible screams had ceased, and no noise save the hooting of an owl and an occasional motor-horn now came to her above the sound of the swift-running water. Ann shivered in her hiding-place, and longed for Austen.

Then there came to her the terrible realization that she had lost Austen. It was not possible for him to marry a murderer's daughter. That she knew; for when the village constable had wanted to marry the barmaid at the Black Horse, a lady with a very lively local reputation, he had been forced to resign the force. However, an old admirer had set them up in a pub, and they were flourishing. But if Ann came to Austen, she came empty-handed. She knew what his career meant to him, that he was wrapped up in it body and soul, and she saw with clear eyes that that could not be done, even if he were willing, and she doubted if he would be.

With the realization that marriage between them was impossible from his side, the last barrier to Ann's love for Austen went down. Now that she had not to face the very practical social difficulties such a marriage would offer, caste feeling no longer made conflict. Ann bowed her head on her knees and had not even the consolation of tears. Murderers kill more than their victims.

CHAPTER NINE

THE moon rose early that night, fortunately for Ann in her thin dress, and when she finally lifted her head from her knees, she saw that a long shaft of cold clear light shone down the little canon in which the river ran below the weir, and that the rocks stood up clear and black amid the white of the rushing water. Ann came to the edge of the river and stepped on to the first of the stones, a slender, wraith-like figure in the colourless moonlight.

The stones were none too close together, and she had to spring from one to another, but it did not seem to her to matter whether she crossed in safety or not; it would simplify matters very much if she didn't! She sprang from stone to stone recklessly in the uncertain light. What did it matter if she missed her footing and fell in? What did it matter if her father saw her and pushed her in? Nothing mattered now. She was the daughter of a triple murderer and her own turn would come soon. Moreover, she had lost Austen. Desperate and indifferent to danger, Ann crossed far more safely in the treacherous moonlight than if she had cautiously felt each step.

Once upon the farther bank she had to move more carefully, for in the shadow of the miniature cliffs the light was very dim. She met with little difficulty, however, and marvelled how free the path was from undergrowth, and wondered how much it had been used to come and go between Deepdene Hall and Thatched Cottage. It was a path upon which no one would be observed.

Once on a level with the weir she found herself back again in the clear bright moonlight. The weir was growling like a hungry animal, and she remembered how nearly it had devoured Austen. The memory of that struggle, and his face as he struggled and felt his strength giving out, came back to her, and she saw that she was standing at the very spot where he had dragged himself out of the water. There was the sapling she had hung on by. There were the marks on the bank left by his struggles. There were the broken bushes where he had dropped unconscious, still clutching her. Ann hastened away. These things had better not be remembered.

But next minute she came out of the little wood into the orchard, and there, in the clear moonlight, was the patch of trampled grass where she and Austen had wrestled together in their rough love-play. Ann started to run and did not stop till she came to the dark, silent house, and let herself in and went to bed.

But sleep was out of the question. She lay awake listening. When would they come home, if they did come home-her father and Austen ? Inspector Saunders, she knew, was away for the night. What had been the upshot of the scene in the cafe?

As she waited, she tried to plan her course of action. She had a very difficult task before her. There was a chance, just a remote chance, that when Austen knew all, he would still want her. She did not know exactly what the police regulations were with regard to marriage of members of the Force. Were they allowed to marry into the criminal classes? She thought not. Yet would the fact that poor Ann herself was blameless be taken to mitigate her offence in being the daughter of her father? Would Austen, who would certainly have his own pride and standards of respectability, care to ally himself to a murderer's daughter in the sight of all his comrades? Ann did not know this either. A man may feel cer-

123

tain things in the full tide of falling in love that he will cease to feel when he has had time to think things over and cool down.

But then, it suddenly occurred to her that nothing might come out about her father after all. She was crossing her bridges before she got to them. Her wisest decision, she felt, was to keep quiet and do nothing; behave as if nothing had happened to bring her world crashing about her ears; keep Austen at arm's length, but not give him his final dismissal (in this matter she was reckoning without Austen). In the warmth and safety of her own familiar little room the idea of her father sending her to join his other victims appeared to her ridiculous. Ought she to betray him to the police for the sake of abstract justice? Austen had said he had never known such a thing to be done. She could not see that it would help the dead, and it would cause dreadful anguish to the living. She thought of poor Mrs. Gregory's frantic screams, her sister's terrified eyes— It would be quite enough punishment for Mrs. Gregory if she married Francis Studley; that would be a judgment on her all right for her complicity in the affair.

Then it suddenly dawned on Ann that her father's punishment would not be imprisonment but the gallows if she betrayed his guilt, and the full horror came home to her. She would be put up in the witness-box as Mrs. Gregory had been, the principal witness against him; the only witness, in fact, for she alone could supply the missing links in the chain of evidence.

But would they believe her if she spoke? That was another pitfall in this maze of unsuspected dangers, a fresh one of which showed up at every step. Supposing she gave this evidence against her father, and in spite of it he were acquitted—Austen said juries were extraordinary things, especially murder juries—what would be his revenge upon her and Austen?

And supposing she were believed? She could see her father watching her from the dock as word by word she made his conviction certain. She could see him standing up to receive the death sentence, still looking at her. She could see herself counting the days, and then watching the clock, till one morning the hands pointed to eight a.m. and she knew that her father was being strangled. Ann had nearly been strangled once in her dressing-gown cord when she was little, and she knew what it felt like—the horrible fighting for air and seeing things go dark—No, it simply couldn't be done. A long sentence, even a life sentence, would have been a different matter, but capital punishment—? No, she would not come forward with her evidence.

She had hardly reached this decision when she heard the motor-cycle return up the lane, and in a few minutes she heard Austen's heavy tread in the hall, and was comforted by the sound. At least he was under the same roof with her. She heard him go round the house, looking into the different rooms, evidently to see if she were still about. Then he came upstairs and stood on the little landing as if listening outside her door. Then he called: "Ann, are you there?" But she did not answer.' With a sudden jump Ann realized that she had not locked her door; she never did; she was not sure if it had a key. Would he walk in to see if she were there? And if he did, how was he to be got out again? But he did not come in. He would have walked into the room of any armed desperado to see if it were occupied or not, but he would not walk into Ann's room.

She heard him go downstairs again, and enter the kitchen. After that all was quiet, but she smelt his cigarette smoke. She wondered what time it was? Pretty late, she thought. She must have been in bed at least an hour.

Then she heard the Baby Austin jugging down the lane,

125

and an awful crashing of gears as her father changed down for the turn into the barn. There was a long pause. Ann wondered whether he was spending the night in the garage, unable to get any farther. She decided that if he did, she would let him stop there, and if he took a chill, that was his lookout.

Then she heard a bump in the hall, and knew that her father had entered.

Immediately she heard Austen's voice.

"Where is your daughter, Mr. Studley?"

"Well," said Mr. Studley with the painful deliberation of the very drunk, "Ash she hashn't come home, I thought she wash shpendin' night with you."

"You say another word, and I'll knock your bloody head off!" shouted Austen.

"Knocked head off—chucked out of police," said Mr. Studley, with more shrewdness than might have been expected of him in his condition.

"Where is she?" snarled Austen. "You're going to answer, or it will be the worse for you."

"I donno, m'dear feller. You more likely to know than me. Shwear I don't. Poor little girl been shedushed."

"You go to bed, damn you," said Austen exasperatedly.

"Go to bed while daughter bein' shedushed? Never. Shtop up all night. Never go to bed." Mr. Studley spoke with great dignity and feeling. "Shay, you tell me shomthing I want to know? Ish she pregnant yet?"

" ! ! !—!—! !——!" said Austen.

Ann thought it time to intervene.

"I came home and went to bed long ago," her clear voice came from above their heads, "and should be asleep now if you two weren't making so much noise. I wish you'd both go to bed and be quiet."

"Are you all right, Miss Studley?" Austen's voice was

126

sharp with anxiety.

"Quite all right, thank you, Mr. Austen," said Ann, and shut the door, wedging a chair under the handle in lieu of the absent key.

She heard the sound of a heavy body being dragged roughly up the stairs, and bumped hard on every step; and between the bumps, her father's voice singing something about the bobby on the beat. Then she heard the door of his bedroom opened, and something flung in, and the door slammed, and Austen's stride crossing the little landing, shaking the house. Then his door slammed too, and all was quiet.

Ann knew who she would find in the kitchen when she came down in the morning, and there he was, in his grey flannel bags and old sports coat, looking extraordinarily normal and everyday after the excitements of yesterday. He came towards her holding out his arms, and she put the table between them. She thought she had never seen anyone look so radiantly happy. He took hold of the edge of the table with his big brown hands and leant towards her.

"Pussy," he said, very quietly, "you know I love you, and I think you love me. Will you marry me and let me take you away from all this? I haven't a great deal to offer you—not like what you've been accustomed to, but it's steady, and it's safe. Will you marry me, Puss ?"

Ann put her hand to her throat and looked into the smiling eyes, bent down to a level with her own.

"I can't," she said. "It's no use. I can't."

She saw the expression go out of Austen's face as if a sponge had been drawn across a slate.

"Why can't you?" he said in a very low voice.

"I—I can't. I can't tell you why. I just can't."

"I thought you liked me, Pussy. You acted as if you did."

"I know; I do like you. It isn't that. I just can't."

127

"Is it because of your father?"

Ann hesitated. "Yes, partly."

"But you've known that all along, Puss, and yet you acted as if you liked me."

"I know," said Ann, miserably. "I hadn't realized."

"You hadn't realized what?" Austen's face suddenly hardened. "You hadn't realized till you saw me with the other coppers that I was a policeman? Is that it?"

If he hadn't been a policeman, it wouldn't have mattered her father being a murderer. Ann hesitated, and was lost.

Austen walked out of the kitchen and slammed the door.

When he met Inspector Saunders at the station a couple of hours later, that worthy took one look at his face and said:

"Had a row with your girl ?"

"Yes," said Austen, and swung the side-car round the bend of the station-yard in a way that caused Saunders to yell and clutch his hat.

When Ann brought in the tea, Saunders saw that she had been crying. He saw her look appealingly at Austen, whose eyes were fixed on his boots. He judged it was an inauspicious time to question his subordinate, who was looking like the devil. Things would come out in due course. He had been Austen's guide, philosopher and friend ever since he entered the C.I.D. He was pretty certain the lad would want an older man's counsel as soon as he felt able to speak of his troubles. For his part, he would be by no means sorry if the pretty Ann gave him the go-by. He'd get over it in time. She wouldn't be a good wife for everyday wear for a policeman. He would be much happier in the long run with a girl of his own class. So he soliloquized, while Austen stirred his tea moodily and stared into space.

When Saunders thought the sulks had gone on long

enough, he broke the silence conversationally.

"I shouldn't be surprised if we had a case of D.T.s on our hands," he said.

"Neither should I," said Austen indifferently. "I don't think it's wise for both of us to be out together and leave the girl alone in the house till the old boy has either bucked up or spotted his first rat. I think we'd better stand watch and watch," said Saunders.

"Yes, sir," said Austen without enthusiasm.

"Dangerous for the girl, you know," continued Saunders. "I seen a woman chased down the road with an axe by a chap that was seeing snakes."

"I've seen one chased with a gun," said Austen listlessly.

"Buck up, my lad. Faint heart never won fair lady."

Austen's face hardened. "I've had my answer. I shan't bother her again."

This was a predicament which Inspector Saunders had not bargained for. He certainly did not want Ann flung away until she had been sucked dry.

"I shouldn't take no for an answer as easily as that, if I was you, my lad. They nearly always say no the first time you ask 'em. All the best ones, anyway."

Austen did not answer, but Saunders saw that the set, stony look had gone out of his face, and judged that his words had taken effect. Then they discussed the case, and Saunders thought his subordinate looked quite well pleased to hear that they were not to quit the trail and move on to other quarters yet. He might not have been so pleased, Saunders thought, if he had known the reasons that had been given at headquarters for persevering with the case.

Mr. Studley had not gone out that day in his car. He often did not, after a particularly bad drunk, his nerve not being equal to the effort of driving it. Ann thought that she had never seen him look so dreadful as he did when she went to his study after supper, and kissing him on the top of his head, said :

"Dad, I want to have a talk with you."

Mr. Studley had a very dim recollection of what had been said and done during his quarrel with Austen, but he had an exceedingly clear and lively recollection of Ann's face when Mrs. Gregory threw back her veil, for he had been in the part of the court reserved for the public, though neither Ann nor Austen had noticed him. So he smiled grimly at his daughter, and felt for a small packet that lay in his waistcoat pocket.

Ann sat down on the hearthrug at her father's feet and laid her hand on his knee, and without looking at him, said:

"Father, I recognized Mrs. Godfrey."

"Did you, my dear?" said Mr. Studley, the paper packet between finger and thumb, and his eyes like those of a jaguar waiting to spring.

"And I wanted you to know that I shan't say anything."

"Thank you, my dear," said Mr. Studley brokenly, putting his hand over Ann's as it lay on his knee. And they sat thus, father and daughter, far into the night, the girl thinking of her lost lover and the wretched man striving to drown thought as rapidly as might be in the whisky that now took effect so slowly and left him feeling so ill.

It was past midnight before he sank into the drunken stupor that passed for sleep with him, and Ann, kissing him again on the top of his head, crept out of the room. The door of the detectives' sitting-room stood open and the room was in darkness. Ann thanked her stars. But at the sound of her step in the hall, out came Austen.

"Pussy," he said, "don't drive me away."

Ann remembered a stray dog, a mongrel spaniel, that used to come round the kitchen door, and was driven away by her father's orders. She remembered how the poor starving thing had looked at her when she clapped her hands and shooed it, not daring to feed it, because her father had said he would poison it if it kept on coming. But it had come again, and he had put the wasp poison, cyanide, she remembered with a shudder, on a piece of meat and flung it out, and the famished creature had sprung upon it gratefully, given one strangled yelp, and died.

Ann could not speak. She pushed past Austen and ran upstairs to her bedroom and flung herself on her bed and wept. How could she explain herself to Austen without directing suspicion on her father?

Austen turned on his heel and re-entered the sitting-room, shutting himself in alone with the darkness.

Inspector Saunders found his subordinate utterly unmanageable next morning, and cursed all women. Austen's eyes were heavy with lack of sleep, and his temper exceedingly short. He handled his precious microscope in a manner that threatened to wreck it, so Saunders demanded the side-car and caused himself to be driven to the back of beyond to a wrong address. There was nothing to be done but hang about till Ann's nerves reached the state when she would deliver the goods.

Saunders had given instructions where she was to be seated during the inquest, and had reserved for himself a seat in a strategical position which would enable him to watch her without being observed. He had seen her recognition of Mrs. Gregory and her dawning horror as the evidence unfolded. He had seen the look of resolution that had come into her face when the coroner explained to the jury exactly what the medical evidence meant, and Ann had taken in its significance, and he had more than half expected to be met by his subordinate with a signed statement. But Ann had evidently made up her mind that nothing would induce her to tell. Women were surprising things. Fancy preferring her tank of a father to a fine young fellow like Austen, who was breaking his heart over her. It would be very awkward if Ann could not be got to speak; his superiors would not thank him for wasting any more time on the case when they were so short-handed. However, he had a shot or two still left in his locker. If Ann would not give herself away for love, she might if made sufficiently angry, or alternatively, if badly frightened. He thought, however, that from what he had seen of Ann she would have to be very badly frightened indeed before anything could be extracted from her, and abandoned the second alternative in favour of the first.

He took his companion to lunch at a roadside pub, to Austen's obvious relief, for meals served by Ann were an ordeal, and once again plied him with beer, wondering whether he were wise, or whether he were starting his comrade on the downward path. Inspector Saunders had a shrewd suspicion that he was raising the wind with his machinations, and must be prepared to ride the whirlwind. He also felt, however, with his peculiar detective's flair, which often accounts for more than Holmeslike logic, though not so suitable for use in fiction, that if there were a thorough showdown and everything about Mr. Studley came out, Austen's path might be cleared. So he felt even less scruple in using his comrade as a cat's-paw than might otherwise have troubled his not particularly tender conscience.

The beer calmed Austen's overwrought nerves, and presently he availed himself of the safety valve that Saunders dangled patiently before him, and began to talk about his troubles.

"It's no use, Chief, she won't look at me. I tried her again last night, after you had gone to bed" (Saunders wondered what time that was, for he was by no means an early bird), "and she just hared past me and up the stairs without a word."

132

Saunders did not like that. A talking woman can be talked round; but a silent one—God only knew what they were up to. They usually meant business.

"What reason did she give for turning you down, lad?" he asked.

"Well, she wouldn't give a reason. She practically admitted she cared for me, and I fancy she does. But when I asked her if she wouldn't have me because I was a copper, I could see I had hit the right nail on the head. So I left it at that. That's a thing you can't argue about with a girl like her, isn't it, Chief?"

"Yes, my lad. I'm afraid it is," said Saunders, feeling intensely sorry for the young fellow, and very angry with Ann, whom he considered had led him on most outrageously.

Now it so happened that Saunders had drunk glass for glass with his subordinate, this being the etiquette among men of his class; but whereas in his present state Austen could have drunk a barrel without its having any effect on him, poor Saunders, who only took about three glasses of beer per annum, and those only when he had to get into conversation with topers, was being very decidedly taken by the head. He saw moisture in Austen's eyes, and was seized by a sudden horror that his companion was going to weep. Anything on God's earth was better than that! It was ten times worse than hysterical women, his especial bugbear. So he launched hastily into conversation in a way he would never have done had he stuck to his rule that police work is best done on water.

"Now look here, my lad," he said dropping his voice to the husky whisper of confidences, "I'm going to tell you what I reely think."

Austen woke up suddenly and paid attention.

"Was you watchin' Ann's face while the evidence was bein' given at the inquest?"

"No," said Austen, "I couldn't. She'd got a hat like a cart-wheel."

"Well, I was," said Saunders, "and I'll tell yer some-think." Under the influence of the beer he was lapsing into the idiom of his youth, very different to the well-spoken man who answered so politely in the witness-box. "Miss Ann, she knew Mrs. Gregory, and knew 'er well."

"Go on!" exclaimed Austen. "Did she? Then that ex-plains it."

"Explains what?" asked Saunders eagerly, feeling that things were at last beginning to move.

"Explains why she looked so queer at tea. She was as white as a sheet; and when she saw her dad, she chucked the tea all over the table. Said she had a headache, and I believed her. The place stank like a stable."

"I bet she had a headache," chuckled Saunders. "And a heart-ache. And a stomach-ache, too, for the matter of that."

"What do you mean, Chief? Got anything definite?"

"Nothing definite, as you might say. But I been watching that old codfish of a father of hers, and the more I see of him, the less I like the look of him."

"Why didn't you tell me, Chief? You never said a word."

"What was the use of saying anything to you, my lad? You was that goofy there was no gettin' any sense out of you."

"Now this puts a different complexion on the matter," said Austen slowly. "But you don't think Ann's mixed up in it, do you? My God, Chief, you don't think Ann's mixed up in it? If she is, you must let me out of this. I can't go on with it."

"No," said Saunders, "I don't think Ann was in it for a moment, and I don't think she even suspected anything until she saw Mrs. Gregory in the witness-box. But she obviously knew 'er, though probably under another name, as the name o' Gregory never seemed to mean anything to 'er. And Mrs. Gregory knew Ann, and was expecting Ann to identify 'er; you could see that by the way she glared at the girl. My bet is that old Studley is the Missing Link."

"You mean the man we've been looking for? Mrs. Gregory's fancy, Gosh, I'll have his finger-prints before he's much older!"

"You've no objection to huntin' old Studley, then?" inquired Saunders.

"Hunt that old—— !" exclaimed Austen.

"Hush," said Saunders, as the waitress came in with more beer.

CHAPTER TEN

"NOW, Jack," said Inspector Saunders, "we've got to watch our step very careful in this matter, or the old boy will try and make capital out of the way you've been hanging round his girl."

"Will try?" exclaimed Austen, with an angry laugh. "Has tried—and managed it—blast him to hell!"

Saunders judged from the badness of the language his subordinate used whenever the subject of his future father-in-law came up that Mr. Studley must have done something particularly outrageous, for Austen was usually a clean-mouthed man.

"What's he been up to? Let's have it all out," he said.

"He came into the cafe where I was giving Ann tea after the show," said Austen, "and he stood up in front of every-body and said at the top of his voice: 'Well, Sergeant Austen, seducing my daughter?' " Austen's face went crimson and he ground his teeth at the recollection.

Saunders looked at him anxiously. "What did you do?" he asked.

"Oh, I gave him police talk. 'Yes, sir. No, sir. Very im-proper observation, sir.' I never batted an eyelid. It was the only thing to do. He was as drunk as a hoot-owl."

"Good lad !" exclaimed Saunders, breathing an audible sigh of relief. "What did the girl do?"

"Hopped it. Best thing she could do. I never saw her go. Just found she was gone."

"How did she get home?"

"Don't know. She didn't come home with me. Nor with him. That reminds me, I must give her back her coat. It's still in the side-car. Must have got a lift from someone she knew. She was back before we were."

Saunders wondered who it was that had given Ann a lift, for according to his inquiries, she knew nobody.

"And how did you get rid of old Studley?" he asked.

"I couldn't get rid of him. I thought I'd have to take him in charge. Luckily for me, Ashcott and another chap came along, and they tackled him; tackled him pretty rough, too. Told him to shut up or they'd run him in. Gave him no choice. Clear off or come along. So he hopped it, too. Into the bar of the Blue Lion. They told me they'd always had a lot of trouble with him, but never like he had been lately. And what do you think old Ashcott said to me. He said, 'That's my fancy for the Gregory Stakes.' I asked him if he'd got anything to go upon; but he said, nairy a thing. Just didn't like the cut of his jib."

"Odd, ain't it, how you know these things?" sighed Saunders. "Wish juries was made like us. "One of these days," he continued, "Old man Studley will ditch that Baby Austin of his and come home feet foremost. What was he like when he arrived home that night?"

"Tanked to a degree you'd never believe, sir. I was scared to death as to what he'd done with Ann. I thought he'd break her neck with his driving. But she wasn't with him, thank God. And then an awful thing happened."

Saunders turned anxious eyes on his subordinate, as the young man paused, evidently experiencing difficulty in getting his confession off his chest.

"I didn't know she had got back, and I was waiting up for her when in he came, blind to the wide, and she wasn't with him. I was scared stiff. It was getting on towards midnight, there was a fair on in the town and a lot of rough characters about, and I didn't know what had become of her. I took him by the collar and upended him, and started to pump the truth out of him. And what do you think he said to me?"

Austen paused, and seemed to have difficulty in getting his lips to frame the words.

"He asked me if she was pregnant."

Inspector Saunders said what he thought of Mr. Studley in the language of the street.

"And that isn't all," continued the unhappy Austen. "I said pretty much what you've said, and a bit more into the bargain. And she was hanging over the banisters watching us the whole time!"

Saunders collapsed in guffaws. It struck him as irresistibly funny that his comrade, leashed in by discipline till he reached bursting-point, and letting himself go when he believed himself alone with his tormentor, should have had Ann for a silent witness. He had not heard Mr. Studley's remark concerning the raw, rough ranker, but something of the same sort passed through his mind, and he wondered what part this outburst had played in Ann's refusal, and he could see by Austen's unhappy face that he was wondering the same thing.

"It's no laughing matter for me, Chief," he said, smiling wryly.

"It's no laughing matter for either of us, my boy," said Saunders. "What was the end of it?"

"I had to put the b—— to bed," said Austen glumly, and Inspector Saunders collapsed again.

"And, gosh, didn't I bump the beggar up the stairs! He won't sit down for a fortnight. I hit him on every step. Good job there was no station sergeant about. And I fetched him such a kosh on the post at the top! He'd got a lump like a hen's egg on the back of his napper this morning. Then I chucked him into his room in a heap and left him, and prayed he'd catch pneumonia. That was the end of that, Chief. He didn't, no such luck. That sort never do."

Saunders had got a pretty good idea of the kind of man-handling Mr. Studley had received, and thought it no wonder he was taking a day off. He had done the same thing himself in his younger days with old chronics who gave the police a lot of trouble. It is no uncommon thing for a prisoner to bump into something hard while the station sergeant is engaged in meditation. To the credit of the police be it said, however, that their patience is long, and no one gets it in the neck who hasn't asked for it repeatedly. But when it does come, there is nothing quite so ugly as the unleashing of disciplined men.

"Now I'll tell you what I advise you to do," said Inspector Saunders. "Hi, miss, more beer, please."

The beer having been duly supplied, Austen lowered his share of it in company with his chief, who was by now beginning to feel slightly bilious, but was convinced that his brain had never been clearer in his life, and was hatching a plan of campaign which, for sheer ingeniousness, he was convinced had never been equalled in the history of the Yard.

"Now look here, my boy," he said. "Miss Ann knows a lot, and either daren't or won't tell. I haven't no compunctions about taking her in hand, because then we can clean the old —— up and give 'er a chance in life. But I can't do it officially, my boy, you see that. The regulations don't allow of it."

And then he expressed his opinion upon the regulations governing the questioning of witnesses by the police, especially the more recent enactments, until even Austen, accustomed to strong language, raised his eyebrows and hoped the waitress was out of earshot. Finally he returned to his muttons.

"Now next time we see the old —— go off in 'is car, you

an' me will go off also. You can drop me at Ashcott's, see? and come back by yourself. Then you get the girl in a corner so's she can't bunk; get between 'er and the door, see? and you put 'er through it properly. Give 'er the third degree, an' let it rip."

"Chief, she'll never forgive me!" exclaimed Austen aghast.

"It's your only chanst, me lad. You've tried coaxin' and that's failed. Your only line is caveman stuff. You beat 'er up like you did 'er pa, an' she's yours. I know women."

The advice chimed so completely with Austen's instincts that he found himself wishing that the C.I.D. were provided with batons. He had implicit confidence in the shrewdness and judgment of his superior, born of many tight corners and intricate cases through which he had steered successfully, and being blessed with a head of teak himself; it never occurred to him that Inspector Saunders's words might be tinged with beer.

He nodded his head. "Right, Chief, it shall be done," and the more he thought over the prospect, the more he liked it. He had no intention whatever of hitting Ann, but he was quite prepared to hold her wrists, and twist them, too, if all else failed, but accidentally, of course; that goes without saying. For the rest, he would rely on such methods as are used when the station sergeant says, "Get on with it, boys," and walks away. The raw, rough ranker was coming to the surface, as Mr. Studley had foretold. But whether it would prove as distasteful to Ann as her father expected was another matter.

It was some time before Mr. Studley afforded them the opportunity to put their plan into action, and he was so careful in the matter of fingermarks that the detectives knew they must be well worth having. He slunk about the house like a sick cat, and Austen eyed him like a basilisk. He had been

140

beaten up with exceeding thoroughness by an expert who had his heart in the job. No bones were broken, but there was hardly an inch of sound skin on Mr. Studley's entire anatomy. Ann firmly believed he had been in a motoring accident, and as he could not remember any of the incidents of his return home, he confirmed her in this opinion, and even went so far as to supply details with daily increasing verisimilitude. In fact, feeling lonely one evening, he had paid a visit to the two detectives in their sitting-room and told them all about it. They had been very sympathetic, and agreed as to the terrible state of the roads, but he formed a very low opinion of the intelligence of the police, with their silly, wooden, expressionless faces. It was just as well that he did not see them the moment the door had closed behind him, with Chief Inspector Saunders swallowing his handkerchief and Detective-sergeant Austen rolling on the sofa and biting the cushions in an endeavour to keep their mirth from being heard on the other side of the door.

"You got away with that, all right, my lad," said Saunders, wiping his streaming eyes.

"Yes, thank God!" gasped Austen. "Gosh, I thought I'd telescoped the beggar's spine! I was certain he was a hospital job. My only regret is that he doesn't know who hit him, and what for."

Finally, one dark and stormy evening, Mr. Studley got out the Baby Austin and drove it carefully down the lane, slowing up for every puddle.

"Now we go off," said Inspector Saunders. "You drop me at Ashcott's, and I'll get him to give me a bite of supper, and you come back home and do your little bit."

They passed the Baby Austin, chugging at a foot-pace a few hundred yards down the road.

Inspector Saunders saluted its occupant. "Good luck, sir, take care of yourself, and don't get smashed up again!"

When Austen re-entered the house he was trembling as he never trembled before a raid on desperadoes known to be armed. He was, he knew, very liable to lose his head and make a fool of himself when he got to close quarters with Ann. In imagination he could feel Ann's soft hands gripped by his, not as a lover, but as a police officer. He had his full share of the streak of cruelty that is in every virile male, and he knew that if he failed to keep himself in hand, Ann was in for a rougher handling than any virago armed with a hat-pin.

He went into the kitchen, but though the lamp was turned up, she was not there; but he knew by the preparations for supper lying about on the table that she could not be far off. Inspector Saunders's teapot was warming on the hob, and the cocoa for himself stood ready mixed in its cup, only awaiting the hot milk that he saw in a saucepan drawn to the side of the fire. Saunders would drink tea, black and thick as floorstain, at all hours of the twenty-four, and be snoring ten minutes afterwards but he could not sleep if he took tea at night, so Ann made him cocoa. It took him by the throat to see all the little details of her domestic cares, the cat purring on the hearth and the kettle singing on the hob. A bachelor feels very forlorn on these occasions. He wanted his woman and his home, and he wanted them badly.

He knew by the sounds that Ann was laying the table in their sitting-room; taking advantage of his absence to get it done, he supposed, smiling grimly. He took his lower lip between his teeth, and walked down the passage and in at the door, closing it behind him. Ann started up from the hearth she was tending with a look of terror on her face, and Austen heard his blood beginning to sing in his ears. He did not know that she had thought it was her father who had come back so unexpectedly. He had left the side-car down at Ashcott's, intending to walk down and collect his chief later, so that Ann might have no warning of his return and he might gain the advantage of surprise.

He put his back to the door.

"Ann," he said, he could not call her by her love-name, in view of what he was about to do. "Ann, you know a lot more about the murder of Mr. Gregory than you have told, and it has got to come out, my girl; and the sooner it comes out, the sooner it will be over, and the easier it will be for you. Now, come on, out with it. You know Mrs. Gregory?"

"Yes," said Ann, "I know her by sight."

"Then why did you deny knowing her when Saunders questioned you?"

"I did not know she was Mrs. Gregory. I did not know her name." Perfectly true, but not as Austen understood it.

"Has Mrs. Gregory ever been in this house?"

"Not to my knowledge." Again perfectly true.

"Does your father know Mrs. Gregory?"

"He has never mentioned her to me. You had better ask him."

Austen paused, baffled. Her frank admission of knowledge of Mrs. Gregory had taken the wind out of his sails. Then he turned on her with a look on his face that not many prisoners had seen, even in the charge-room.

"Ann," he said, "you're lying. You're trying to shield your father. You can't shield him. We've got too much against him. All you can do is to bring suspicion on yourself as his accomplice."

"In that case," said Ann, "I had better wait to see a solicitor before I make a statement."

Austen saw her through a red haze of anger. He had overreached himself badly this time, and he knew it.

"There are no solicitors here, my lass, there's just you and me, and I mean to have the truth out of you if I half kill you to get it."

Ann thought of what her father had said about the raw, rough ranker coming out.

"Do you want reporting, Sergeant Austen?" she asked him.

His teeth were bared like a dog about to bite, but Ann remembered what Saunders had taught her about handling him when he got worked up, and stood perfectly still. In the silence she heard something moving in the kitchen, and hoped and prayed it was Saunders, come back to control his subordinate, and not her father, bent on more trouble. But no one came into the sitting-room, and the sounds died away.

The slight diversion, even if it were only caused by the cat jumping on the table, as Ann thought probable, served to recall Austen to something approaching his senses, or at least to give his lunacy another turn.

"Ann," he said, "I love you so desperately! You are simply breaking me up. Won't you tell me what the difficulty is between us and let me try to put it right? Why won't you marry me?" And with a sudden flash of insight he added, "Is it because you know your father has done this job?"

Ann, caught on the raw, turned on him savagely, "It is because I don't like your trade, Sergeant Austen. Stand away from that door, I wish to leave the room, and you have no right to detain me."

"I have a right to ask you to hear me, loving you as I do."

"I don't wish to hear you. Stand away from that door."

"I won't!"

She hit him one stinging smack in the face; he stepped back and opened the door for her.

"That finishes it," he said, and closed the door behind her.

* * *

When Saunders entered Sergeant Ashcott's house, he was welcomed by Mrs. Ashcott, the sergeant not yet having come in, though expected momentarily to his supper. Mrs. Ashcott was deeply flattered at entertaining the great man, and immediately killed the fatted calf with a can-opener. As soon as Ashcott appeared, they sat down to a substantial meal, and the Gregory case was discussed intermittently, during Mrs. Ashcott's absences in the kitchen.

Ashcott was immensely intrigued that the detective made no rebuttal when he himself referred to his suspicions of Studley, and began to wonder where he would have got to if he had joined the Metropolitan instead of the County Police, and had had a front seat for the C.I.D.

"There's one bit of comfort I've had to-day, anyway, sir," he said. "I'm going to have old Studley up before the beak at last."

"What for ?" asked Saunders.

"Leaving his car in the highway without lights. Not fifty yards from his own house, too. I suppose he ran it into the bank and was too drunk to back it out again."

Inspector Saunders sat up and took notice. If Austen was giving the girl the third degree and Studley returned and overheard, there would be the devil to pay. He rose from the table.

"I don't like that," he said, "I must get back."

"Would you like me to come with you, sir?" asked the eager Ashcott.

No, Saunders would most decidedly *not* like Sergeant Ashcott, who might hold conventional views on the questioning of witnesses, to come with him. He set off up the dark lane at a good round pace, almost a trot, leaving Mrs. Ashcott divided between regret at his precipitate departure,

145

and pride that her husband had supplied him with information important enough to occasion it. Ashcott, it may well be believed, did not neglect to improve the shining hour of domestic esteem.

Saunders found the Baby Austin, as Ashcott had said, parked at the side of the road under overhanging trees, with its lights out, and unquestionably a danger to navigation if any other traffic came along, though there was not much likelihood of its doing so in that quiet lane.

Nevertheless, Ashcott had Studley on a technicality, and could hardly be blamed for using it to square outstanding accounts, wherein Studley had taken advantage of the technicalities on his side.

Anxious as he was to get back to the house and see what was happening, Saunders spared the time to examine the little car sufficiently to assure himself that there was nothing the matter with it; its handbrake was on and its windows closed against rain, and it showed none of the signs of having been abandoned by a drunken man.

He redoubled his speed up the lane, and achieved over a short distance a pace that would not have disgraced Austen.

He arrived at Thatched Cottage thoroughly blown, but fetched a compass round it to see what was happening before he made his presence known, for in certain circumstances it might be better for him to be able to plead ignorance of his comrade's doings. All was quiet, however; Ann was not weeping, nor Austen shouting at her, nor was there any sign of Mr. Studley. There were no lights save in the detectives' sitting-room, and the kitchen. Inspector Saunders did not like the look of things at all.

In order to guard against any sudden appearance of Studley, and to prevent his getaway if he were lying hidden somewhere, Saunders took out a pair of handcuffs and linked them round the latch of the gate, thus securely padlocking it, knowing that Mr. Studley's love of privacy was such that the fences all round his little domain would take a good deal of negotiating, and he was quite sure that that gentleman, at his age, and in his battered condition, would not achieve the feat without audible groans.

Then he went in at the door with his catfooted detective's prowl, so different to his heavy, policeman's tread, and entered the sitting-room.

For a moment he thought it was empty, and then he saw Austen standing bolt upright, just behind the door, with his face the ghastly yellow colour a bronzed skin goes when the blood leaves it, and a red mark on his left cheek which the experienced policeman knew to be the sign of a well-smacked face. He shook with suppressed laughter. So this was the end of Austen's boasted capacity for hazing a prisoner! But he dared not twitch a muscle. His junior was in no mood to be laughed at, and discipline or no discipline, he would probably get his head punched if he dared even to smile, and a head punched by Austen was not a pleasant possession; he had seen one or two, and he knew.

"Well, my lad, how did it go?" he inquired placidly.

"Finished, Chief," said Austen. "I throw in my hand. You will have to let me out on this. I've had all I can stick. I'm going to report sick. I am sick. I've had no sleep for a week."

"Tut, tut, lad," said Saunders, genuinely concerned, not only for the way in which the case was going, but also for the way in which Austen was taking things. He had guessed he might take them hard, but not as hard as all this. "See how you feel about it all in the morning. If you still feel like that, I'll send you back." He saw it was the only thing to do. Austen, in his present condition, was no use for work. "Now come and sit down by the fire and tell me what you got, or didn't get."

Austen ignored the invitation to sit down.

"I got nothing. She admitted she knew Mrs. Gregory by sight, but denied she knew she was Mrs. Gregory. I'm certain she was lying, though she never batted an eyelid. That girl's case-hardened, if you ask me."

Saunders did not think she was, but he was pleased to hear his subordinate say so, considering it a hopeful sign, pointing to a speedy recovery.

CHAPTER ELEVEN

ANN dropped into the hard chair beside the kitchen table and laid her head on her arms among the crockery. Austen's words, and even more his manner, had been a terrible shock to her, but the thing that appalled her most was the fact that she had struck him in the face. She had seen his expression, and heard his words, "That finishes it." It is a terrible thing for a woman to do to any man because he cannot retaliate, and the blow festers in his very soul, and a particularly bad thing to do to a man in Austen's position, very much her social inferior, and very much in love with her. There was only one thing she could do; she must go and apologize at once. And abjectly. Even if she had to do it in front of Inspector Saunders. It would never do to let that blow rankle till morning.

She raised her head from her arms, and in so doing, capsized the cup in which the cocoa for Austen's supper stood ready mixed.

"Damn!" she said, with emphasis, for it was all the cocoa she had in the house, and with a teaspoon tried to scoop it up from the clean, scrubbed wood of the kitchen table and restore it to the cup, arguing as many cooks do, that what the eye does not see, the tongue does not taste. It would never do to deny Austen his cocoa this evening of all evenings, and let him feel neglected.

Her eye was suddenly caught, as she scraped, by a white sediment at the bottom of the cup. She inspected it narrowly. Was she scraping up Vim, or something from the surface of the table? Impossible. The table, like all Ann's utensils, was spotless. She looked at the white sediment again, and then, as a sudden horrible suspicion occurred to her, jumped up and ran into the scullery, and took from the highest shelf of the cupboard a rusty cocoa-tin, opened it, and looked inside. It was empty! Ann leant against the sink, her knees giving way under her. That tin should have contained an ounce packet of cyanide of potassium, obtained at her father's instruction for the destroying of wasps' nests.

Ann could not think. Her mind worked in a series of pictures, as minds do when life is driven down into its foundations. She saw her mother fall back on the pillows, the fatal cocoa streaming all over the coverlet. She saw Austen's face looking at her as he looked when he still loved her. She felt the pressure of his arm about her as she had felt it that afternoon in the coroner's court, and she felt the nearness, and warmth, and the breathing of the living man. And she saw him, struck down and falling with one strangled cry, as her father's hand reached out at him, through her. Ann did not stop to think. She picked up that cocoa-tin and started down the passage.

When she entered the detectives' sitting-room she thought, as Saunders had done, that Austen was not there. Then she heard a quick in taking of breath behind her, and turned, and found herself looking up into his ravaged face, clay-coloured, with the scarlet mark of her hand still upon it, still standing where she had left him.

Forgetting the presence of Saunders, forgetting even the poisoned cocoa, she raised her hand and laid it very gently on that mark.

"Jack," she said, "I am so sorry, so very, very sorry. Please forgive me."

He sprang towards her. "Pussy!" he cried.

But she slipped away from him, quick as an eel. "No!"

she said. "Hear what I have to say first."

She turned to Saunders and held out towards him the cup with the dregs of the cocoa in it.

"I think there is something the matter with this cocoa," she said huskily.

"Do you, missy?" said Saunders, peering at it, but unable to see much without his spectacles. "And what do you think is the matter with it?"

Ann never hesitated. "I think there is cyanide of potassium in it," she said.

"Phew!" said Saunders. "Do you, now? Jack, test it for cyanide."

Austen came forward and took the cup from her hand. They looked into each other's eyes, but they did not speak. He saw that hers were blazing with an anger that came up from the very depths of her soul, and that her lips were held in a narrow line. He thought she was through with Mr. Studley for good and all now, and whatever she knew would be told.

He worked among his bottles for a while, and finally said, "It's cyanide, all right, sir."

"How much of it ?"

"I couldn't say that without doing a quantitative analysis. Any amount of it. Enough to kill an army corps, as they said at the inquest."

He left the table in the window and came over to the fire, and saw that Ann lay curled up face downwards in the chair in which he was about to seat himself, with Inspector Saunders staring down at her pityingly. She looked like a small and tired child, with her tossed golden hair and crumpled frock.

"Now, lassie," said Saunders, "we must get to business. The sooner it's done, the sooner it's over. Got your notebook, Austen?"

151

"Yes, Chief," said Austen, taking his fountain pen from his pocket and settling down to his notes. He felt as if he were operating upon his beloved without an anaesthetic.

"Now, dearie, begin at the beginning and tell us all about it," said Saunders, making a feeble endeavour to soften the process by his endearments. He was exceedingly sorry for Ann, for they had got to know her well during their residence at the cottage, and he had taken a great fancy to her, apart from her treatment of Austen.

But Ann did not stir.

"Go into the kitchen, Jack, and make her some tea," said Saunders, applying his universal solvent and infallible consoler.

Ann raised her head suddenly.

"No, not that, not that !" she cried, hysterically. "It's dangerous. It's dangerous. Everything's poisoned in this house."

"Now, now, dearie, come along," said Saunders, feeling himself threatened by his bugbear. "All the cyanide there is, is in that cocoa. People don't sprinkle it."

All the same, he whispered to Austen to keep his eyes skinned; and Austen, not relishing the contents of the larder in that house of death any more than Ann did, helped himself to a fresh packet of tea and an unopened tin of condensed milk from Ann's store-cupboard.

He saw the spilled cocoa on the kitchen table, and realized that but for the chance of this upset, Ann would never have seen the white sediment. She would have poured in the boiling milk, and all would have been dissolved and invisible, and he realized with something of a shock how near he had been to eternity. It was obvious that the poison was meant for him and for no one else, for he was the only person who took cocoa.

The kettle was boiling furiously, and he made the consoling tea and bore it off to Ann, whom he found having her head patted by Saunders as if she were a dog, in an endeavour to comfort her.

"Now, lassie," said Saunders, "let's make a start."

"Oh, dear," said Ann, putting her hands over her face. "Where am I to begin? There is so much of it. I had better begin at the beginning. It mayn't all matter, but you will be able to sort it out."

She took her hands from her face and stared into the fire, while Austen waited with his pen poised above his notebook, watching her. As soon as she started he had no more time for thought. The man who is taking down shorthand verbatim cannot pay much attention to its meaning.

"This house used to belong to Grannie," said Ann, at length. Saunders sighed. He thought they were going to hear all the family history before she would cut the cackle and come to the 'osses, but he knew better than to check her till she got going.

"And father and she fell out about it because he wanted her to mortgage it and raise money and pay off his debts, and she wouldn't. She said there was going to be a roof over our heads, whatever happened.

"Father sulked and rowed, and rowed and sulked for ages: and then one day he suddenly cheered up and became quite normal. And he began to do a thing he had never done before, he took an interest in the garden. I used to help Granny with the garden, and I made him keep all his cigarette-ends for me, and we soaked them in a bucket of water, and they made a splendid insecticide for the roses. I had got the recipe out of the Sunday paper. He said that he had also seen a recipe in the Sunday paper for making weed-killer out of foxglove leaves."

"Phew !" said Saunders. "So that's how the milk got into the coco-nut !"

"I collected a big armful of foxglove leaves in our little

153

wood by the river," continued Ann, "and I chopped them up as he told me to, and stewed them in an old saucepan and strained the liquor off. It is dark brown, and it smells not unlike cocoa."

Ann paused, and looked round the room into the shadowed corners uneasily.

"What's the matter, dearie?" asked Saunders.

"I don't know," said Ann. "I've got a feeling I'm being watched."

"Well, Jack ain't watching you, duckie 'es got 'is short 'and to attend to." Inspector Saunders's h's always went astray in times of excitement.

Ann continued: "Father took the stuff I'd made for him, and poured it on the flagged path leading to the gate. At least, I thought he did. At any rate, all the weeds curled up. And almost at once Granny began to complain of her heart. She had always been so strong and well before, and no great age, under seventy. She felt so bad we sent for the doctor, and he said it was high blood pressure, and due to her age, and she would be all right if she took things quietly.

"But she wasn't all right. She felt wretched. Isn't it awful," she lifted her head suddenly and looked from one man to the other, her eyes full of horror, "to kill a person by inches, watching it hurt them all the time?"

"Poisoners is the very worst, miss," said Saunders. "The very worst of a bad bunch. And the hardest to convict. The only thing that hangs 'em is the fact that they are seldom content with one murder, once they've found out how easy it is to kill a feller human. That's what's done your pa in, miss. If he hadn't tried for Jack, here, he could have cocked a snook at us."

Ann shuddered at the word hang, but as Saunders passed on to refer to the attempt on her lover, her heart hardened. Her father should never murder anyone again. His daughter

154

would see to it that her evidence hanged him.

She went on: "But Granny didn't die. She was too tough for that. And father's temper got shorter and shorter, and men began to call at the house about his debts. And then, one day, we saw a queen wasp in the kitchen, and Dad said we had better take the nest at once, before the little wasps hatched out, and told me to go into the village, to Watson, the chemist, and get an ounce of cyanide of potassium. I asked him to write it down for me, lest I should forget it, and I remember now how angry he was with me, and how surprised I was. That was in the days before his temper got so bad, and he was generally jolly, at least with me."

Ann paused, and her face twisted up like a child's in distress as she remembered the happy days with her father, before evil came upon them. Saunders hastily started her off again with the first thing that came into his head.

"What date was that, miss, can you remember?"

"I can't, for the moment," said Ann. "Somewhere about now, or a little earlier. At any rate, it was after the foxgloves had grown their big leaves and before they flowered. They flower in May and June. You can find out, however, for it was the day before Grannie died."

"How did she come to die ?" asked Saunders.

"She always had cocoa last thing at night, and as mother and I liked to go to bed early, father always made it for her. We left it ready mixed for him, just as I left—Mr. Austen's cocoa this evening."

Saunders wondered if a Christian name had been on its way when Ann hesitated.

"Was anyone with her when she died?"

"No, no one. We found her in the morning, quite cold; we thought she must have been dead some hours. Dad said she was all right when he took her the cocoa about eleven, but she must have died as she was drinking it because it was

155

all over the bed."

"What became of those bedclothes, my dear?"

"The blankets and sheets we washed. The sheets came clean, because we boiled them, but there are traces of the stain on the blankets; I saw it as I made up the beds for you two, but it is practically gone, now, after several washings. The eiderdown we could not boil, and the stain would not budge with sponging, so we re-covered it."

"Where is it now?"

"On Mr. Austin's bed."

"Think you'll be able to do anything with it, Jack?"

"Might do. Depends how thoroughly they cleaned it before they gave it up as a bad job. I might not be able to, with my little outfit, but they probably could at the central lab: I think I had better leave it alone for them."

"Yes, missie? Go on. What did the doctor say?"

"He said it was heart disease. I forget what he called it."

"He made no difficulty about the certificate?"

"None at all. He said he had been expecting her to die for some time. He did not even come to see her after she was dead, but took our word for it."

"That's what I call first-aid to murderers," said Saunders, bitterly. "Yes, missie?"

"Father put on a black tie and said how much he missed her, and what a good mother she'd been to him; but when the will was read he nearly had a fit, and made a most dreadful scene, and quarrelled with the lawyer and shocked everyone because the house was left to him for life, and then to me, and he couldn't mortgage it any more than he had ever been able to, as I was under age, and couldn't give my consent to a mortgage. It was dreadful. The funeral only just over, and father swearing at the lawyer; we were so ashamed, mother and I."

"Well, and did he succeed in mortgaging it?" asked Saunders, eager to see if anything was left of Ann's little inheritance for Austen's sake.

"No," said Ann. "And he never has. As soon as ever I was twenty-one he began about it. I was quite willing to do whatever would help him, I was very fond of him in those days. And he took me to see Mr. Watford, the lawyer about it. And Mr. Watford made him wait in another room; he did not like it a bit, but he had to do it. And as soon as we were alone, Mr. Watford said to me that it would be a very bad thing for me to mortgage the house, because my father had always been so unlucky in business, and it meant everything to mother and me to have a home, just as Grannie had said. And he was sure Grannie would have been very grieved at the idea of Thatched Cottage being mortgaged after it had been in the family so long, and the best thing I could do was to make a will and leave everything I had to my cousin Wilfred; and if I did that, Wilfred would probably be willing to help me if ever I was in trouble. So I made the will then and there, and he got two of his clerks to witness it; and then he sent for father back again, and told him what he had advised me to do, and showed him the will, and then put it away in a safe; and father couldn't say a word, because there were the two clerks looking on."

"You probably owe your life to that will, young lady," said Saunders.

"I don't know," said Ann. "He often used to threaten to murder me."

Austen sat up so hurriedly that he dropped his notebook.

"Did he, now?" said Saunders. "In so many words?"

"Well, not in so many words," said Ann, "but he used to say, 'You'll never make old bones, you'll die of heart disease, like your mother and your grandmother. It's in the family.' And you know what kind of heart disease it was that they

157

died of."

"Did your ma die of it, too?"

"Yes, she did, in exactly the same way. I was just coming to that."

"Cor!" said Saunders.

"It was the whole story over again. I hardly need repeat it, it was so alike. A year ago this month. Two years after Grannie. And she died drinking a cup of cocoa, too; gave a kind of squeak and threw her head back, and was gone. Just like the butler said it was with Mr. Gregory. I knew that squeak at once when he described it. And father once poisoned a stray dog in the same way, and it squeaked just like that as it died."

"Very characteristic, the strangled cry of cyanide poisoning," commented Austen, thinking how nearly he had come to uttering it.

"Yes," said Ann, "and there were the other things, too." Shyly, but frankly, she referred to the sordid details that had enabled the doctor to distinguish with certainty between death by cyanide and death by heart disease. Saunders rejoiced at the kind of witness he had got to put in the box.

"That was what first opened my eyes," said Ann. "I never suspected a thing before; why should I? The doctor was quite satisfied."

"He won't be so satisfied when he has to tell us about those deaths in court," said Saunders, with relish. The police have a profound contempt for the doctor who has allowed a murdered person to be quietly buried.

"He's dead, too, himself, poor man. He died soon after mother."

"He didn't die of heart failure, by any chance?" asked Saunders.

"No, he committed suicide—oh, my God, he committed suicide with cyanide! Could it possibly have been—?"

"Were they friendly?" said Saunders. There was no need for names.

"Yes, very. Father was the last person to see him alive."

"Worth looking into," said Saunders.

"Gosh, what a slaughtering!" exclaimed Austen. Even the case-hardened police officers were startled out of their philosophic acceptance of the vagaries of human nature by the chronicle of Mr. Studley's achievements.

"I told you poisonings never came singly, didn't I, missie?" said Saunders. "Now if your pa had been content to stick to the sawbones what didn't know one end of his stethoscope from the other and never bothered to view the corpse, he'd have had no trouble. He overdid it, that's what he did, and it's been the downfall of many a better man than him. Now, missie?"

"That's all," said Ann.

"And quite enough, too," murmured Austen, *sotto voce.*

"No, my dear, it isn't quite all. What about Mrs. Gregory?"

"Oh, yes," said Ann. "I'd forgotten all about her," she turned to Austen. "You remember when you asked me if Mrs. Gregory had ever been to this house, and if I knew who she was, and I said no ?"

Austen nodded.

"Well, that was true, and yet it wasn't true."

Austen grinned. "I knew you were fibbing, you little puss."

" 'Mrs. Gregory' never came to this house to my knowledge, as I told you, but a Mrs. Godfrey did. In fact she came so often that she always kept some things here, and I used to wash her nightgown for her, and put it ready for her next visit. But I knew her as Mrs. Godfrey, and I never suspected that Mrs. Godfrey was Mrs. Gregory until I saw her in the witness box."

159

"Gosh, Chief!" exclaimed Austen. "Haven't we got 'em tied up tight?"

"Don't halloo till you're out of the wood, my lad," said Saunders. "Where are her things, missie?"

"In the bottom drawer in your room," said Ann.

"Cor!" said Saunders, "and I shoved my Sunday trousers in on top of 'em! I thought they was your traps, missie."

"I don't run to dressing-gowns like that," said Ann regretfully.

"I'm very glad to hear it, missie," said the virtuous Saunders. "Respectable women never do."

"You can see now why I looked old and plain when you took me out to tea, can't you?" said Ann, turning to Austen.

"You poor kid," said Austen. "You'd had a jugful!" He thought it was no wonder she had been glad to feel his arm around her and to lean up against him. Then he suddenly remembered her questions about the case, and wondered how much she had given away to her father.

But he saw at once that Ann must have been faithful, or Mr. Studley would have taken a dose of his own cyanide.

"Tell me, Pussy, how did you get home that night?" he leant towards her anxiously. Was there another admirer with a fast sports car—a Daimler—a Rolls Royce? His lover's imagination presented them all, moving in procession.

"I took the bus to Datley," said Ann, "and crossed the river by the stepping-stones."

"Cor!" exclaimed Saunders. "Are there stepping-stones? We've been looking for something of the kind. Where are they?"

"Just below the weir," said Ann.

"And you never told us? You little divil! Why didn't you tell us? And there was Jack swearing the Archangel Gabriel couldn't have crossed that river!"

"Neither he could, Chief, if he'd had to swim it. He'd

have gone back to heaven, quick," said Austen.

"Why didn't you tell us, missie?" said Saunders.

"Well, you see, it was this way," said Ann, twisting her handkerchief uneasily. "Dad's alibi depended upon your not knowing that there was any way of crossing the river nearer than the bridge. It never occurred to me for a moment he had had anything to do with poor Mr. Gregory, and I thought there would be such a fussdoodliation if you found out about the stepping-stones and began to look into his alibi, for I knew that Dad was in all sorts of petty mischief, which would all come out and be so beastly."

Saunders nodded. He had come across that sort of thing so often, the innocent person who has got a perfectly good alibi that does him no credit.

"Well, missie, I think that's all," said Saunders. "You can go to bed, my dear, you look tired out."

As Ann crept away thankfully, Austen rose to open the door for her, which was something new for him, and just touched her hand as she went out.

CHAPTER TWELVE

"WELL, lad, how do you think the job was done?" said his chief, as Austen returned to the fireplace and dropped into the chair that Ann had just vacated; the warmth of her body, that still lingered in it, sending his wits all astray, so that Saunders had to repeat his question before he took it in.

"The old boy brewed foxglove soup and used it to make the cocoa with till their hearts were groggy, and then polished them off with cyanide. The old country sawbones was deceived; it looked exactly like heart trouble at first sight, but the smart young chap, fresh from the hospitals wasn't, and Studley was in the soup himself."

"Now I see," said Saunders thoughtfully, "why we never could trace where the poisons came from. We were looking for tincture of digitalis having been bought at a chemist's, and all the while little Ann had been brewing foxglove tea by the gallon in the back kitchen!"

"And cyanide, too," said Austen, "I saw her signature in the poisons book at old Watson's. She'd bought it regularly, on and off, every spring and what more likely than that it would be for wasps? Can't people get hold of poisons easily? I wonder there's anyone left alive on earth. Fancy letting 'em get stuff like cyanide for a job like that! Why can't they use a rag dipped in paraffin, or swat the brutes?"

"It's my belief," said Saunders unctuously, "that nowadays people use more weed-killer on their relatives than they do on the garden paths."

There was a sound of someone moving in the

kitchen.

"I've got a warrant in me pocket. Go on, boy," said Saunders.

Austen took a pair of handcuffs out of his pocket and Saunders chortled to see that they were still decorated with blue ribbon, and went cat-footed down the passage towards the kitchen. In a moment he was back, however.

"It's Ann," he said. "She's making supper."

"Now, ain't that fine of her !" said the gratified Saunders, who was feeling very empty, and wondering what they would do for a meal if they had to haul a kicking Mr. Studley to the local lock-up. "She's the right kind of wife for a policeman, lad, she knows that when a chap's done his work, he's got to have his food, whatever hour it is."

Austen beamed. He felt that at last his chief had accepted the situation.

"What's going to happen to Ann if the jury let the old boy off?" he asked.

"Well," said Saunders, "I wouldn't be surprised if she was thankful to marry any nice young feller that asked her. This spot certainly won't be healthy for her."

Ann came in with an omelet. "I made this," she said, "I thought that eggs would be safe, anyway."

They all sat down to the meal, and even Austen took tea after his exertions, for shorthand for long spells is hard work, and Ann had a quick, eager manner of speaking that could only be taken down in full by an expert.

No one spoke. Saunders was busy shovelling the food down; Austen was tired after his emotional storms and long spell of shorthand; Ann was preoccupied, thinking of her father, and what the next move would be on either side. Suddenly she lifted her head and listened.

"What is it, Pussy?" said Austen, alert to every movement she made, in spite of his fatigue.

"I feel I'm being watched," said Ann.

He put his hand over hers. "Try to think of something else, Pussy. It's no use letting your nerves get the upper hand. I know you're going through a bad time, but it won't last for ever. Happier times coming," and he smiled at her. But she was disturbed and distraught, gazing into the shadows in the far corners of the room and twisting her fingers about his absent-mindedly, oblivious of Saunders, who winked at his comrade and made him blush.

"Now then, missie," said Saunders, at the conclusion of the meal, "let's have those eiderdowns, if it isn't too much trouble. It was because he was smart after eiderdowns that Ashcott got us a nice bit of evidence."

Ann rose, and with her quick light step, passed out into the darkness of the hall, leaving the door open to give her light. She went up the stairs to Austen's room to get his eiderdown, opened the door, and came face to face with her father.

Ann screamed, the short, harsh scream of intense terror. There was a crash in the room below as a chair went over and in one bound Austen was up the stairs, seized Mr. Studley by the throat, shook him as a terrier shakes a rat, smashed his head against the wall, and dropped him senseless at her feet.

"Good God, Austen, have you killed the feller?" exclaimed Saunders, gaping in the doorway. "Ann, my dear, go downstairs. Get out of this."

Ann fled to her room, horrified. She could see before her eyes Austen's face as he took her father by the throat, and hear his head crack against the wall, and she experienced a terrible revulsion of feeling. Austen was the raw, rough ranker, as her father had said. Why, oh, why, had she ever betrayed her father to the gallows? Blood was thicker than water. She had loved her father before she had ever heard

164

of Austen. Her father was more sinned against than sinning. He couldn't help his nature. There was a lot in him to love, in spite of all. Why, oh, why, had she betrayed him in a moment of madness? She ought to have thrown the cocoa down the sink and said nothing about it. Ann sank in a heap on the floor, half under the bed, and it was there that Mrs. Ashcott found her, sent up by Saunders to look after the girl, whose state of mind he could guess.

* * *

Saunders phoned to the headquarters of the County Police to report the arrest and ask for an ambulance, as the prisoner had resisted arrest and got damaged in the process. Fortunately for all concerned, Mr. Studley had recovered consciousness before it arrived, but the lump on the back of his head was coming up nicely, rising like Mount Everest among the minor peaks left behind by the previous beating-up that Austen had given him. This bruise, at any rate, thought Saunders, could not be attributed to a motor smash, and he did not like the way Studley was eyeing Austen and keeping quiet.

In the end they all went off together in the ambulance, Mr. Studley securely handcuffed. Saunders was amused to observe that Austen steadfastly refused to look at his future father-in-law, seeming to consider him something obscene and unfit to be gazed upon. Studley, however, was constantly looking from one to another of his captors out of the corners of his eyes, like a mule getting ready to kick. Saunders, who always watched his prisoners steadily till they were taken over from him by the station sergeant, did not like the look of him at all.

As soon as details began to be taken in the charge-room, the kick came.

165

"I have a complaint to make against the way in which the police have behaved in this matter," said Mr. Studley, who for once in his life appeared to be completely sober, though whether he owed this happy state of affairs to self-denial or the shock of his arrest, was not clear.

"Yes, sir?" said the station sergeant, who was bound to take note of all such complaints.

"I have an only daughter," said Mr. Studley, sighing and looking soulful, and a chronic inebriate can look very soulful indeed when he gives his mind to it. Saunders and Austen stiffened; they knew what was coming.

"I had reason to believe," continued Mr. Studley, "that all was not well with her. I kept my eyes open, and made in-quiries among neighbours" (Saunders thought of the ditcher who was supposed to have heard Ann's screams) "and I learnt that a state of affairs existed between her and this young man to which any father would take serious exception, and which was particularly undesirable between a police officer and the man whose crime he was investigating—if he were investi-gating it."

The station sergeant looked at Austen, and saw by his demeanour that the charge was no surprise to him.

"In my anger, and I think you will agree, sergeant, if you have daughters of your own, that it was righteous anger, I charged this young man to his face with his offence when I found him with my daughter in a resort of doubtful reputa-tion one evening.

"I admit I acted unwisely; but you will appreciate, if you are a father, that I did not act altogether unnaturally. How unwisely I acted, remains to be seen. At any rate, the upshot of the matter is this charge against me, in which this young man and my daughter are the only witnesses. I leave the rest to your imagination."

"Did you report the matter in the proper quarter, sir?"

166

asked the sergeant without emotion.

"No, my man, not yet. I have been trying to get my daughter to undergo a medical examination, but so far she refuses."

"Will you kindly step this way, please, sir?" said the sergeant politely, ushering Studley towards a door other than that by which he had entered. He cast a leering glance of triumph at Austen as he passed, for he thought that he was being conducted to some senior official for his charges against Austen to be inquired into, but he found to his chagrin that he had been conducted to a cell.

The station sergeant came back and looked sharply at Saunders and Austen.

"This is a nasty business, sir," he said to the senior man.

"Very," said Saunders shortly, for the matter reflected on him nearly as much as it did on his subordinate. "Ever had anything to do with the prisoner at this station?"

"No, sir," said the sergeant.

"Well, they know him well enough in his own district, and they'll soon tell you what a statement of that sort is worth from him."

"Yes, sir," said the sergeant dutifully, but all the same he privately thought there might be something in the charge, for the younger of the two detectives was a man to get away with it with any woman. Jealousy is not an exclusively feminine prerogative.

The Chief Constable came in at the door, a mackintosh over his evening dress, just as Mr. Studley had been safely disposed of in the cells, and heard Saunders's story of the arrest and Ann's evidence. No one said a word about Mr. Studley's complaints. The rank and file of the police force are apt to regard their chief executive officers with suspicion until they have been some time in their appointments, for they are never drawn from the force, but from the commissioned ranks of the Army and Navy. Consequently, a complaint against a police officer was a family matter within the force, and not readily to be communicated to them.

Major Seward, therefore, suspected nothing, and offered to drive Saunders and Austen back to Thatched Cottage in his car, as the house at which he had been dining was in that neighbourhood, and he wished to return for his wife. Saunders, however, declined, saying that they must go straight back to the Yard immediately, now that they had handed their prisoner over to him. Major Seward demurred at such zeal in the pursuit of duty, as they would have to get on the milk train, which stopped at every station and arrived only an hour ahead of the fast morning mail train. Saunders, however, was adamant. Under no circumstances was Austen going to be seen in the neighbourhood of the girl until the case was safely over and Studley hanged and his mouth shut for ever. He would go down to Thatched Cottage next morning in a police car, tuck in all the loose ends of the case, and collect their belongings. If Austen wanted a toothbrush, he could buy it at Woolworth's. He himself was above such fripperies. Austen would be "returned to store" in the police barracks and dared to show his nose in the neighbourhood of Ann, or to put pen to paper.

Saunders slept peacefully all the way to London, but Austen never closed his eyes. But his thoughts were by no means altogether worrying ones. Ann had shown her feelings unmistakably with regard to him. He felt that the present unpleasantness was a thing to be endured till it blew over. He had a clear conscience in the matter of his behaviour towards Ann. A fellow had the right to court a girl if she were willing. He did not think his career would be adversely affected by the unpleasantness Mr. Studley was bent on making; the police stand by their comrades and wash their dirty linen in private unless it is so spoiled that nothing but an air-ing on the the line will restore its colour, as in the Goddard case, when it was his own comrades that cleaned Sergeant Goddard up. He gritted his teeth, however, when he thought of the dragging of Ann's name in the mud.

* * *

Inspector Saunders, inquiring of Sergeant Ashcott on the phone next morning, learnt that Ann had been in such a state the previous night that the doctor his wife had called in had ordered her removal to the cottage hospital. So he decided to take Austen down with him by train, collect the side-car and their things, and generally tidy up the case. But when he saw Austen wandering round the familiar rooms like a dog that has lost his master, he wished he had let well alone. He did not understand this sort of police officer. Austen was not like the lads he had worked with in his young days. Unless they got run over on their points, or picked up pneumonia on night patrol, they seemed to thrive on anything, like Army mules. Austen, with his tantrums and his insomnia, was beyond his power of calculating. The post-War brand of police recruit was a very different quantity to the pre-War vintage.

Saunders and Austen, having been borrowed from Scotland Yard by the County police, any serious complaint concerning the conduct of either or both of them naturally had to go to headquarters, and the station sergeant, being the man to whom the complaint was made, had to give his version of it, and his impressions of the man who made it, and the man concerning whom it was made. The County police station knew nothing about Mr. Studley and his habits—if he had made his complaint to Sergeant Ashcott, he would have got short shrift—and human nature being what it is, and an older man in a junior position having to report on a younger man in a senior position, in the version of the affair which reached the Yard, justice was not tempered with mercy. As every photographer knows, although he cannot alter the actual face of the landscape, a great deal can be done with the lighting. It was a sore point with the County police that their new Chief Constable had so promptly called in the C.I.D., instead of letting the local detectives have a try; and when the station sergeant and the divisional superintendent realized how big the case was going to be, the story of Austen's misdeeds lost nothing in the reporting; neither did Mr. Studley's injuries; and as his health was by no means improved by the sudden and unaccustomed sobriety that was imposed on him, for there is no bail for a man charged with a capital crime, his physical condition left much to be desired. In twenty-four hours Austen found himself on the mat in front of a disciplinary board, which could get no sense out of him. He simply denied everything and would explain nothing, putting on what he called his police face, and contriving to look like one of those heathen deities which represent the less amiable aspects of divinity. They got rid of Austen and had Saunders in, to ask him his version of the affair. They knew from Austen's manner that there was more in it than met the eye, and that it could not be dismissed as pure drunken malice on Studley's part.

Saunders was too old a hand, and too experienced as a witness under cross-examination, to attempt to mislead them.

"It's this way, sir," he said to the president of the board, "the young lady and the young feller got sweet on each other, and it may be they larked about a bit, as young folk will, but nothin' that I would have minded if the girl had been my daughter. As soon as this case against her father is cleared up, he wants to marry her, and I think she means to have him. A man doesn't seduce the girl he wants to marry, and he doesn't want to marry the girl he has seduced."

170

They saw the sense of this at once, and the charge of immorality against Austen was wiped off the slate. Then they inquired into the question of the state of repair in which Mr. Studley was received by the County police, and concerning which they had also had something to say in their report.

Saunders was on safer ground here.

"He was smashed up in a motor accident a few days before, sir," he said, thanking his lucky stars for the blank memory of the very drunk. "Most of those bruises was old bruises. I saw the prisoner's head hit the wall as he struggled, but I think the doctor will tell you, sir, that that is the only fresh mark on him."

And so Austen was left with his spotless record still intact.

When Saunders got to his little office at the top of the big building, he found Austen waiting for him. They sent the young constable who acted as office-boy to get his tea, and Saunders had a heart-to-heart talk with Austen and impressed on him the need of excessive caution between now and the time that Studley came up for trial.

"Don't you go near the girl," he said, "and don't you put pen to paper."

"I quite see your point, Chief," said Austen, "and I will do as you say about keeping away from Thatched Cottage, but I have simply got to write to Ann, otherwise she will think it so odd, seeing how friendly we have been, and her in such trouble."

"I shouldn't, if I was you. Not for a few days, at any rate. She must have had a shakeup when she saw you bash her father. I saw her face. You mayn't get a civil reception, and that will leave a nasty taste behind."

Austen looked mutinous. "She can't be very keen on the old —— since she turned King's evidence on him."

"That may be, my lad, when she was scared at finding

171

cyanide in your tipple. But you'll find she'll run backwards and forwards, like a hen in traffic, between you and him till he's safely hanged. I know women. I order you not to go near her, my boy, and if I find you've been, I'll send you up to the board myself. I can't order you not to write, because I can't enforce the order, but if you are a wise man you'll leave her alone until she's had time to simmer down."

Usually Austen had the greatest respect for his chief's wisdom, but in this case the counsels of his own desires prevailed, and he wrote.

Consequently Ann, lying in bed in the little cottage hospital, dazed with bromide, had an official-looking communication handed her by the nurse, with the remark, "I hope it is nothing to worry you. Would you like me to deal with it?"

Ann very nearly handed it to her then and there, to be spared the effort, which she felt quite incapable of making; but it suddenly occurred to her that it might contain something concerning her father, and as she now deeply regretted she had ever betrayed him, she felt she must make an effort to cope with this document herself, and not make bad worse. So she took it from the nurse's hand, and opened it, but when she saw that it commenced, "Pussy, my darling," she realized that it could not be as official as it appeared.

She thrust it hastily under her pillow, determined to read it at her leisure after the nurses had done working at her end of the ward and had moved down to the other end. As she lay waiting for them to finish with her next-door neighbour, she wondered what sort of a letter it would be. She had read "The End of the House of Alard," by Sheila Kaye-Smith, and she remembered the wonderful epistle of the young farmer, proposing to the squire's daughter, and with a sick feeling wondered what Austen would produce. She was tempted to destroy it unread. She felt that she had completely got over her infatuation for him. The sickening crack as her father's head hit the wall was constantly in her ears.

But something prevented her from carrying out this drastic resolution. After all, it was the first love-letter she had ever received. Moreover, curiosity is highly developed in females, and they never do with anonymous letters as judges say they do, and destroy them unopened. Though how they know they are anonymous until they have opened them, is a curious problem. Consequently, Austen got a hearing, though not a very favourable one.

Ann commenced to read, with a sharp eye for solecisms of grammar; for she had not realized that Austen was a man who had been educated to university standard, and was within a hand reach of his degree when fortune turned him into another channel; nor that he spent a large portion of his time writing reports, for Saunders was incapable of doing anything with a pen except sucking it. She shared her father's concept of the working classes, and had not the slightest realization of what public education does nowadays for its brighter pupils. Consequently, Austen's letter was a revelation to her. She knew that, as far as speech went, he had two or three argots, and that he spoke quite a different language to her to what he did to Inspector Saunders when he believed himself alone with him. He could speak correctly when he chose, or he could use the language of the streets. They were like different tongues to him, and he employed one or the other according to whom he was addressing.

The letter was short, but it had its own dignity. Ann had always noticed that Austen had a very keen sense of personal dignity, and woe-betide anyone who did not respect it, whatever his rank.

> Pussy, my darling [it ran], I know
> what you must be going through, and I
> want you to know that I love you, and that

173

as soon as things are cleared up [Ann
shuddered at that phrase] I shall come to
you again and ask you to marry me. I
think we could be awfully happy together.
I know I could. I will not say any more
now, except that I have never looked at any
girl except you, and never shall—Jack.

Ann was not able to think clearly owing to the clouds of
bromide in her head, but somehow the letter soothed her,
and she pushed it back under her pillow, glad to have it there.
Next time the nurse came that way, she asked for pencil and
paper. The nurse demurred. Ann was to be kept absolutely
quiet. The sister was appealed to. Ann, who was fast becoming nearly as expert as Saunders himself in the use of half-
truths, told her that the letter was from Scotland Yard, as she
could see for herself by the envelope, and must be replied to
at once.

So Ann got her paper and set to work on her letter. But it
did not prove an easy task. How she envied Austen his terse,
clear style. She did not know how many drafts that letter had
had, nor the amount of official stationery that had gone into
the waste-paper basket in the course of its final copying. Her
mind was too clouded for anything but a few brief words,
and anyway, she only had one sheet of paper at her disposal;
so she wrote the first thing that came into her head.

How should she begin? "Dear Sergeant Austen?" No.
Too official. "Dear Jack?" No, darned if she would! Dear
Mr. Austen? Yes, that would have to do. "I was glad to get
your letter." Ann wished she had not put that, but not having
an india-rubber, she could not erase it. "I cannot write very
much now, because I have had a lot of bromide and cannot
think clearly. Later on, if I feel I can, I will write to you, but
you must not count on it," and she was his sincerely, Ann

Studley.

It was this letter which was flung down in front of Inspector Saunders with a demand for an opinion on its significance by a distracted Austen, who had sat up with it all night, trying to read between the lines what poor bromided Ann had never put there.

Saunders raised his eyebrows when he read it. But when he re-read it, he was not quite so sure. He knew that Ann was as straight as a die, and dealt squarely, like a man. He thought that her yea would be yea, and her nay would be nay, and that she would not say one thing to mean another.

"You can't make much of this, lad," he said, handing the missive back to Austen. "The girl's sick and don't know what she wants. The thing I should bank on if I was you, is this—when she had to choose between you and her pa, she never thought twice about it. She didn't mind his murdering Gregory, or her granny, or even her ma; but the minute the old —— touched you, she rounded on him."

Austen saw the sense of this; and all through his dark days it was his sheet anchor to windward, and it probably saved the Metropolitan Police a lot of disciplinary trouble.

Nevertheless, Inspector Saunders had a dog's life of it. He reluctantly chose simple confidence tricksters instead of interesting forgeries when the choice was offered to him as a senior man, because he knew that he could not rely on his subordinate. Austen developed the temper of a fiend as the days went by, and station sergeants looked at him askance as he brought in battered prisoners. Finally even Inspector Saunders could stand no more, and sought out the head of the disciplinary board in his private office, and conversed with him unofficially; and the upshot of that conversation was that Austen was asked to call at his office, also unofficially, for there is always reluctance to put the first black mark on a clean record.

A highly-disciplined body of men like the London police are not brought to their state of perfection by brute force. Skilled manhandling, of a different kind to that which Austen applied to Mr. Studley, goes to the making of them, and they are not as hard done by as they like to think themselves because the highest posts are always given to non-policemen. The man who has risen to senior position from the ranks has no mercy on the weaknesses of his fellow-rankers. The man who comes in from outside takes a broader view. Austen was too good a man to be lost to the Force if it could be avoided, for the Metropolitan Police is always hard put to it to obtain sufficient brains along with the indispensable brawn.

As soon as Austen sensed the sympathetic attitude, his mercurial temperament responded, and he told the quiet-voiced soldier what he would not tell the board of superintendents. He asked him whether there would be any difficulty about his marriage to Ann, from a disciplinary point of view, if her father were convicted; and was assured that as the prosecution were raising no question whatever of the complicity of Ann, and as, in fact, she had done a very great public service by coming forward, there would be no difficulty whatever. He found, to his surprise, that his superior officer knew Ann's uncles, and this gave him a better realization of the social gulf between them than all Saunders's talk of dukes and earls could have done.

Austen asked whether it was likely that the state of affairs between himself and Ann, and Mr. Studley's shameful accusations, would come out at the trial.

"Improbable," said the official. "I doubt if even Murgatroyd, who is briefed for Studley, would risk a defence like that, which can be so easily disproved by medical examination. In any case, even if you were carrying on with his daughter, it would not justify him in trying to poison you."

"Do you think I ought to be legally represented?" asked

176

Austen.

"I should advise you not to be," said the official. "It will only draw attention to the charge, and might give Murgatroyd a hint. You are an experienced witness, and I will ask Sir James Morris, who is to lead for the Crown, to look after you. If anything comes out, it will be incidentally, and you will get rid of it quicker if you live it down, and let it die a natural death . than if you cry 'stinking fish.' "

Then Austen told him frankly and without being questioned, about Studley's behaviour in the tea-rooms, and the official's comments did not differ greatly in point of pungency, though they varied in vocabulary, from those of Inspector Saunders. But when Austen told him about the eavesdropping of Ann and the bumping of Mr. Studley, he was amazed to see the impersonal official throw back his head and go off in roars of laughter. The humour of the situation struck Austen himself for the first time; hitherto he had only seen the tragedy of it, and he joined in the guffaws, and the official was pleased to see his man looking a very different person to the one who had come into the room, reminding the old cavalryman of a shying horse with flattened ears. He saw that Austen was now ready to eat out of his hand, and asked him how he came to have these uncontrollable outbursts of temper, a most dangerous and undesirable thing in a police officer, and Austen explained that he was getting little or no sleep. The official was a shrewd judge of men, and he knew that in a man of Austen's highly-strung temperament intractable insomnia is a dangerous thing, and there was no knowing where he might land himself, and incidentally his superiors, in the course of his intricate work. So he told Austen that he had better apply for sick-leave, and he would get him sent down to the police convalescent home at Hove, for he knew it to be unwise for a man in Austen's state to go off by himself to lodgings or a boarding-house. Austen demurred indignantly, and began to shy again; he held, in theory at least, Saunders's view that a policeman, in matters of stamina, can give away points to an Army mule; but he soon responded to the skilled hand that was handling him, and agreed to see one of the famous specialists who act as consultants to Scotland Yard. The Metropolitan Police Force has never been stinted in medical matters.

That worthy, however, failed to gain Austen's confidence, although primed with a case history; the policeman regarding him as a member of the general public, and as such only fit to be either shepherded through traffic, or run in. Austen attributed his insomnia to watching night after night on the roof of a warehouse in an east wind. He was recommended psycho-analysis, and when this was rejected as impractical, a trip to Paris; and when both these twin remedies were scorned, the specialist wrote a prescription, which Austen threw in his waiting-room fire as he went out. Prescriptions were no use to him. He knew what was the matter with him—he wanted Ann, and he would be no use to himself or anyone else till he got her. And if he didn't get her—well, it wouldn't bear thinking about. And he reminded himself for the thousandth time of Saunders's words, "When she had to choose between you and her pa, she didn't think twice about it—as soon as he touched you, she turned on him." The old detective was a better psychotherapist than the Harley Street specialist.

Austen went down to Hove, and disgraced himself by picking up a girl on the Brighton pier who, seen from behind in a dim light, looked not unlike Ann. Seen from the front, in a good light, she was an entirely different proposition. He met her two or three times, taking good care to keep from her knowledge his name and profession for fear of blackmail; and then, undergoing a sudden revulsion of feeling, insulted her grossly, and went back to the police convalescent home and flung himself face downwards on his bed, Ann's letter clutched in his hand, and indulged in a hymn of hate against the entire world, and wished that well-tried remedy were open to him of going out and getting drunk and assaulting the police. The superintendent of the convalescent home came to the conclusion that Austen would do best on medicine and duty.

CHAPTER THIRTEEN

THE police court proceedings, and the trial before the grand jury, who brought in a true bill without leaving the box, were even more formal and devoid of news interest than usual, the bulk of the evidence being put in as depositions, medical certificates being produced on behalf of the two chief witnesses, Ann and Austen, one of whom lay in her high white bed in the cottage hospital, torn between her love for Austen and her memory of the sickening crack of her father's head against the wall; and the other, picking up the girl who looked like Ann, back view, and then insulting her.

Ann had written to her father from the hospital, offering to go and see him, but received no answer; and when Saunders came to see her and get her deposition signed, he dissuaded her from visiting him unless he sent for her, for Mr. Studley was bombarding Scotland Yard with the vilest allegations regarding his daughter and their officer, and hints were even leaking into the papers, presumably via Mr. Studley's solicitors, for it was difficult to know how else they had passed outside the prison doors. Saunders did not tell this to Ann, but he rubbed Austen's nose in it with extreme thoroughness, and redoubled his commands that his subordinate should steer clear of Ann till after the trial.

* * *

Shortly before the case came on, Ann insisted on returning to Thatched Cottage, which she adored, and although the rooms were full of memories, they were not all by any manner of means unhappy memories. She went into the room that had been Austen's, and that still smelt of his cigarettes, and knelt down by the bed and prayed for guidance; and then made up her mind definitely that as soon as the case was over, and all that was likely to come out had come out, if Austen still wanted her, she would marry him; and Ann was a little person who, once she had made up her mind, stuck to it. But it also seemed to her possible that by the time everything had come out, with all the ghastly publicity, Austen might be of a different mind. In any case, she felt she ought not to call him to her until it was known whether he was to have as father-in-law a hanged murderer, or a live poisoner whose hand had not lost its cunning.

Ann had not been back at Thatched Cottage many hours before callers began to find her out. The first was Mrs. Ashcott, who came almost daily to see that the girl was all right, sometimes accompanied by her husband, who was always most careful to change into plain clothes lest the sight of his uniform should be painful to Ann. Ann became very fond of motherly Mrs. Ashcott, who was unremitting in her care of the motherless girl, and came to the conclusion that she was a vast improvement on Aunt Maude, who had never been near her, after reading in the papers of the nature of Ann's evidence.

The next caller was the vicar (not his wife, to leave cards, Ann noticed). He administered spiritual consolation to Ann, which she accepted politely, but without enthusiasm. As he took his leave, he said to her:

"I hope, dear young lady, that your father will come through his trial safely."

"I don't," said Ann, who was in a very pro-Austen mood at the moment, having just found and washed a pair of her lover's socks. "If he does, I shall be the next victim."

The vicar hastened away, horrified at her callousness, for he, too, was a father, though not such a father as Mr. Studley.

The third caller was a Miss Smedley. Ann thought, when she saw Miss Smedley coming up the path, that she was evidently going to be received into local society on the strength of her father's notoriety. She soon found, however, that this lady was district-visiting, and not calling; and she also found that the C.I.D. could teach her nothing when it came to questioning unwilling witnesses. Fortunately for Ann, Inspector Saunders had warned her what to expect when he had called at the hospital to get her to sign the statement that Austen had decoded from his shorthand; and had told her always to reply that she had been forbidden by the police to say anything to anybody; for once she talked, she was lost, and would be subjected to endless annoyance.

Then the reporters discovered that Ann had returned to Thatched Cottage, and there was a race to be the first to interview her, knowing that she might talk to the first man, if he were sympathetic and personable, but she was hardly likely to say anything to the fourth or fifth.

Ann received them, and gave them tea out of politeness and because she was lonely, and most of them were very nice, and the nice ones chased off the nasty ones; but talk about the case she would not, saying that the police had told her not to, and the subject was a very painful one to her. She also firmly refused to be photographed, and as she promised to make a very pretty picture, and just the one to appeal to the readers of illustrated Sunday papers if she could be persuaded to pose, this was a serious loss to the pressmen.

But Ann would not. And finally it was decided to resort to a ruse to get a picture of her. She evaded their efforts by refusing to come out of the house while they were about, though she would let them in and give them tea in reasonable numbers; but it was impossible to snapshot her in the low-ceiling rooms with their diamond-paned windows, and a time-exposure was out of the question with an indignant Ann, who was as quick as an eel. So the young men of Fleet Street sank their rivalries, and agreed that the one of their number who appeared to be highest in favour with her should call unexpectedly, at an hour when the sun was shining in at the front door, and beguile her with conversation, while the rest, hidden in the bushes, took their chance of a snapshot.

This plan worked admirably. Out came Ann in the gay cretonne overall Austen particularly admired, with a great bird of paradise flying all over her skirt, and when the young man whom she liked the best of the highly amusing bunch, for reporters are not dumb-bells, demanded of her to show mercy and give him some crumb of news for his paper, she said with a laugh:

"Well, all I can think of is that the cat has had kittens!" And they both laughed heartily, and the other reporters snapped them.

It was this photograph that capsized all that was left of Austen's equilibrium.

It was the same reporter who had the bright idea of stealing a march on his fellows by coming down early on the morning that the Gregory poisoning trial opened, and offering to escort Ann up to London and look after her through the trial, as she seemed to be a very friendless little person—and a very attractive one, though he did not mention this consideration to his chief when he suggested that he should be detailed for this task. The editor was delighted, for young Tuke was the son of one of the directors of the paper and was being made to learn the business from the bottom, and his chief thought privately that that was the only aspect he would ever have seen of it if it hadn't been for his pull. Therefore it was considered a blessed mercy that the young man was at last beginning to take an intelligent interest in his work, and would not have to be returned empty to his father; so Tuke got his assignment.

He worked out the trains that Ann would have to catch in order to be at the Old Bailey by the time the trial opened—for Mr. Studley had preferred to be tried at the Old Bailey rather than the local assizes, where the jury would be composed of men to whom his reputation might be known—and he arrived at Thatched Cottage in his fast sports car just before she was due to start for the station, and found to his surprise that Ann had no intention of going up that day.

Inspector Saunders had been through to her on the phone, and had told her that as there was not the remotest chance of her evidence being required on the first day of the trial, when the opening speeches would be made and the technical witnesses heard, she could ignore the summons she had received, and he would take the responsibility. He knew what an ordeal it would be for the girl to sit in court, watching her father and being watched by him. He told her that there would probably be a long wrangle as to whether the four crimes, the three murders and the attempt on Austen, should be taken together or separately. The accused had a much better chance of getting off if they were taken separately, and Murgatroyd would not yield this point without a struggle. So long as she was ready to come up the moment he sent for her, she need not leave home until he phoned. To this Ann thankfully agreed.

All this she explained to young Tuke on his arrival. Far from being displeased at this thwarting, he decided to take the day off with Ann, with whom he was considerably enamoured, and invited her to go for a motor-run with him to pass the time away while she kept her anxious vigil. At this she opened her mouth concerning the case for the first time, and told him that she was busy getting her especial treasures

184

stowed in a safe place against the possible acquittal of Mr. Studley, when flight would be imperative if she desired a long life. Tuke was nearly off his head with excitement that this, his first big assignment, was going so well, for Ann's words were minted gold to him. He took her boxes in his car and transported them for her to the house of the family solicitor in the neighbouring country town, who had been to see how Ann was faring in her trouble, and invited her to come to him and his wife in the event of Mr. Studley's acquittal, for he knew well what manner of man his client was.

Tuke then put through a trunk-call to London, and his newspaper came out with a special edition bearing the head-lines: "PRISONER'S DAUGHTER MAKES ARRANGE-MENTS FOR FLIGHT IN EVENT OF HIS ACQUIT-TAL. From our special correspondent." There was also a character sketch of Ann, in which Austen, grinding his teeth as he read it, suspected a lover's eye.

In addition to the anguish he inflicted on Austen by this journalistic scoop, Tuke, whose lucky star appeared to be in the ascendant, also secured himself another day with Ann in the country, for Mr. Murgatroyd, the counsel for the defence, wrangled so long with the judge, demanding the newspaper's blood for these headlines, and the judge took so long to tell him he couldn't have it, and why, that the court's brief working day had worn to its close before the case even got started.

It was not until the afternoon of the third day that Saunders sent for Ann, and Tuke ran her up to town in his fast sports car, and as luck would have it, Austen, who had been stretching his legs during the luncheon interval, saw them arrive, though unseen by them, and recognized Ann's companion as the young man in the picture with whom she had been laughing so gaily, instead of pining for him, as he was for her. Austen immediately jumped to the conclusion that

Ann's secret place of refuge, at which the newspaper had hinted, was in marriage with this young man and his sports car.

He returned to the court; he had no choice; but instead of going to the seats reserved for witnesses, he took his place among a number of other policemen standing around the walls, at a point from which he could watch Ann without being seen by her. He found it impossible to deny himself that painful pleasure; and when Ann came in, shepherded by Saunders, and took off her coat, and he saw that she was wearing her blue linen frock, he felt that death had no sting left in it for him. When he saw the young man of his abomination follow her in, and sit down beside her, and be introduced to Saunders, who, however, received him none too well, being resentful, for Austen's sake, the only hope he had left in the world was that death had some sting in it for other folk. He leant back against the panelled wall, his hands in his trouser pockets, his reefer jacket bunched up over them like the feathers of an angry hen, looking most unprofessional, ignoring the shocked glances given him by his brother policemen, and daring anyone to tell him to behave himself.

He watched Inspector Saunders whispering to Ann, and knew that he was giving her instructions as to how she should comport herself in the witness-box during her impending ordeal. The trial was not going well for the Crown. Murgatroyd, counsel for the defence, refusing to take the weak and vindictive line suggested to him by his client, had diluted Mr. Studley's statements till they became plausible, and was attacking the police witnesses, Saunders and Austen, on the ground that Ann had been intimidated by threats to charge her as an accomplice. His special line of country, which he took in case after case, was that the police had brow-beaten their prisoners, or obtained statements from them by dubious means, and when the judge heard him gather himself together for the first familiar fence, he rolled up his eyes to heaven, tapped his teeth with his pencil, and registered extreme boredom by every means available to a judge in full canonicals, and wished that the jury had a whole-time job and knew Murgatroyd as well as he did.

But as he heard the evidence unfold, he came to the conclusion that there might be something in it for once, for there was a good deal of independent testimony. The hedger, for one, who had heard Ann's screams on the occasion of the famous handcuff adventure. A servant at Deepdene Hall for another, Mrs. Gregory's personal maid, who had heard Ann screaming near the river upon another occasion. But the greatest surprise had been the testimony of the wife of a local publican, who had apparently been accompanying Mr. Studley on his return to the house on the evening of his arrest, and who had heard Sergeant Austen giving the girl the third degree and actually threatening her with a charge of complicity in the crimes if she did not tell all she knew. This witness was offered to the court as being, like Caesar's wife, above suspicion, for she was the wife of a retired policeman. Ann knew well for what purpose that witness was accompanying Mr. Studley to the house at a time when he believed it to be empty of all but his daughter, and gave a shudder of disgust as Saunders whispered an epitome of the evidence into her ear. She knew that the retired policeman lived to a far greater extent on the earnings of his wife than on the profits of his pub.

Neither Saunders nor Austen had made their usual good impression on the jury because they were both straining every nerve to prevent Ann's fair name from being sullied, as well as to defend themselves against the aspersions that were being heaped upon them; and the lack of frankness and general restiveness and obvious bias of the two detectives, and particularly of Austen, were apparent to the jury even before they were used as window-dressing by Murgatroyd.

The official who had counselled Austen to do without personal legal representation, and who was present in court listening to the case, cursed himself for the advice he had given, and determined that everything his influence could do should be done to clear Austen if either judge or jury censured him. He was thankful, however, that there were no charges of immorality, thus justifying his forecast; but he had never foreseen Murgatroyd taking quite this line. He was glad, however, that Austen, with whom he had been very favourably impressed during his interview, was spared the worst, for he knew how terribly keenly the young fellow would have felt any aspersions coming through him on the fair name of the girl he wished to marry. He had seen that expressionless countenance suddenly flick into mobility, and knew what manner of man lay behind the wooden police exterior.

He watched with interest for the entry of Ann Studley into court, for he was curious to see what manner of girl she was, this daughter of an old schoolfellow, who proposed to marry a policeman. He hoped for the man's sake that she had sufficient guts to see the job through, this marriage out of her station, for he was too good a fellow to be played about with. He also hoped she had sufficient guts to stand up in the witness-box to that bullying brute of a Murgatroyd, whom not only the police force but also the Bar, hated with a deadly hatred.

Ann was the last hope of the prosecution, and if she failed to keep her end up in the witness-box, a very dangerous criminal was going to be turned loose on society. The police, also, were going to be in for serious unpleasantness, for the disbelief by the jury of Ann's evidence would carry with it the implication of their belief in the charges against police methods in general, and those ofSaunders and Austen in particular, which were being handed out by Mr. Murga-troyd, by means of innuendo and direct statement, with an exceeding freeness. Judges are very slow to pull up a counsel when he is working along this line of country, lest the news-papers accuse them of bias in favour of the prosecution, so they let the police take their chance; their backs are broad, and to have dirt flung at them, both literally and metaphori-cally, is all part of the day's work to them. To do the police justice, they care very little for abuse from prisoners' counsel, though they are more sensitive to a bad press, as actors call it. What they really dislike is the permitting of their witnesses to be heckled, because it is very difficult to get people to come forward and give evidence in serious crime, especially capital charges, and if the ordeal of the witness-box is made too terrible—it is had enough in any case—it becomes increas-ingly difficult to get witnesses to give the kind of testimony which would provoke attacks from the defence. To subpoena a witness is one thing, but to get him to stand up to a bullying counsel and stick to his story in a case out of which he has nothing to gain, is quite another.

Austen and Saunders were not particularly concerned about a bad press; they did not think they were very likely to get one, as Austen was very popular with Fleet Street, partly because he photographed so well, and did not mind being photographed, and partly because he was on terms of per-sonal friendship with a good many of the more influential pressmen. He liked the society of men with a wider outlook than the average run of his comrades; and the reporters, who had cultivated Austen at first as a potential source of news, for they always like to keep in with the police, had come to like him for his own sake when they got to know him. There were, of course, the papers which appealed to very demo-cratic tastes, and which keep columns of abuse of the police permanently set up in type. But they did not matter; their

189

steady stream of abuse was like the noise of traffic, which one soon learns to sleep through, and would wake up if it stopped.

But the high official had no knowledge of these personalities, though they make a great deal of difference to the efficiency or otherwise of individual detective work. He slipped into a seat beside the counsel who was leading for the Crown, and begged him to look after the police witnesses to the best of his ability, and at least to let them feel that the Crown was not indifferent to their sufferings. Austen watched Sir John Morris, his two bewigged juniors, and the high official, all with their noses close together, and occasionally glancing at him, and he felt that he need not worry unduly; there would be nothing worse than public unpleasantness in store for him; the things that really mattered, which went on in the bleak brick building on the Embankment, would not happen.

Finally the jury were packed away in their box like sardines, everybody rose, the judge came in, and the business of the afternoon commenced.

Ann heard her own name called. Saunders delivered her with a push into the hands of a large sergeant with a well-greased forelock, who shooed her before him down a narrow alley; she stumbled up some wooden steps and found herself in a position of vantage overlooking the court. She had not had a good view of the court before, because the reporters' box blocked her outlook, and although she had kept on looking round for Austen, she had not been able to catch sight of him. But that did not mean that he was not there, for only a small section of the crowded court had been visible to her from where she sat. Neither had she seen her father, for which she was truly thankful, for she dreaded the moment when she would have to meet his eyes. The shadow of the gallows hung over her imagination the whole time, and the dreadful morning, in three weeks' time, when she would be watching the clock till its hands pointed to eight a.m. Something in her still clung to her father, though she had made up her mind to sacrifice him to Austen, and had no intention of weakening or turning back.

She looked round the court in perplexity; she was slightly short-sighted, and it was not too well lit. She saw the judge in his scarlet robes in a great chair, sitting high up. And also seated high up, she saw her father, Mrs. Gregory and Mrs. Gregory's sister. She wondered why they all sat together up there, and supposed that the two women were his witnesses. It never occurred to her that they were all three prisoners, being charged with capital crimes. Her father looked extraordinarily well and dapper in his smart suit of summer grey; Ann might make her own frocks, but Mr. Studley never lacked the best tailoring. She thought she had not seen him look so well for ages. A period as one of His Majesty's guests often does wonders for the health in certain cases. Mrs. Gregory, however, looked ghastly. Either from policy or compulsion she had washed her face, and her skin, bereft of the stucco frontage of make-up that usually decorated it, looked like that of the women who sell clothes-pegs at the door. Ann thought that nothing would have induced her to buy clothes-pegs from such a dreadful-looking harridan had she come selling them at her door. She thought that her father must be thoroughly disillusioned by now as to Mrs. Gregory's charms, but perhaps he still retained his affection for her bank-book.

Ann peered round with her short-sighted eyes, but still she could not see Austen. It all seemed unreal, like waxworks. Then she found that someone was trying to attract her attention, and was offering her a book. She took it politely, to oblige him, not in the least knowing why it was offered to her. And then the swearing of Ann Studley as a witness for the Crown against her father in a capital charge began, and she found herself being called upon to inform the assembly that she would tell the truth, the whole truth, and nothing but the truth, and startling them by saying in conclusion, "And may God have mercy on my soul." She heard with surprise the rustle and murmur in court as she said these words, quite innocently, for her mind had been so obsessed by the thought of the hanging of her father that they had come to her lips unbidden.

She looked round for Austen again, and still she could not see him. Surely, surely he would have been near her in this ordeal if he still cared for her? Love is very quick to suspect itself unloved, simply to save itself from the worse hurt of compulsory disillusionment. Then she saw that someone else was trying to attract her attention; a man who had risen from his seat just under her, and turning his back on the court, was speaking to her, asking her questions. His face was aquiline and sallow under his grey horsehair wig, and his dark eyes were extraordinarily bright. Ann was specially interested in the funny little curls on his wig, and wondered if he put them up in curlers at night, and wore a slumber-cap over them, as Mrs. Gregory did. Still she could not feel that the scene before her was anything but a drop scene at a theatre.

The manner of this man was simple and kindly, and his dark eyes smiled at her in an encouraging fashion. He asked her her name, and she told him. Ann's voice, though soft and sweet, was rather high-pitched, as the voices of the petite often are, and it sounded like a child's voice, shy and startled, in the big, silent court. The man in the wig looked at her in surprise, and asked her how old she was, and she told him twenty-three. Austen seized on this information with avidity: He had often wanted to know how old Ann was, but had never dared to ask her. He was twenty-eight himself. That would do nicely, just five years between them, as there should be. Then he thought of the young man with the sports car and set his teeth.

Ann heard another voice speaking to her, interrupting the questioning, the voice of a very old man, cracked and creaking. She looked in surprise in the direction from which the voice came, and saw that it was the judge. He asked her to be good enough to remove her hat. She had on the same large, drooping hat that had tantalized Austen at the inquest, and it hid her face from anyone who was not directly in front of her. Courts like to have a good look at their witnesses while they are giving their evidence.

Ann took off her hat, and looked round for somewhere to put it. It was taken from her by a very large policeman, whom she found was her companion in the witness-box. She turned back again to the court, tidying her ruffled hair with little quick pats and strokings of her childlike hands, for she was an entirely unselfconscious little person. Austen, watching her every movement, felt the blood surge into his head as she performed her innocent little toiletings. He had always been fascinated by Ann's soft, fluffy fair hair, and longed above all things for the time when he should have the right to stroke it.

Ann finally gave her attention to counsel.

He led her by patient questionings through the long and involved history of her father's crimes. Ann hesitated at describing them. The ordeal was evidently going to be painful. It was like going to the dentist. The drill does not hurt at first, but as it goes deeper and deeper the pain becomes sharper and sharper. Ann hesitated, and looked miserably round the court for a friendly face. Saunders was out of her sight, and she saw nothing but strangers, staring strangers, and no Austen. Her voice cracked like that of a child about to cry.

Then the judge took her in hand, and added his probings to those of counsel.

"I know this is very painful to you," he said, his manner reminding her of a dentist, "but you must try and tell us all

193

about it, and no harm shall come to you."

Ann looked at him piteously.

"Not even if my father gets off?" she said, and the silence in court could have been cut with a knife. There were two ways in which that remark could be taken.

It was not so difficult, once you got started, thought Ann. She tried not to think of her father, or of Austen, and concentrated on the man in front of her; his bright, dark eyes held her attention more and more as she began to warm up to her work, till finally she could think of nothing but those bright, glittering eyes, and she seemed to be alone with him in a circle of darkness, and every question he asked pressed a button, automatically eliciting the right reply.

He asked her if the police had ever threatened or coerced her in any way.

"No, never," said Ann, with emphasis. "They have been very kind. We liked having them in the house." It never occurred to her that she was hardly justified in using the plural pronoun; it was unlikely that her father concurred in that sentiment.

Then he sat down, indicating that he had finished, and Ann felt as if she had lost a friend.

Suddenly there rose before her a figure that looked like Watts's *Minotaur* in a wig. Its face was dark and congested, and its eyes bulged like those of a Pekinese. She looked at this vision in horror, and wondered if it were going to put its head down and charge her, and felt thankful for the stout barrier on which she leant. It looked at her loweringly for a long moment, and then it levelled a menacing forefinger at her, and said :

"I want the truth!"

"Certainly," cried Ann, who resented his manner.

The high official from Scotland Yard noted with anxiety that Murgatroyd made no attempt to cross-examine Ann on the evidence she had already given. It was too horribly damning to be picked at piecemeal; it had to go bodily, if it went at all. He wondered what was coming. The Minotaur, as Ann christened him, waved his hand round the crowded court. "Do you see anyone here that you recognize?" he asked, in his portentous voice, as if he were demanding whether there were hemlock in his drink.

Ann peered. "I cannot see anyone I know from here," she said. "But there are people I know in court."

"Who are they?" demanded the dreadful, bull-like creature, in a voice that sounded as if he were charging her with unspeakable crimes.

"Inspector Saunders and Mr. Tuke, the reporter of the Evening Record.

"Anyone else?"

"My—my father, and Mrs. Godfrey—I mean, Gregory, and I also know her sister by sight. I saw her at the inquest."

"Anyone else?" continued the implacable voice.

"No, there is no one else."

The menacing forefinger rose again.

"That is a lie."

Ann, being a person who respected the truth, did not like being called a liar, and she drew herself up to the full of her little height, tossed her golden head, and said to the menacing cross-examiner:

"I am not going to put up with rudeness from you, or any other man. If you want civil answers, you must ask your questions civilly."

Cheers from the gallery, which were hastily hushed into silence by innumerable policemen and ushers.

The bull cast an indignant glance at the judge, appealing for protection, but the judge merely gazed back blandly at him and left him to take care of himself.

He looked like murder, but changed his tactics. His scowl

195

gave place to a rather sneering smile.

"Look behind you," he said.

Ann looked round, and saw Austen immediately behind the witness-box, within hand-reach of her. Her face lit up radiantly, oblivious of the crowded court. But his face, though he looked steadily into her eyes, never moved a muscle. He was facing the court; he dared not show anything. Ann felt completely crushed. So this was the end of her romance. Austen had finished with her. Tears came smarting into her eyes, and a lump in her throat nearly strangled her. She turned back to face the menacing counsel, utterly dispirited, and he saw at once that all the kick had gone out of her. He gathered himself together; he felt that he was on the right lines.

"You have seen Sergeant Austen before?"

"Yes," said Ann, hoping she was not going to weep.

"He resided in your house for several weeks?"

"Yes,'" said Ann, her mind going back to the days of the first happiness of her dawning love, and the tears getting nearer and nearer to overflowing.

"During the time he was at your house did he ever threaten you, or speak menacingly to you?"

"Never," said Ann, unable to imagine what all this was leading up to.

"But Miss Le Bas, Mrs. Gregory's maid, states on oath that she heard you screaming on the river bank after she had heard your voices talking together angrily?"

"I was screaming on the river bank because he was being carried over the weir by the current, and I was badly frightened."

"He does not appear to have come to much harm," sneered counsel.

"No, 1 was able to pull him out. But it was touch and go."

"And what were you quarrelling with him about prior to this?"

"I was not quarrelling with him," said the indignant Ann.

"But Miss Le Bas said she heard your voice raised in anger."

"Well," said Ann, "I was rather cross with him, but we were not quarrelling."

"And what were you cross with him about?" persisted Murgatroyd, seeing the way opening up as he advanced in a most gratifying fashion. He had had a run of failures recently, desperate cases, entirely indefensible, for he took all corners, and he did not want to obtain a reputation for being unlucky, for the criminal classes are very superstitious.

"He wanted to show me how life-saving was done, and I did not want to have my life saved. I hate being mauled about. I did not know him very well in those days, and I thought he was rather cheeky, so I came out. It was very cold, anyway." ("The little—" said Saunders, to himself, "she side-tracked me properly about that bathing!")

"We are not surprised to learn that this young man is cheeky," said Murgatroyd, with emphasis, giving the jury a look to call their attention to this admission on Ann's part. "So you admit that Miss Le Bas was correct when she said that you ,first spoke angrily to Sergeant Austen, and then began to scream?"

"Yes," said Ann, "and it would have been very much more useful if she had fetched help, instead of just listening."

"Kindly limit yourself to answering the questions you are asked," said Murgatroyd tartly. "Now, with regard to the screams heard by the hedger working in the road the day before the inquest—"

"What hedger?" said country-bred Ann, in surprise.

"There is no hedging going on at that time of year."

"Neither there is, Mr. Murgatroyd," came the cracked, weary voice of the judge, who was a landed proprietor.

Murgatroyd gave him a hasty glance and pressed on quickly with his questioning.

"Well, the man Guppy, who states on oath that he heard you scream."

"Oh, Guppy!" said Ann, with profound contempt.

"Yes, Guppy. He states that he heard you screaming intermittently and imploring Sergeant Austen to let you go."

"Then why didn't he come to the rescue?" said Ann promptly. .

"Will you limit your answers to what you are asked?" snarled Murgatroyd.

"Guppy is not a hedger. What was he doing, working on the road?"

"That is not our problem. You are here to give evidence concerning the case that is being tried."

"But it may be our problem, Mr. Murgatroyd," came the weary voice from the bench. "Who is Mr. Guppy, and what is his profession?"

Ann saw that she was being addressed by the judge, and, delighted to have the opportunity of turning her back on Murgatroyd, raised her voice as she saw the old man cupping his hand round his ear and leaning forward, and said:

"Guppy is our local bad lot. He minds cars during race-days, and watches the horses from the training-stables, and comes up before the magistrates once a month for poaching. He is no hedger. Hedging is skilled. He never did anything so much like hard work in his life. Sergeant Ashcott can tell you all about him. No one ever employs him except my father."

"What does your father employ him as?" inquired the judge.

"I don't know. But he comes to the door from time to

time, and father gives him money, so I presume he employs him."

No comment was offered on Ann's remarks, but as the judge handed her back to Mr. Murgatroyd with a gesture, she felt that the atmosphere in the court had undergone a slight change for the better.

Mr. Murgatroyd returned to the attack.

"What was this screaming that was heard from the road?"

"It wasn't serious," said Ann. "It was only fun." And under Murgatroyd's persistent pressure the story of the decorated handcuffs was slowly extracted from Ann, amid giggles and hushings from the gallery.

"Well, Mr. Murgatroyd," came the cracked voice of the judge once again, "I do not think we need take that as evidence of intimidation. That is a common joke with policemen, to handcuff their young ladies in play."

"But not young ladies of the social position of the witness," said Murgatroyd acidly.

"And what did Inspector Saunders say to all this?" was his next question.

"He was very angry," said Ann.

"With whom?"

"With both of us. He told Mr. Austen he would report him if he ever did it again; and he said it was just as much my fault as his, and I deserved all I got, and I ought to have had more sense, and I was to go to my room and stop there."

The line of blue round the walls had its collective hand before its collective mouth.

"In fact, he adopted a fatherly attitude towards you?" said the judge.

"Very," said Ann. "I felt as if I had been spanked," and the hushings broke out afresh.

Murgatroyd was not making quite the progress he

199

hoped. But there was evidently something in Mr. Studley's complaints about the behaviour of Austen, after all, and he wished he had taken the line his client desired. Still, it was not too late to shift his ground.

CHAPTER FOURTEEN

MR. MURGATROYD'S next move surprised everybody.

"Will you oblige me by turning round and looking at this young man?"

Ann did as requested, taking a hasty glance at the blushing Austen, who glared into space, as red as a turkey-cock, while she herself went a vivid and painful pink and felt her temper going.

"How does he impress you?"

"I am afraid I do not understand your question."

"Do you consider him a handsome man?"

Ann considered him a very handsome man, but she was certainly not going to admit it.

"Some people prefer moustaches," she said, and the court exploded with one accord, cracked cackles even coming from the bench.

It was impossible for the judge to threaten to clear the court, as he was still wiping his eyes, that were streaming with merriment, so he looked appealingly at the gallery and said, "Do try to behave up there. We mustn't laugh. This is a very serious matter."

Then as things quieted down, Murgatroyd returned to the attack again, and began to cross question Ann concerning the happenings when Austen gave her the third degree. Now Ann had known all the time that Austen had no right to question her in the way he was doing, and she had seen how he reacted when she told him so; consequently, she guessed that if she admitted what had really happened she would be doing Austen a great deal of harm, and she made up her mind that, oath or no oath, she would admit nothing. It is doubtful if the oath has a great deal of influence over witnesses while they are actually in the box, though it may cause the conscientious a few twinges afterwards.

No, Austen had not bullied her. Neither had he threatened her.

"But Mrs. Hewitt states on oath that she heard him say, 'Unless you tell all you know, you will be charged as an accomplice,' and that you replied, 'Then I had better consult a solicitor before I make any statement.' "

Ann did not relish a deliberate lie, so she resorted to her old trick of side-tracking.

"Do you know who Mrs. Hewitt is?"

"She is the wife of a retired policeman. Kindly answer questions, instead of asking them."

"Do you know that he had to retire because he married her?" Ann had turned cross-questioner now.

"What grounds have you got for making that statement?" said the judge.

"She is well known round our way. Ask Sergeant Ashcott."

The judge lifted his finger. Ashcott was produced like a rabbit out of a conjuror's hat.

Yes, he knew the witness in question, and she was a woman with a very bad record. Murgatroyd objected to his evidence because he was not on oath.

"Then we will recall him presently," said the judge. Mr. Murgatroyd might get plenty of rope, but not much small change, from him.

But Murgatroyd pressed the attack. His experienced cross-examiner's ear, as sensitive as that of a musician to a false note, had told him of the change of timbre in Ann's voice when questioned concerning this third quarrel. There was something to go upon here, he felt certain, and he chiv-vied Ann from pillar to post and back again, tripped her up, made her contradict herself, and flurried and worried her till there was no sense left in her. Ann was lying desperately, and the court knew it; even the jury knew it.

Finally the judge said, "You must be frank with us, Miss Studley, remember you are on oath."

Ann threw up her head and looked round the court like a trapped animal. She knew she would not be allowed to go until she had answered, even if they kept her there all night. It was so rotten for Austen, with all the other police-men about. But out it had to come.

"He asked me to marry him, and I wouldn't, and I was beastly to him about it. That was why we had the row."

"Oh?" said Murgatroyd, "So the young man made him-self unpleasant?"

"No," said the wretched Ann. "It was I who made myself unpleasant."

"And what did you do?"

"I slapped his face," gulped Ann. "But I apologized im-mediately after."

"And what cause had you to slap his face?"

"None," wailed Ann. "It was an awful thing to do. I only did it because I was so upset."

"And what were you upset about?" went on the inexo-rable voice.

"I was upset because I thought it was all going to come out about my father."

"What made you think that?"

"Mr. Austen said they knew all about him."

"But you have just been telling the court that the trouble between you and Sergeant Austen had nothing to do with your evidence in this case."

"I know, I know," wailed the miserable Ann. "It's all a

muddle, an awful muddle. I don't know where I am. You have tangled it up till it's all behind before. It's quite simple, when you understand it."

"Let me see if I can disentangle it," came the kind voice of the judge. He had begun to wonder when protests would be coming from Sir John Morris at this treatment of his witness; but Sir John had had the story of Austen's romance from Saunders, and knew that it was the best possible thing for the case that Ann should confess the honest and honourable love affair between herself and the young detective, for it was the complete answer to all Murgatroyd's charges against the police, whether of immorality or brutality; so he cast poor Ann to the lions, feeling very sorry for her, but quite satisfied that neither she nor the young fellow would take any serious harm from the process to which Murgatroyd was subjecting them.

"Now supposing you tell me, in your own words, just exactly what all this difficulty is about between you and the police?" said the judge.

Ann was truly thankful. In her evidence concerning the actual facts of the crimes she had been steered by the skilful hand of Sir John Morris, but neither he nor anyone else had expected that Murgatroyd would take the line he was doing in order to discredit her testimony. Sir John was making furious notes with a view to the re-examination of what was left of Ann after Murgatroyd had done with her, but he could not break in upon the cross-examination to come to her rescue. Only the judge could do that. The game is played according to the rules.

Ann turned to the face like a wizened apple which looked out at her, half buried under a full-bottomed wig.

"There was no trouble," she said, feeling like a swimmer who comes to the surface again after being entangled under the water. "It is quite simple when you understand it. You see, I was pulled first one way and then another between my father and Mr. Austen. I know I acted sillily, but I was so upset. It is a dreadful position to be in," added Ann pathetically.

Someone in the gallery began to sob audibly, . and was led out.

"The position is this, then," said the judge, "that there has been no coercion on the part of the police, but you came forward to give evidence against your father voluntarily because of your affection for this young man, Sergeant Austen?"

"No, no !" wailed Ann, feeling her self-control leaving her.

"Then what was your motive?"

"He was too dangerous to be left loose any longer. He couldn't go on killing people right and left as the fancy took him."

"When did you first suspect your father?"

"When 1 heard the evidence at the inquest. I never suspected anything before, I swear I didn't."

"How was it you came to be attending the inquest? It is not a place where young ladies usually go."

"Inspector Saunders told Sergeant Austen to take me."

"Did you go willingly?"

"Yes, quite willingly. I thought it would be interesting. I didn't know what it was going to be like."

"Were you engaged to him then?"

"No," shrieked Ann, "I'm *not* engaged to him!"

"I think you had better get on with her, Mr. Murgatroyd," said the judge.

So Murgatroyd started again. But the judge had given him an invaluable lead, and he shifted his ground from seduction as he had shifted it once before from coercion. He would throw doubt on Ann's good faith because she had not come forward promptly with her testimony. What was such delayed testimony worth? Could it be relied on when it at last arrived? Why was she running with the hare and hunting with the hounds?

"Why did you not come forward promptly with your information?" he inquired.

"Because of my father," said Ann.

"You were fond of your father?"

"Yes, and am still, for that matter."

Ann cast a pitiful glance at her father, who smiled unpleasantly.

"Then, in that case, what made you, shall we say, reverse your policy?"

"He tried to kill Sergeant Austen," said Ann, in a low voice.

"Well, we may not agree on that point. At any rate, you thought he wanted to kill Sergeant Austen. And you considered that a sufficient reason for handing him over to the gallows, although you did not mind him killing your mother, your grandmother, and William Gregory?"

"I did not think it would help the dead, and capital punishment is a very terrible thing."

"A powerful argument that, for the abolition of capItal punishment," said the judge. "Witnesses will not come forward."

"I felt it would be no better than murder on my part," said Ann. "And I felt it was not altogether my father's fault, because when he got drunk he never knew what he was doing, and I was sorry for him."

The judge observed that she always spoke of her father in the past tense, as if he were already executed.

The light was growing dim in the court, as a thunderstorm passed overhead; the electric lights were switched on, and the court saw how Ann's small, oval face had changed since she entered the box.

"I think the witness had better have a chair," said the judge, kindly.

It was brought, and Ann sank into it thankfully. She had not realized how tired she was. She wished she dared to ask the judge to let her have a cup of tea. She was sure he would have done so, he was so very kind and considerate.

Then her weary *via dolorosa* began again.

"Why did you choose that particular moment to communicate your evidence to the police? Why keep silence for three days?"

"I hoped things would blow over about my father. It never occurred to me he would try and do another murder."

"You must not say that, Miss Studley," said the judge, "We have not yet decided that he has committed any murders."

"Why first run a very considerable risk to shield your father, and then go out of your way to betray him? You need not have given that cocoa to Sergeant Austen if you suspected it of being poisoned. You could have thrown it away."

"I thought he would try again," said Ann faintly.

"And you thought it was better to betray your father to the gallows than to let the Sergeant run any risk?"

"Yes," said Ann, still more faintly.

"So you preferred a sergeant of police whom you had only known a few days, to your own father?"

Ann was heard to murmur something indistinguishable.

"What does she say?" said the judge, cupping his hand round his ear and leaning forward.

Austen felt his heart beating to suffocation in his throat.

"She says YESSSSSS!" shouted Murgatroyd, spitting the word at the judge in his wrath. It was not the answer he had expected.

But he had still got a shot or two left in his locker. He was a popular advocate with the criminal classes largely because he struggled for his client so gamely to the last. Ann wondered if he were ever going to finish, and what it had all got to do with the case.

"You knew this young man was the son of a builder's foreman?"

"I knew his father was a working-man. I did not know exactly what he was."

"Your father is a man of good family, I take it?"

Ann agreed. Murgatroyd led her through her pedigree. She agreed.

"And yet you want us to believe you have a love affair with this working-class youth?"

Ann did not answer.

"That makes very little difference to the young, Mr. Murgatroyd," said the judge, who thought privately that Austen was one of the finest looking young fellows he had ever seen, in uniform or out of it.

"But then you also tell us that you refused to marry him?"

"How could I?" wailed poor Ann.

"Because he was a policeman?" pressed Murgatroyd? This would go down well with the democratic Press, with which he was popular.

"Yes. How could I?"

The judge looked at Austen's face, and pitied him. So did everyone else in court. Austen knew it. He kept his face tense and immobile, but of all the bad times he had been through, this was the worst.

"How could I marry him?" Ann's voice rang through the hushed court like a cry of pain. "I had just found out about my father. How could I marry anybody? Least of all a policeman. They can only marry women of good character. Look at Mrs. Hewett!"

She thought she heard someone behind her say, "Pussy!" very softly.

"So although you had decided not to marry him," Murgatroyd thought he would see what a sneer could do, the situation called for desperate remedies, "you also decided not to spare your father?"

"Yes," said Ann.

"You had no objection to his killing your mother, as you thought, and yet when this young man, whom you do not wish to marry, is threatened, you change your mind?" said Murgatroyd sarcastically.

"Yes," said Ann, lifting her head defiantly. "I did not see that it could help the dead to punish my father, but when he struck at the man I loved, that was another matter. I let him take his punishment then." She gazed desperately round the hushed court that hung on the drama of her words, wondering how she could justify her illogical behaviour and save herself from being charged as her father's accomplice, which was what she thought was coming. "The Bible says, 'A man shall leave father and mother, and cleave to his wife,' and I suppose it is the same with a woman."

"But you have just told us that you refused to become this man's wife?"

"Yes, but I might have been, if things had been different," and to her intense surprise and mortification, Ann collapsed into floods of tears.

She felt a pair of hands take her under the arms and lift her bodily out of the chair. Austen who had pushed aside the policeman in charge of the witness-box, was bending over her, oblivious of all the staring eyes.

"It's all right, Pussy, they have finished with you. It's me. It's Jack. Come along," and he gathered her up, and with his arm round her, half carried and half supported her out of the box and into the little room that is reserved for collapsed witnesses, where she leant against him, oblivious of her surroundings, sobbing unrestrainedly.

"Sorry, sir, but you're wanted in court," she heard someone say.

Austen said "Damn!" with exceeding heartiness, and thrust Ann into the arms of the nearest policeman where, discovering his tunic instead of Austen's jacket under her cheek, she looked up hastily, and saw a very large red face looming over her—gratified, but embarrassed. Its owner deposited Ann carefully in an arm-chair, to their mutual relief, and a woman in semi-nurse's uniform produced sal volatile.

Now sal volatile is such an excellent remedy for hysteria largely on account of its flavour, for no one who has had one dose risks a second. Ann gasped, spluttered, and pulled herself together. She heard Austen's voice in court, taking the oath. She heard Murgatroyd say to him, "You have not been altogether frank with us, Sergeant Austen," and Austen reply, "I answered your questions, sir. If they were not relevant, that is no fault of mine;" and the judge's voice: "You must not talk to counsel like that, Sergeant."

Then someone closed the door and she could hear no more.

She sat for a little while with the police matron beside her. Then she rose rather shakily.

"I think fresh air will do me more good than anything else," she said. "Is there anywhere near here where I can get tea?"

They encouraged her departure. They are not fond of having murderers' next of kin on the premises when sentence is pronounced, and they had no doubt whatever in their minds what the sentence would be in Mr. Studley's case, even allowing for the known vagaries of juries.

CHAPTER FIFTEEN

ANN found herself bowed out of the Old Bailey by a perfect bevy of smiling policemen. The news of her testimony had gone round the building like wildfire, and they felt individually and collectively flattered. It was as if the very attractive Ann had declared her love for the entire Metropolitan Police Force.

She was met on the steps by Tuke, who had apparently been waiting for her for some time, for his shining mackintosh testified to the fact that he had been out in the thunderstorm. He greeted her sympathetically, and talked loudly and continuously to drown the sound of a volley of clicks going on all round them as the cameramen got to work.

"Poor old kid," he said. "Thank God that's over. Now come along round to my little place and have a meal in peace, away from all the starers."

Ann jumped to the conclusion that he had missed the end of her evidence, for he was looking, in the words of Inspector Saunders, nearly as "goofy" as Austen. His wet mackintosh bore this out, for the rain had started before Ann's poor little secret was dragged from her. He was shepherding her towards his car as he talked, the pressmen snapping like fury and a cinematograph camera whirring in the background. For the rest of the week Tuke was infuriated by the appearance in the news gazette of all the cinemas of this film, with himself labelled as Austen; which was a judgment on that young man for his duplicity. But it did not suit Ann's book at all to be taken to tea by Tuke. She was hoping that any minute Austen might make good his escape from court and come to her, and her heart was beating furiously in anticipation of this moment. She had ears and eyes and thoughts for nought else, and was looking all round her as Tuke took her by the arm and led her toward his car. She was completely oblivious of his presence. He might have been the Angel of the Day of Judgment, for all she knew or cared.

She suddenly woke up to the fact that she was being put into his car by Tuke, and backed away hastily. She was shrewd enough to know that Austen, being very much in love with her, would be correspondingly jealous, and she did not want to upset or hurt him. Moreover, she had taken great care to blaze a very wide trail for him to follow, asking the police matron in the witnesses-room where would be a good place to get tea, announcing her intention of going to the place recommended, and telling the sergeant on the door of the Old Bailey the same thing. Consequently, Austen could easily find her if he wanted her, and Ann was daring to hope that he would want her, with occasional quivers of doubt.

It was her intention to wait in the teashop till Austen joined her, have a talk with him, and—well—but—? Ann quavered off into queries. She knew her own mind all right, but would—could Austen want her after all that had happened?

"I am going to a teashop just round the corner to have some tea," said Ann, pulling her arm out of Tuke's grasp. The movie man cursed himself for having used all his celluloid on Ann's descent of the Old Bailey steps, arm in arm with Tuke, whom he thought was Austen. Here was still further drama, and he had nothing to take it with!

"I shouldn't do that, if I were you," said Tuke, "You'll be horribly stared at. Your photo has been in all the papers."

"Yes," said Ann tartly, "and who put it there?"

"Come on round to my fiat. It's quite near here, and I

212

can give you tea quietly."

Ann could as soon have seen herself going to tea in hell with the Devil, but she could not bring herself to tell the young man the truth, for it was all so very embarrassing. So she hummed and hawed, and turned pink, and Tuke took her embarrassment as a tribute to his irresistible charms. After all, it is not altogether insulting to a young man when a young woman will not trust herself alone with him.

"All right," he said, "I'll take you to tea at a teashop, if you prefer it. I know a nice quiet one near Ludgate Circus."

Again poor Ann had to manoeuvre. "Thank you so much," she said, "but I am going to this one," and set off at a brisk pace in the direction of St. Paul's. Tuke had no option but to follow if he did not want to lose sight of her.

The teashop was very full when they arrived there, and they could only get a table round a corner, from which the door was invisible, and Ann was on tenderhooks lest Austin should look in, and not seeing her, go away again. However, there was no choice, it was that or nothing. Tuke tried to put her into a chair facing the wall, for he saw that she was being recognized all over the crowded room, but she would have none of it, and pushed him aside so vigorously that he nearly sat down in someone else's tea.

He attributed her distracted air and the tense way she gazed at the incoming stream of people, to anxiety as to her father's fate, and sought to divert her mind with conversation.

"That swine of a Murgatroyd gave you a poisonous time in the box," he said, with cheerful tactlessness, for the one thing of which Ann did not wish to be reminded of was that ghastly experience. "He's famous for it. The police hate him like poison because he always takes that tack about them; it may comfort you to know that. I only heard the beginning of your evidence, but I saw he was playing his usual opening.

The police didn't really bully you, did they? I suppose what happened was that that young detective chap got a bit fresh. Rotten for you having that sort billeted on you. Pity he didn't go over the weir, I say."

He paused, but got no answer out of Ann, who wasn't looking at him, and hardly heard him.

"I say, was there anything in that handcuff yarn?" he asked curiously; partly because, being rather partial to Ann, he wanted to know, and partly because he had suddenly remembered that he was a newspaper man, and that this tea with Ann was a scoop of scoops for him if she could be got to talk unguardedly. He had been turfed out of court halfway through Ann's evidence by the senior reporter of his paper, and told to wait for her at the witness's exit as it took some time to get round to that side of the building from the court, and no one could say how long she would be under cross-examination.

"Was there?" he asked again, getting no reply.

"Was there what?" asked Ann, waking up to his existence with an effort.

"Any truth in that handcuff yarn?"

"No, none," snapped Ann, wishing him dead.

"Was the whole thing a put-up job? Were you never handcuffed at all?"

"Oh, yes," said Ann, impatiently, "I was handcuffed, all right, but not in the way they made out."

"What happened?" asked the pertinacious young man, wishing he could get out his notebook, but not daring to, lest he put Ann off her stroke.

"I found them, and played about with them, being a fool, and they clicked shut on me, and couldn't be got off because nobody had the key. Inspector Saunders was trying to get them off when my father came in. We told him what it was, but he chose to try and make capital out of it. He doesn't care what becomes of me," she added bitterly.

Tuke was disappointed. He had hoped for something much better than that, but unfortunately for him, Ann, in her turn, had discovered how much can be done to a landscape by the lighting.

"Hullo," said Tuke suddenly, "there's the very chap."

"Who?" asked Ann, looking round, but seeing no one she knew in all the crush and stuffiness of the big multiple teashop with its crowded tables.

"That detective fellow, the big one. The chap who made himself a nuisance. Hope he doesn't see us here. I should think you had had about enough of him."

Then Ann saw him. He was looking round at the crowded tables, seeking for her; she saw that people were staring at him as they had stared at her, for he had fallen a victim to the picture papers. She felt perfectly certain that the account of her evidence was out in the evening papers by now, from the way that a fat female with a sentimental face, who happened to be sitting at the next table with an Evening Mercury propped against her teapot, was gazing enraptured from one to the other of them. But Ann cared for none of these things. The one thing that mattered was that she should not miss Austen. She saw that he was turning towards the door, evidently having failed to locate her.

"Catch him for me, will you?" she said to Tuke.

"I shouldn't, if I were you," said Tuke, rather annoyed by this request. "You know the sort of chap he is. If you once get mixed up with him again, you may have an awful job getting rid of him."

"I want him! I must speak to him!" cried the frantic Ann, who saw that Austen was on his way out, looking worried. Everything would go astray if she missed him now. What would she do if her father were acquitted? She rose from her seat and regardless of the staring restaurant, waved her handbag at him. But even this Austen would have missed, if a waitress who was watching the little drama had not touched him on the arm, saying:

"There's a lady wants you."

Austen looked round and saw Ann, gave her a beaming smile, raised his hand to the policeman's salute, and came striding across the restaurant.

Tuke, who had not had Austen's experience of standing up to be stared at on point-duty, squirmed at the attention they were attracting.

Their table was for two, but Austen picked up a chair from another table and sat down at it without waiting to be asked. Tuke froze. He was the son of a City magnate who had "arrived" during his son's adolescence. Consequently Tuke had very clear-cut notions of class distinctions, and considered a policeman distinctly below the salt, especially such a very large one, and in a public place. He had expected Austen to take his stand alongside Ann's chair, address her as "miss," hear what she had to say, and take himself off.

"This is Mr. Tuke, of the *Evening Record*, who has been very kind to me," said Ann to Austen,

"Ah, yes," said Austen, "I saw you in court."

Tuke noticing the absence of the "sir," which he considered his due, made no sign of having heard the introduction, but merely stared steadily at Austen in the hope of keeping him in his place and preventing him from getting fresh with Ann.

An awkward silence fell upon the little table. The sentimental female's neck was stretching out like a piece of rubber in her eagerness to see and hear what was going on. The one thing Ann wanted was to get rid of Tuke. Austen did not care a damn whether he was there or not, he guessed that the reporter had fastened himself on to Ann willy-nilly, and felt quite equal to brushing him off as if he were a fly; the only

216

thing he cared about was to do it as discreetly as possible, and not let Ann in for any public unpleasantness.

"Well," he said to Ann, "are you ready to come along?"

Ann knew at once what he was trying to do, and gathered up bag and gloves, but Tuke misunderstood and exclaimed:

"Look here, my man, what are you driving at? You can't order a witness about like that unless you have a warrant. There has been quite enough third degree in this case already, we're not standing for any more. Miss Studley is having independent legal representation. She will do nothing further until she has seen her solicitor."

Ann, knowing Austen's tendency to quarrelsomeness, was terrified of a scene, and seized his hand under cover of the table—but not out of sight of the sentimental female, whose eyes were popping out of her head, and whose countenance was wreathed in a beatific smile.

But Austen, being sure of his Ann, was all right, and the Tempter himself could not have provoked him. His hand closed on Ann's so that she could not withdraw it, and he proceeded to amuse himself by teasing Tuke.

"Yes, sir," he said politely, putting on his wooden police face, "Wisht, miss? Menu, please," and he put his slouch hat on top of Tuke's Homburg, which occupied the only available space on a radiator. Tuke looked as if about to burst.

The delighted waitress instantly popped a menu in front of Austen. They knew him well there, for the detectives appearing in cases that were being tried at the old Bailey often used this restaurant when for any reason they did not wish to use their own meal-room in the big building. The entire staff was thrilled to the marrow at having this romantic comedy played out under its eyes, having taken the measure of the situation on the strength of Tuke's infuriated countenance.

Tuke never spoke. Austen's tea came, and he tried to cope with it with his left hand, because he knew if he once let go of Ann's hand with his right, he would never get hold of it again, for she had already tried to wriggle until a decided squeeze had made her aware of the futility of such attempt. He saw that she was shaking in a repressed fit of the giggles, and thanked God for it, for it would take her mind off the terrible ordeal she had undergone, and the even more terrible ordeal which lay ahead of her as she waited for her father's fate to be announced to learn whether he were to be hanged as a result of her testimony, or whether she would be in flight for her life from a man who was little better than a homicidal maniac. Detectives learn to be good psychologists. Austen saw what the present situation was worth in therapeutic value for Ann, and determined to play if for all he was worth.

Scone and butter are elusive things to deal with single-handed, and Tuke watched Austen's table manners in disgust. Ann, more and more overcome by hysterical laughter, momentarily expected Austen's tea to end on the floor. She had given up trying to recapture her hand by now.

Tuke addressed her stiffly. "If you have finished, shall we go?" he said.

"No," said Ann. "I am interested in Mr. Austen's score for the hole."

"Ah," said Austen, "I am doing this one in bogey," and neatly flicked the butter off the side of the hot-water jug.

Tuke looked as if on the point of walking off and leaving Austen to settle the bill, but he suddenly remembered once more that he was a newspaper man, a fact he frequently forgot when he got interested in the subject he was supposed to be reporting, and seeing that the detective and the girl obviously knew each other better much than either of them had admitted in court, determined to sit tight and see what came of it, his editor's praise being sufficient compensation for a heart slightly broken by Ann, and dignity outraged by Austen.

Seeing that Tuke meant to stick closer than a brother, Austen soon tired of his game. He let go of Ann's hand, dealt with his scone, gulped his tea down scalding hot, and called for his bill. Out they went. Austen shepherding Ann, and Tuke trailing behind.

Austen, hoping to shake him off at the cash desk, had the exact sum ready. But Tuke, not to be outdone, threw down half a crown for a one and tuppenny bill, and abandoned the change.

Once outside the restaurant, Austen, determined not to mince matters. He stepped forward into the streaming traffic and held up his hand. The traffic instantly responded to the air of habitual authority. Luckily for all concerned, the road had dried since the thunderstorm. Austen dispatched Ann across to an island with a thrust of his hand at her back, turned to Tuke, and said, "This is where you get off, sir," crossed the road himself, and beckoned the traffic on behind him. On came the traffic obediently, and Tuke, skipping for his life from a lorry, lost sight of his quarry in the crowd.

Austen found Ann waiting for him on the opposite kerb, laughing immoderately; and liking this laughter none too well, led her into a quiet little tea-room up a long flight of stairs, which had only recently been opened, and had not yet collected a clientele. He wanted somewhere away from curious eyes, where they could await the verdict. Until that was announced it was impossible for Ann even to know where she would spend the night. Return to Thatched Cottage she dared not, if Mr. Studley were let loose on society by an imbecile jury. The judge had announced that he meant to finish the case that evening, and sit as late as might be necessary. When the judge says that, counsel do not play to the gallery in their final speeches, but get on with the job.

He settled Ann at a table by the open window, overlooking the seething tides of Ludgate Hill, and asked the little proprietress, who appeared to be single-handed, if he might use the telephone. She had recognized him from his photo in the papers, but paid no particular attention to him, not having followed the Gregory case closely, being no lover of horrors. He had to speak loudly into the telephone, however, and she was puzzled to hear him ask to be informed of the verdict on Mr. Studley the moment it was announced, giving her telephone number to the person he was talking to, saying in explanation, "I have got to get the girl away, sir. Her life won't be safe if he gets off. The man isn't sane, in my opinion."

She realized at once that something was afoot, and that her little venture, started in such hope, and struggling so hard for a footing, might be the scene of happenings that would give it some much-needed publicity, for amazing numbers of people will flock towards anything even remotely connected with a murder as if it were a holy place where their souls could be saved by pilgrimage.

Austen came out through the flimsy cotton curtains that guarded the privacy of her sanctum, and addressed her formally and officially.

"What time do you close, madam?"

She told him she closed at seven, as there was no evening trade in that district. He looked at his watch. It was now half past six. The verdict might not be out for hours.

"Might I ask a favour of you, madam?" he said.

She readily acquiesced. The police seldom ask in vain, especially when the policeman has Austen's looks.

"I dare say you have seen about the Gregory case in the papers. The young lady I have got with me is the prisoner's daughter, and has only just come out of the witness-box after a very trying cross-examination. She wants to wait somewhere for the verdict. Would you permit her to wait here after you close? It would be a great kindness if you would;

she is in a very terrible position, as I am sure you will understand."

Ann had taken off her big hat, and had leant her head back against the dark woodwork, utterly exhausted, looking like a tired child. The proprietress went over to her.

"My dear," she said, "I am so very sorry to hear about your trouble. I shall be delighted if you will wait here as long as you like. I will fasten the door now, in case anybody else comes in."

Ann smiled at her with a smile that was very near tears, for speech was not in her power.

Austen sat down at the little table opposite Ann. It was the first time that they had been alone together since she had slapped his face. Both were thinking of that incident, and both were embarrassed. Ann's hands were lying lightly clasped on the table as she leant back in her corner. Austen placed his over them and smiled into her eyes. Ann tried to smile back, but her eyes faltered and fell, and she blushed till even her ears were crimson. Then the proprietress appeared with an unordered tea, and relieved their embarrassment.

Returning to her corner she caught sight of an evening paper someone had left in a chair, and picking it up, read the account of Ann's evidence, which as may well be believed, had lost nothing in the telling. Newspapers are not often so happy as to get hold of anything quite as juicy as that. There were photographs, too. She at once identified Ann's big hat. Austen and Saunders had been snapped going into the Old Bailey that morning. Saunders very sulky, for he hated pictorial publicity, holding that it greatly increased the difficulties of a detective's work when his face became known to the general public. Austen amiably allowed his friends of the Press to make any use of his face which was of help to them, for the only disguise that he could use, with his strongly-marked features, was a three days' growth of beard and no collar, which turned him into the most villainous looking tough it was possible to imagine.

The proprietress was thrilled to the marrow. She looked at Austen and Ann, smiled, sighed, and went into her sanctum and drew the curtain, leaving them alone.

CHAPTER SIXTEEN

AUSTEN knew that if there were a sentimentalist or two on the jury that were trying Mr. Studley, they might haggle half the night over their verdict, and what to do with Ann would be a difficult problem; he, moreover, would have to watch his step very carefully, owing to the publicity that had been given to their relationship. However, it was no use meeting trouble halfway. There were several quiet little hotels where he had got to know the proprietors personally in the course of his work, and into the hands of some decent, motherly manageress he could deliver Ann to be looked after till morning, when even the most sentimental of juries ought to have made up what passes for its mind one way or the other.

Meanwhile, the problem was to kill time, and the usual resort of an hour at the pictures seemed to him about the last thing that either of them would care for under the circumstances. Watching celluloid sorrows while your father was awaiting the verdict on a capital charge hardly seemed the thing to do. They were lucky to have found this quiet little place and the sympathetic proprietress, but they could not go on eating teas indefinitely. This one was already their second. Austen was liable to sudden attacks of shyness with Ann, and he felt a bad one coming on at the moment, and could find nothing with which to break the silence that had fallen between them.

Ann spared him the trouble, however. She never seemed to be shy with him, he noticed with envy.

"I am so awfully sorry about all the beastly publicity I

have let you in for," she said.

"Puss," said Austen, "it was worth every bit of it to hear you stand up in front of all of them and say, the man I loved."

"O-oh," groaned Ann, wishing she had her big hat on and could duck behind the brim, "that was the worst bit of all! I never intended that to come out, but it had to."

"But you meant it, didn't you, Puss?" asked Austen anxiously.

"I meant it all right," said Ann, "but I did not mean to admit it. I had no idea what cross examination could do to you."

Austen laughed. "I think old Murgatroyd has been a good friend to me for once. I don't believe I should ever have got that admission out of you myself, not even if I had given you the third degree in the way they said I had."

Silence fell between them again. Austen did not want to talk seriously to Ann of marriage between them while she was so exhausted, and while they were liable to be interrupted at any moment by the ringing of the telephone bell announcing the verdict on her father. So they sat together quite happily in silence, as many other lovers have done, tranquilly holding hands in the gathering dusk.

The room was lit by nothing but the glare of the street lamps when at last the sudden ringing of the telephone bell cut across it. Austen rose hastily and went to the manageress's sanctum, and she handed the receiver to him. Ann heard him say to the inaudible interlocutor, "Couldn't very well have been anything else, could it?" Pause. "And what did Mrs. Gregory get?" Pause. "Ten years? She was lucky. And her sister?" Pause. "Poor woman, I think she was let in for this thing. I don't believe she had any hand in it. Still, perjury is perjury."

Austen came back to her and put his hand on her shoulder. "It's all over, Puss," he said.

Ann could not speak, and he hung over her anxiously, wondering if she were going to faint.

The manageress came out of her sanctum with a medicine-glass in her hand.

"I think you would feel better if you would take this, dear," she said, and Ann got her second dose of sal volatile that day. Austen gathered her up and led her out while its effect was still on her.

By some means known only to himself he had got hold of one of the Scotland Yard cars, a smart blue limousine, and had disposed of its lawful driver. Into this he put Ann, and the City being comparatively free from traffic at that hour of the evening, they were soon clear of the houses and among the orchards and nursery gardens of a by-pass. Austen, who had spent some time in a garage while waiting to join the police, and could drive anything that had a wheel left hanging to it, put the powerful car along at a pace that would certainly have led to his arrest if the motor-patrol had not recognized the car as it flashed past them. Ann, who had been made nervous in a car by her father's driving, could only brace her feet and bear it as best she might. Austen was wondering whether he could get Ann to let him kiss her in the privacy of Thatched Cottage, and drove accordingly.

In an incredibly short space of time, so it seemed to Ann, they reached home. Austen put the big car into the barn, beside his battered baby namesake, for he had no wish to draw the attention of the district to his presence in the cottage, alone with Ann, at that hour of the evening.

As they walked down the rutted lane he remembered the previous occasion when he and Ann had walked back from the garage to the house together, and he had thought he had never met a girl who could snub quite so drastically, but was so infatuated that he didn't care what she did to him.

They came through the rose-arched gate into the garden, the scanty second blooming of the ramblers colourless over their heads in the moonlight. Ann had sown night-scented stock beside the path, and its flowers were open and full of moths, and exhaling their heady scent in the still, damp, evening air, for it was now late summer, just as it had been early spring when he had walked up this path with her before. He could hear the voice of the weir, and the hoo-hoo of an owl in the wood. No other sound broke the absolute silence of this little place of secret solitude, so near the great city.

Ann raised her hand to the low eaves and felt for a key, and Austen guessed that the key was there in order that the other occupant of the house might have got in if the verdict had been different, and Ann in flight for her life from her beloved home. His heart was beating hard, and he was striving to get a good grip on himself because he knew that he was liable either to lose his head when he came to close quarters with Ann, or to get an attack of panic shyness. Ann opened the quaint, low door, and a stream of moonlight flooded the little hall of the old house, revealing the staircase where he had bashed Mr. Studley so thoroughly.

Ann went in; but overcome by shyness, Austen hesitated on the threshold. Ann turned to look for him, and seeing him hesitating, took him by the hand and led him in like a child, and he bowed his head to the low lintel and followed her. He felt that, for all his toughness in his rough, dangerous work, this was how he and the small Ann were destined to go through life together.

Ann led the way to her own little sitting-room, Austen at her heels, cogitating how he was going to get that kiss. She lit the lamp, and he saw that supper was laid for one, all ready; the bread wrapped in a clean white cloth, eggs in a basin, tea-caddy beside pot, evidently put ready for a person who might not know where to find things. Austen wondered what would have been in Mr. Studley's mind if he had come home to that meal, and in what condition he would have sullied the little room with his presence.

Austen noticed that Ann seemed to have recovered her poise marvelously during the brief journey from town, and realized that most of her strain and distress had been due to her terror of her father and his vengeance, should he escape from the justice to which she had delivered him, and thanked God that that dipsomaniac ghost was not going to be invited to haunt their marriage by any futile self-reproach on the part of its daughter. He also marvelled at Ann's self-possession. He himself was half-dead with embarrassment, and she must have known that a proposal was due just as much as he did. He did not realize that Ann's matter of factness was her defence against her own emotion.

She knelt down in front of the unlit hearth and held out her hand. "Matches, please, Jack," she said.

He knelt beside her, and set light to the small brushwood that served as kindling.

They knelt together, watching the flames burn up, priest and priestess of that most ancient rite of the home—the ceremonial kindling of the sacred hearth-fire. Austen put his arm round Ann as they knelt, watching the flames, and she put her head on his shoulder.

"These are our own apple-logs," said Ann at length.

"Do you cut down apple-trees for burning?" asked Austen in surprise.

"Oh no, of course not," said Ann. "This one blew down last autumn. They are very old; we badly need some new ones planting."

Austen wondered if he would do that planting.

"Jack," said Ann, "do you think it would be possible for us to live here after we are married? This house really belongs to me, you know, and it is very handy for London."

Austen nearly fell in the fire with his amazement and delight that his difficult task should thus be done for him.

"I'd love it, Puss," he said. "It's a heavenly little place. I don't see why not. The Yard won't worry where I live so long as I can do my work all right."

He had had in his mind for some time a job in the new police staff college, and he thought that he had a very good chance for it. He knew that he came half-way between the old type of thief-taker, like Saunders, and the new type of university man that they were trying to recruit, and he reckoned that the "powers that be" would want someone who could keep the peace between both parties and persuade the lion to lie down with the lamb and the rest of the scriptural menagerie to get on together; and it wasn't going to be any little child that would lead them either, if he knew his comrades. Much as he liked the newcomers as men, he despised them as police, and reckoned that they would take more licking into shape than the authorities had bargained for. He knew he could work with men of both types, and he fancied the authorities had spotted the fact and intended to make use of him in that capacity. For he had had the vision to see that the change of recruiting method, and the consequent change in the type of men who were recruited, meant that the higher grades of the police were eventually going to rank socially with the Army and Navy, but that the door between commissioned and non-commissioned rank would still stand open to the man who started at the bottom. There never has been any hard and fast line drawn in the police between officers and men, for everyone had had to start at the bottom hitherto, and the distinction could not be made now. The newcomers, in fact, far from trying to draw distinctions, were almost apologizing for drawing breath. The Metropolitan Police has always been recruited from the cream of the working-classes, whereas the fighting forces, in the old days at any rate, had all too often got the scum. A skilled craftsman is a man of brains as well as a man of his hands, and the son of the engine-driver, the pattern-maker, the lens-grinder—is not apt to be a clod. It was about time, thought Austen, that the public gave up thinking of the policeman as a lout in uniform and the detective as a tough in mufti. He did not think that their own generation would regard the marriage of himself and Ann as any very desperate enterprise.

Ann broke in upon his meditations. "What about a meal?" said she.

"God help us !" said Austen. "We'll be sick! I've done nothing but eat since I left the Old Bailey."

Ann looked at him, and she saw that his face bore the same peculiar, indefinable look that her father's bore the morning after a bad debauch, and a horrible fear closed like ice on her heart. A drunkard's womenfolk panic at the very smell of alcohol.

"What is the matter with you?" she demanded, looking at him hard, dark tides of horror flowing over her very soul. If it were so, this was the end.

"Old age creeping on, I expect, Puss," said Austen. "Do you know, they sent me down to Hove for a fortnight for insomnia. Think of it, Puss, a copper with insomnia! They generally consider themselves lucky if they keep awake on their beats. You should have seen old Saunders's face when I told him!"

Ann went off to the kitchen and brewed hot milk. She handed it to Austen with the command that he should drink it whether he liked it or not, and he took it like a lamb and lapped it like a kitten. This was a new kind of thief-taker, and one that Bill Sykes was not used to; nevertheless, the thief-taker was quite used to Bill Sykes, and quite capable of dealing with him, despite his milk-drinking. The hardness of a man's shell is often in inverse ratio to the softness of his core with the woman he loves.

"Puss, you have the right idea," said Austen, stretching out at his ease; and reaching up from the low chair, he put an arm round Ann as she bent over him, and accidentally catching her behind the knees, toppled her over. He got his kiss.

Ann settled down on the hearthrug at his feet and put her head on his knee. He laid his hand on the bright hair that had always fascinated him, and began to stroke it. It was infinitely softer and more silky than he had expected. He had never touched a woman's hair before, unless, it had been that of some greasy harridan in the Harrow Road, when the hair had acted as a handle to pull her off some other harridan whom she was fighting.

So this was what married life with Ann was going to be like, he thought, with infinite satisfaction. It amazed him to find that, whereas when there was a great gulf fixed between them, close contact with Ann had always gone to his head like strong drink, now that Ann was wholly his, there was nothing but happy contentment and affection, together thus in the firelight after a hard day's work.

* * *

Something white moving in the shadows caught Austen's eye, and the cat came silently in with a kitten in her mouth. She was an old friend of his, and she settled herself in front of the fire, propped her back against his foot, and got to work on the kitten's toilet, emitting intermittent purrs between the mouthfuls of fur. Austen watched the little furry mother, busy with her baby, and then for the first time it occurred to him to wonder whether this also would be part of his life with Ann at Thatched Cottage.

"Puss," he said, "I hate to disturb Sophonisba and her family, but I have got to get back to barracks some time to-night. We C.I.D.s can come and go pretty much as we please, but I solemnly swore to Saunders I would get back p.m. and not a.m., out of respect for your reputation"

"Oh, dear," said Ann, "My poor reputation! I am afraid there is not much left of it after all that has happened. I don't suppose a little more or less will make much difference to it."

Austen smacked her lightly on the head.

"Come on, Puss. Turf me out," he said.

In the hall she put up her face to be kissed as naturally as a child. There was no longer any embarrassment between them. He kissed her and held her close. With his cheek against hers he said:

"One of these days you won't be turfing me out, will you, Puss? This will be my home too—our home." She felt his cheek grow hot against hers.

Ann laughed softly. "Go on, hop it," she said. "Even my reputation is capable of being a little blacker than it is now, and then the vicar will stop calling altogether. He only district visits me as it is."

Austen laughed also, and reached for his hat. "You know how to handle me, don't you, Puss?" he said.

She went down the pith with him to get the car from the garage, and he held her so closely that she trod on her favourite pinks at the path edge. He risked his neck to wave to her as he turned the corner of the lane and saw her standing there, ghost-like in the moonlight in her blue linen frock that had seen so much of life in its short existence.

The powerful car ate up the miles with a peaceful snore. Austen thought that he, too, would sleep to-night. No more insomnia for him. He only hoped he would keep awake till he got to the Yard, and not fall asleep at the wheel like a lorry driver.

Suddenly he remembered that he had entirely forgotten

to ask Ann to marry him.

THE END

84657256R00128

Made in the USA
Columbia, SC
30 December 2017